Was Mr. Shepard th[...]
prayers?

He took a deep breath, then blurted, "I'm looking for a nanny for my daughter, Grace. If you take the job, you'll need to move out to the ranch. I will make sure that you make more than what you do now as a teacher. I'll double what they are paying you to teach."

Laura needed the money. If she could work until planting season was over and school started back, maybe she'd make enough money to buy her own house.

She swallowed. "Mr. Shepard, I have no desire to give up my teaching position. School is closed for the summer until the end of the harvest planting. My goal is to obtain a house for myself and Hope by that time."

Clint nodded. "I see. What if I promise to help you look for a house and you work for me until school resumes?"

Laura's gaze moved to the two little girls sitting on the floor at their feet. Grace's small voice was speaking in low tones to Hope. Hope sucked her thumb and nodded as if in agreement with Grace. Would Hope become attached to Grace if Laura took the job and they moved to the ranch? Or worse, would *she*?

Rhonda Gibson lives in New Mexico with her husband, James. She has two children and three beautiful grandchildren. Reading is something she has enjoyed her whole life, and writing stemmed from that love. When she isn't writing or reading, she enjoys gardening, beading and playing with her dog, Sheba. You can visit her at rhondagibson.net. Rhonda hopes her writing will entertain, encourage and bring others closer to God.

Books by Rhonda Gibson

Love Inspired Historical

Saddles and Spurs

Visit the Author Profile page at Harlequin.com.

RHONDA GIBSON

Baby on Her Doorstep

HARLEQUIN® LOVE INSPIRED® HISTORICAL

Recycling programs for this product may not exist in your area.

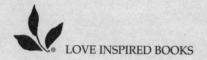

LOVE INSPIRED BOOKS

ISBN-13: 978-1-335-36967-3

Baby on Her Doorstep

Copyright © 2018 by Rhonda Gibson

www.Harlequin.com

Printed in U.S.A.

Have not I commanded thee? Be strong and of a good courage; be not afraid, neither be thou dismayed: for the Lord thy God is with thee whithersoever thou goest.

—*Joshua* 1:9

This book is dedicated to my readers—
thank you so much for reading my books and
supporting my writing. You are the reason I write.

James Gibson, I wouldn't be able to write the stories
of my heart without your help.
Thank you, Michelle Matney—you pulled
my bacon out of the fire this time. You're the best.

Above all, thank You, Lord,
for letting me write for You.

Chapter One

Glory, Texas
March 1884

Something placed beside the door, wrapped in a blanket, was the last thing Laura Lee expected to see when she arrived at the steps of the one-room schoolhouse. Laura swallowed hard. Her eyes narrowed, and her heart pounded in her chest. She whispered to herself, "What is that?"

Ignoring the chill that lingered in the morning mist, Laura looked up the steps. She pulled her shawl tighter about her shoulders. "Well, standing down here won't answer my question, now, will it?" she asked, reminding herself mentally that she was doing it again. Talking to herself.

Laura raised her chin, squared her shoulders and climbed the steps, keeping her focus on the bundle at the top. "Jess Parker could have left some sort of wild animal in that bundle to scare me," she muttered, thinking of one of her favorite students. Jess was older than the other boys and always full of mischief.

Once at the top of the stairs, she looked down into the face of a sweet, rosy-cheeked child. Long blond lashes feathered under its eyes. The blanket rose and fell gently as the child slept peacefully.

Laura looked about but saw no one. Bending, she unpinned a note from the soft blanket. Her fingers itched to touch the child's soft blond curls. Instead she unfolded the paper and read.

"Mrs. Lee, please take care of my little girl. Her name is Hope and she is a year old. I know you are kind and will make a good mother for her. She is a good eater and in good health. Thank you."

Laura turned the note over in her hands. Was this real? Had someone, perhaps one of her former students, just given her a child? Her gaze moved back to the sleeping little girl.

Hope.

How many times had she asked God for a child? And now ironically was given one named Hope? Laura picked up the little girl who continued to sleep deeply. She was small to be a year old. Was that why her mother had pointed out she was a good eater and in good health?

Laura cuddled the sweet bundle close. She couldn't just take her home. Could she? She looked about once more, searching for Hope's mother. Was the letter legal? Could she keep her? What was her landlady, Mrs. Potter, going to say if she returned to the boardinghouse with the child?

Laura looked down the dirt street at the small town. It was growing every day. Thanks to the lumber business, it had two sawmills, a general store with a built-in pharmacy, two churches, a bakery and a saloon. If only it had two boardinghouses, but it didn't. If Mrs. Potter held to her rule of no children allowed, Laura didn't know what she'd do with Hope.

The baby squirmed in her arms. Hope continued to sleep as she worked an arm out of the blanket and stuck two fingers in her small mouth. Then she snuggled against Laura once more.

Motherly instinct swelled in Laura. She gently rocked the baby and sighed. Then Laura straightened her spine and whispered, "You stop right now, Laura Lee. Dreaming and wishing has never gotten you anywhere." Her gaze returned to the bundle in her arms. "Oh, but I do want to keep you." She hugged the child closer.

It seemed odd that four years after her husband Charles's death, she'd been given a child to raise. Laura looked about once more, then started back down the schoolhouse steps. Before she got her hopes up, she'd make sure that she could truly keep the baby.

Thinking of Charles brought about fresh hurt to her wounded heart. He'd wanted children so badly. And she'd disappointed him. How many times after they'd realized she could not bear children had he told her of his disappointment? Too many to count. It wasn't just his words but the look in his eyes that had cut her to the core. The references that never having a son to carry on the good Lee name was a crying shame. It was her shame that he referred to.

Laura pushed the pain aside and hurried her footsteps toward town. She decided to take the side streets to avoid the many questions that would arise at the sight of her holding a child. Her gaze moved to the sleeping face. Little Hope must be very tired to sleep through the jarring of being held while Laura walked down the dusty roads.

She rushed to the sheriff's office and slipped inside. Closing the door quickly, Laura turned to find a bemused lawman sitting behind an old wooden desk. For the first time in her life, she was at a loss for words. How did you explain to the town sheriff that someone had dropped a child on your doorstep?

"Good morning, Mrs. Lee." The sheriff stood and came around the front of the desk. "Please, have a seat." Once she was seated he continued. "What can I help you with?"

Laura looked down at the child and into the purest blue eyes she'd ever seen. Hope smiled around her fingers. Laura's heart melted. Someone had given her this sweet child. She knew she'd do all in her power to take care of little Hope and give her a good home. She sat Hope up. "Sheriff, I'd like for you to meet Hope." She wished with all her heart that she knew where the child had come from. Could she be the product of one of her former students?

He didn't blink an eye. The sheriff reached out and took the little girl's small hand. "Nice to meet you, Miss Hope."

Hope continued to look up at him with big eyes and a grin.

"I didn't know you had a little girl, Mrs. Lee. Where have you been hiding her?" He leaned a hip against his desk and crossed his arms.

He was teasing her and she knew it. The sheriff was a good man who enjoyed a smile or two wherever they could be found. Laura wondered why the child hadn't asked for her mother but hugged her closer. "Well,

I can't claim her just yet. This morning I found her sleeping on the school porch." Laura pulled the note from Hope's blanket and handed it to him. "This was pinned to her blanket." She held her breath as he read.

His gaze moved to hers. "Mrs. Potter isn't going to let you keep her at the boardinghouse, you know."

The sheriff lived at the boardinghouse also and knew Mrs. Potter's rules just as she did. "Well, I'm going to ask, but if she says no, I'll have to find a new place to live. I don't think she's so hard-hearted that she won't give me time to find us a new home."

He nodded.

"What I need to know is—" She paused. "Can I keep her?"

His gaze moved over the paper once more. "Well, the letter is addressed to you, and the request is clear. I'd say yes. But I've a feeling there is more to this than meets the eye. I'll need to do some investigating. I'd hate to think this young lady's ma is in danger, but it's odd that a mother would just abandon her child like this."

Laura wanted to argue it happened all the time in the big cities, but this wasn't a big city, and people didn't drop off their children on doorsteps here. No, he was right. She couldn't just claim the child, even if she had been delivered like a sack of potatoes.

He sighed deeply. "I'm sorry, Laura. You can't just keep her. Judge Miller will be coming to town around the first of next month. He'll make the final decision as to if you can keep her."

"Are you going to keep her until then?" Laura asked, looking about the dusty jailhouse.

His gaze followed hers. "Naw, I don't reckon I am.

You can keep her with you, if you want to, until the judge arrives next month."

Joy jumped in her heart. He'd said she could keep Hope, at least until Judge Miller arrived. By then the judge would see just how attached she and the child were to each other. He was a kind man. He'd let her keep Hope. Laura was sure of it.

Now all she had to do was convince Mrs. Potter to let her keep Hope. Or she'd have to find a new place to live that would let her keep the child with her. But where? She was a schoolteacher on a small budget. Could she afford more than the boardinghouse's fee of two dollars a week?

Clint Shepard held his daughter, Grace, close. The little girl was sound asleep, something he was grateful for. The two-year-old was a chatterbox. She'd talked most of the way to town. If he could have understood half of it, Clint would have been a happy man.

He pulled the wagon up in front of the jailhouse, hoping his friend the sheriff could help him find a nanny for Grace. Normally, he left Grace with her wet nurse when he came to town, but once those services were no longer needed, she and her husband had moved to Colorado. Since his housekeeper refused to watch the child, Clint had brought her with him. Besides, he'd decided along the way that it would be good for Grace to meet her nanny before he hired her.

His housekeeper, Mrs. Camelia Murphy, had warned him that he'd better come home with a nanny for Grace or she was quitting. She'd said she was too old to be chasing after a toddler. Unfortunately, Clint had to agree. She was a great housekeeper and cook, but when it came to running after a small child who raced around the house like the barn was on fire, well, Mrs. Murphy just didn't have the stamina to do so.

Clint held Grace to his chest with one hand and tied the horse to the hitching post in front of the jailhouse with the other. He heard the door open and looked up, expecting to see his friend. Instead, a pretty woman with brown hair and red highlights that caught the noonday sun stood in the doorway. Big green eyes looked in his direction. She held a little girl on her hip and smiled.

The sheriff followed her out on to the porch. "I'm looking forward to hearing what Mrs. Potter has to say about the little one."

"I'll let you know." She turned and walked down the boardwalk away from him.

To Clint her voice sounded almost like a song. It was soft with just the right cadence to make him pay attention. He watched her walk down the wooden walkway. Grace stirred against him, reminding him that he had better things to do than stare after a pretty lady.

He turned to find the sheriff watching him. "What brings you into town, Clint?"

"I need a nanny, Matt. Mrs. Murphy is threatening to quit. This little girl can be a handful."

The sheriff laughed and stepped back inside his office. "Come on inside. I might have just the person you need."

Clint followed. "Who?"

Matt walked to his desk and sat down. He propped his boots up and pushed his hat back. "Well, that lady who caught your eye a few moments ago comes to mind."

Caught his eye? No, Clint had vowed after his wife
Martha's death not to become involved with a woman
again. Martha had died from an infection shortly after
having Grace. Clint didn't think he could go through
that heartache again. And no pretty face was going to
change that.

Clint frowned. Instead of dwelling on his wife's
death or his fear of being hurt again, he asked, "What
makes you think she'd like to be a nanny?"

"Well, for starters she's the schoolteacher here in
town and loves children."

Clint rubbed his chin where Grace's hair tickled
it. "That is nice, but does she want to stop teaching?"

The sheriff shrugged. "I'm not sure. But the school
is closed for the next couple of months for planting
season. She might be interested in earning some extra
money, and it would give you more time to search for
a real nanny."

Clint thought for a few moments. Did he want a
temporary nanny? She could be a quick solution to his
current problem, but he'd have to find a replacement
for her. Still, like his friend said, it would give him
more time to find a suitable nanny, and Mrs. Murphy
wouldn't quit if he brought home a nanny for Grace.

The sheriff chuckled. "What have you got to lose,
Clint? Or, you could ask any of our unwed women to
come out to your ranch. I know of at least two who
would love to marry you, and then you wouldn't need
a nanny for little Grace."

Clint ignored Matt's joke about the other women
and focused on the one he'd just seen. The last thing
he wanted was another wife. "Do you know if she's

looking for work?" Clint shifted Grace into a more comfortable position.

"There's only one way to find out. Go ask her." He picked up a faded wanted poster and studied the picture.

"Where does she live? I'll tell her you recommended her." He waited to see what kind of reaction Matt would have.

Matt looked up. "She lives at the boardinghouse on the corner of Elm and Third Street." He pushed his hat back on his head. "I don't reckon you noticed she was carrying a little girl, did you?"

So, they lived at the same boardinghouse. It was his experience that only single people lived in boardinghouses. He couldn't help but wonder if Matt might be interested in the pretty green-eyed lady romantically himself. Maybe that's why she'd been visiting his office. It was possible she was sweet on the good sheriff. But then again, like Matt had just pointed out, she had a small child with her. "I did. Is she married?"

Matt chuckled and leaned back in his chair. "No, she's a widow now. Her name is Laura Lee. Laura's a fine woman who loves children."

"That's good enough for me. I don't mind her having a child." He rubbed his chin across Grace's feather-soft baby head. "I like them."

Matt grinned. "I'm glad."

Clint realized how silly his words must sound to the bachelor sheriff, who had no children. "Well, I'll be heading over to the boardinghouse. Is it all right if I leave Shadow and the wagon tied to your hitching post for a while?"

The sheriff nodded. "How long are you in town for?"

"I'll be here as long as it takes to get a nanny. Mrs. Murphy has threatened to quit if I return home alone." He hugged Grace close. "In her words…" Using his best imitation of Camelia's Irish accent, he continued, "'A two-year-old is too active for a woman in her six-ties who has a house to run and meals to cook. You'd best be sure to find someone, Mr. Shepard, or I will be going to live with my cousin, Darby. And you know I'll do it, too.'"

Matt laughed. "I can just hear her. Did she shake her finger at you?"

"Yep. So I'm hoping it doesn't take more than a day or two to find just the right person. I want someone who will be good to Grace. If she doesn't like Mrs. Lee, I'll keep looking."

Concern filled Matt's face. "What about the ranch?"

"It will be all right for a couple of days. I left Rich-ard Turner in charge."

Matt rubbed his chin. "Yep, Rich is a good man."

Richard was a good man. He had lost his wife to the fever that had swept the town the year before Grace had been born. If it hadn't been for Richard, Clint wasn't sure how he would have continued running the ranch after Martha's death. Grief had seemed to fill his brain with a dense fog, and he'd had a new infant to care for.

Clint opened the door. "I'll let you know how it goes with Mrs. Lee when I come back for the wagon."

Matt nodded and returned his focus to the wanted posters. Clint closed the door and turned toward Elm Street. He grinned, pleased with the fact that finding a potential nanny hadn't been so hard after all. And if Mrs. Lee took the job, he felt pretty sure that she'd be more interested in taking care of his daughter than landing a rancher husband for herself.

Matt didn't seem to view her as a potential bride, but Mrs. Lee might have her heart set on the sheriff. He remembered the look of happiness on her face as she'd left the sheriff's office. It was the expression of a woman in love. And if she was in love with Matt, it was a sure sign that she wouldn't be looking to him as future husband material.

Chapter Two

Laura had been trying for the last thirty minutes to persuade Mrs. Potter to let her keep Hope at the boardinghouse.

The older woman touched a strand of Hope's hair. "I'm sorry, Laura, but even as sweet as she is, I can't have a small child living here."

"I understand. I'm paid to the end of the week. Can we stay until then? I need time to find another place to live." Laura watched as Hope silently played with a ball of yarn that Mrs. Potter had pulled from her knitting basket for her. She calculated the amount of money she'd saved from teaching and knew it wasn't enough to buy a house. Perhaps someone would have one she could rent, although Laura doubted it.

"Yes, but no longer. I don't mean to be hard-hearted, but I'll need to rent your room out as quickly as possible." She returned to her knitting.

Laura picked up Hope. The child had played silently at their feet. It worried Laura that Hope hadn't asked for her ma or even attempted to communicate since she'd woken from her nap. "Thank you." She carried Hope up to her room.

She'd lived at the boardinghouse for four years. After Charles had died, Laura tried to make their little farm her home but without him selling cotton, she'd had no income to pay the land payment. She'd been forced to return the farm to the bank and take the teaching job in town.

Her gaze moved about the small space she now called home. When she'd moved in, Laura had sewn new curtains for the windows, added a colorful quilt to the bed and braided a nice-looking rug for the floor. Pretty dollies lay on the dresser and side table. Her writing desk rested under the window. Laura had created many lesson plans there. Laura sighed, aware of just how much she was going to miss this room.

Hope laid her head on Laura's shoulder. The little girl still clutched the yarn ball in her tiny hand. Her stomach growled loud enough for Laura to hear it. "Oh, my! I think there is a bear in your tummy," she teased the little girl. Hope raised her head and grinned. She pointed to her mouth, indicating she was hungry.

Laura frowned. "Can you say you're hungry?"

Hope pointed to her mouth again and smiled as if pleased that she'd done as Laura had asked.

She sat the little girl on the bed. "We'll go to Pearl's restaurant for lunch. Do you want to go eat?"

Hope continued playing with the ball.

Laura sighed. Hope hadn't heard her. She feared the child couldn't hear. She folded Hope's blanket and set it on the chair. Then she pulled a small shawl from the closet and wrapped it about Hope. "Come on, sweetie. We are going to lunch and then go to see Dr. Stewart."

She picked up Hope and headed down the stairs. The little girl held tightly to her yarn ball. Laura heard Mrs. Potter in the entryway speaking in low tones to a man. His voice carried up the stairs that she was swiftly descending.

Laura bitterly thought that the older woman was probably interviewing someone to take her room. She continued down the steps. Worry ate at her. Where was she going to find another place to live? She had money tucked away, but there wasn't enough there to purchase a small house. Maybe in another year she'd have enough, but not today. Perhaps the bank held a small farm house that she could rent.

As she stepped off the bottom stair, Mrs. Potter and the man turned to face her. Laura paused. Wasn't this the gentleman who'd arrived at the sheriff's office just as she'd been leaving?

"Oh, good. I won't have to send for you, Mrs. Lee. This gentleman has asked to see you." Mrs. Potter glanced from her to the man waiting.

"Thank you, Mrs. Potter." She turned to look at him. Did he know something about Hope? Who she belonged to? Had he come to claim Hope as part of his family?

A little girl stood beside him, holding his pinky finger in her small hand. Big brown eyes looked from her to Hope. She tugged at his hand and chattered something, but the language was baby gibberish.

He smiled at the child. "I don't know, Grace. You'll have to ask Mrs. Lee." Dark brown eyes rose and met hers.

He'd understood what the little girl had said?

Hope began pushing away from Laura, trying to get

down to Grace. Laura hung on to her tighter. She jiggled the child against her hip to get her attention and then looking her in the eyes, said, "Hope, be still." Her tone was that of a schoolteacher.

The child immediately stopped and laid her head on Laura's shoulder. Laura rubbed her small back. Hope seemed to be a well-behaved child.

The handsome man nodded. "That's a nice trick, Mrs. Lee. Maybe you could teach it to me someday."

Laura frowned. "You seem to know me, sir, but I don't know you." She'd seen him around town before today, but they had never spoken. Had someone pointed her out to him?

Mrs. Potter's head swung from one to the other. Laura wanted to ask her to leave but at the same time was happy that she'd stayed. This man was a stranger to her and yet knew her name.

He stepped forward with his free hand extended. "I'm sorry. I'm Clint Shepard. I'm looking for a nanny for Grace here, and the sheriff suggested you."

Laura shook his hand, just as she would one of her students' fathers. She tilted her head and gazed at Mr. Shepard. Was he the answer to her prayers? The sheriff wouldn't have sent a dangerous man to look for her, if he didn't think Mr. Shepard could help her with her current situation.

"If you are interested, it would mean moving out to my ranch." He shifted his booted feet as if wanting to leave and yet knowing he needed to stay.

She indicated the bench that rested against the wall beside the stairs. "Perhaps you'd like to explain what you are offering, Mr. Shepard." Laura sat Hope down.

Hope waited until Mr. Shepard had sat down and

then toddled over to the other little girl who stood in front of her father.

He took a deep breath and then blurted, "I have a housekeeper and cook, but she refuses to take on the care of my daughter, Grace, too. So, if you will take the job, you'll need to move out to the ranch. You and your little girl will be given a room next to Grace's, and I will make sure that you make more than what you do now as a teacher."

Did he know that she made forty dollars a month as a schoolteacher? "Do you have any idea what this town pays a schoolteacher, Mr. Shepard?"

He grinned and nodded. Grace jabbered something to him, while tugging at his leg. Clint reached down and touched the top of her head. "We'll go in a moment, Grace."

Laura needed the money. If she could work until planting season was over and school started back, maybe she'd make enough money to buy a house in town or at least rent something. "How much more are we talking?"

His head came up and a look of hope entered his eyes. "I'll double what they are paying you."

She swallowed. "Mr. Shepard. I have no desire to give up my teaching position. As you are aware, school is closed for the summer until the end of the harvest, but as soon as harvest is over, I'll resume my job." For some reason, Laura found herself sharing more than she normally would. "My goal is to obtain a house for myself and Hope by that time."

Clint nodded. "I see. What if I promise to help you look for a house and you work for me until school resumes?"

Laura's gaze moved to the two little girls who were sitting on the floor at their feet. Grace's small voice was speaking in low tones to Hope. Hope sucked her thumb and nodded as if in agreement with Grace. Would Hope become attached to Grace, if she took the job and moved to the ranch? Or worse, would she?

Clint held his breath while he waited for Mrs. Lee to make up her mind. If she accepted his proposal, he'd have to find another nanny to replace her, but at least he wouldn't be rushed, like he was right now.

"My board is paid until the end of the week here. I'd like to pray about it." Laura studied the children at their feet.

He nodded. "I realize you need the time, but I also have a ranch to run. I'd planned on staying in town until tomorrow, and even though I'd love to give you the extra days, I really can't stay longer than that."

"I'll have an answer for you in the morning. Is that satisfactory?" Laura asked.

He heard the schoolteacher tone in her voice. If he didn't miss his guess, Clint was pretty sure it didn't matter if it was agreeable to him or not, she'd not have a solid answer until then. Clint turned his attention to the boardinghouse owner, put on his most charming smile and asked, "Would it be possible for me to rent a room for the night?"

The older woman frowned. "I don't normally allow children to live here, Mr. Shepard."

His mind raced. Where else could he rent a room? The hotel was still in the process of being built, so that wasn't an option. He looked down at Grace. Why hadn't he considered that the boardinghouse wouldn't accept children? Since he'd never had need to stay overnight in town before, he'd not considered that the boardinghouse might be full or not have room for children within its walls.

Mrs. Potter sighed and looked down at the two children. "I suppose one night won't hurt, but I'll not allow it again." Mrs. Potter gave him a stern look.

"Thank you. I promise I'll keep Grace as quiet as I possibly can." Clint looked down at his chattering daughter and wondered if he'd be able to keep that promise.

Grace prattled up at him and pointed to Hope. Hope pointed to her heart-shaped mouth and pointed inside. It was obvious his daughter and little Hope were hungry.

"All right, Grace." He looked to Laura. "Would you ladies like to join us for lunch?"

Grace pulled on Hope's arms until she stood steadily on her feet. The two children looked up at Laura expectantly. Did she understand the children were waiting to go eat?

Laura grinned. "I see that I am outnumbered. We are going to go over to Miss Pearl's for lunch. You and Grace are welcome to join us." She picked up the ball of yarn Hope had been playing with and dropped it into her handbag. Then Laura scooped up Hope and swung the child on to her hip.

Grace tugged on his shirt. Clint lifted his daughter up and set her on his shoulders. "Then that sounds like a nice place for us to go, too. I've never eaten there. I usually do my business and get right back to the ranch."

Mrs. Potter snorted. "Dinner is at six." She left the room with her skirts swirling around her.

Clint followed Laura and Hope out the door. Why

hadn't Laura had lunch at the boardinghouse? Maybe the food wasn't as good there as it was at Pearl's.

He stepped into place beside Laura when she made room on the sidewalk for him. Grace giggled and chattered above his head. "She really is a talker, isn't she?" Laura grinned up at Grace.

"That she is. I just wish I understood more of what she's saying." Clint patted the little girl's leg. In return, she patted the top of his head.

Laura laughed.

Clint grinned. He had to admit that he'd not heard a woman's rich laughter in a long time and to be honest, he'd missed the sound. His gaze moved about the town of Glory.

It was growing. Lumber and farmland were both plentiful, and men from all over were coming to Glory. The sound of hammers pounding a steady beat filled his ears as they passed the construction of the new hotel.

Laura stopped in front of the restaurant and opened the door for him to pass. He ducked low, so as not to hit Grace's head. Once inside they were immediately greeted by a redheaded woman with green eyes and a rich Irish accent.

Clint pulled Grace from his shoulders and set her on the floor beside him. He held tight to the little girl's hand and smiled at the lady. Grace chattered happily, probably telling him that this woman had an accent just like his housekeeper, Mrs. Murphy.

"Hello, Laura." The woman reached out and touched Hope's fine blond curls. "Who is this sweet little lamb?"

Laura's lips tipped into a soft smile. "Pearl, I'd like you to meet Hope."

"Hope?" Fine red eyebrows went up into the woman's hairline. "Now that's a pretty name."

What was this? If Laura really was the schoolteacher, wouldn't everyone know the child? Especially since this little girl was at least a year old? He'd assumed Hope was her daughter. Had he assumed wrong?

Chapter Three

Laura smiled at her friend. "Yes, Hope. I'll tell you more about her tomorrow morning. Maybe we can grab a cup of coffee and a sweet roll?"

Pearl looked to the handsome man standing beside Laura and nodded. "I would enjoy that."

Confusion lined Clint's forehead as he looked from her to Pearl. His gaze shifted to Hope and then back up to Laura. She sighed, knowing he had questions about the little girl who snuggled against her as if seeking assurance that she wasn't going anywhere.

"If you two will follow me, I'll get you a quiet corner in the back." Pearl grabbed two menus and began leading the way.

Laura followed Pearl, aware that Clint and Grace followed her. She wondered how much Hope and Grace would understand when she explained Hope's circumstances to the rancher.

Pearl stopped beside a small square table with four chairs and asked, "Is this all right?"

Clint nodded. He helped Grace into one of the chairs. Laura was aware of the muscles that worked across his shoulders as she helped Hope into her chair. She pulled her gaze away from him and focused on the place settings in front of her.

Pearl ran a respectable restaurant and made sure that each table had nice place settings. The linens were clean and the food always good.

Once they were seated, Pearl handed them menus. "Today's special is roast beef sandwiches and fried potatoes. What can I get you to drink?"

Laura answered, "Hope and I will have milk, please." She looked to Clint.

He grinned up at Pearl. "I'd like a hot cup of coffee for myself and a glass of milk for Grace."

For the first time, Laura allowed herself to really examine him. His rich brown hair curled about his collar as if it had a mind of its own. The deep richness of his hair seemed to pull the bottomless blue from his eyes. He was muscular and lean. A working man.

Laura's gaze moved to Pearl, who still stood beside their table. The other woman seemed captivated by the blue of his eyes, as well. She smiled like a schoolgirl at him. A soft pink filled her cheeks in just the few moments she'd been standing there.

Laura cleared her throat. "Hope and I will share the special. Can I substitute mashed potatoes with gravy for the fried potatoes?"

As if taken by surprise, Pearl jumped. "I'll, uh, go get your drinks."

Pearl hadn't heard anything she'd said. Laura shook her head in amusement. Mr. Shepard was a nice-looking man, but personally she didn't see him as a distraction.

Laura turned to make sure Hope was behaving. The little girl had decided to stand up in the chair and reach across the table to take Grace's hands in hers. "No, sweetie. We do not stand in chairs." Laura gently sat her back down. She handed Hope the ball of yarn from her handbag, then gave Grace a spoon that rested on a napkin beside her plate. The little girls immediately began to play with their items.

Clint chuckled. "You have a way with children, Mrs. Lee."

"I'm a schoolteacher, Mr. Shepard. It's my job to have a way with children." She smiled to take the sting out of her words.

Pearl returned with their drinks and a basket of bread. She placed each person's drink in front of them and the bread in the center of the table. "I have your order going in the kitchen, Laura, but I seem to have forgotten to take yours, Mr.—?" She turned and smiled sweetly at Clint.

"Shepard. Grace and I will share the special also, but I'd like to add a steak to my order." He smiled up at her, flashing white teeth in her direction.

Laura noticed a small gap in his front two teeth and thought it charming. She quickly turned her attention to the girls. Grace had decided to stand up in her chair and help herself to the bread. Laura took the bread from her and frowned. "Grace, sit down, please."

Clint turned at the sharpness of her voice. He started to say something, but Laura stopped him with a stern look. If he wanted her to help him with the child, he'd have to let her do it her way. He turned back to Pearl. Grace was a handful, and because she'd never had a mother, he'd let her get away with much more than he probably should have. "I'd like that steak cooked medium well."

Laura focused on Grace. When the little girl was seated once more, she tore the slice of bread in half and gave each of the girls their portion.

Grace babbled, "Tant too," then tore into the bread with her tiny teeth.

Hope smiled and did the same.

"I'll be right back with your orders," Pearl stammered as she backed away from the table.

Laura giggled. Pearl was clearly smitten by Clint Shepard.

He turned and looked at her and the girls. "What is so funny?"

She leaned forward. "I do believe you have an admirer, Mr. Shepard."

Clint frowned. "I'm not interested."

Laura sat back and studied him. "Why not? Pearl is an attractive woman with her own business. Most men fall all over themselves for her attention."

He shook his head. "I suppose I'm not most men." He pulled the napkin off the table and tucked it into the front of his shirt.

"I suppose not." She looked to where Pearl could be seen pouring coffee into one of the local lumbermen's cups. The man looked as smitten with Pearl as she had with Clint.

"Mind if I ask you a question?" Clint asked, reaching for a slice of the bread.

Laura knew what he wanted to know. "Does it have anything to do with being Grace's nanny?"

"Yes and no." He bit off a chunk of the bread and chewed.

She smoothed her napkin on her lap and nodded.

Clint leaned across the table and asked in a very low voice, "Is Hope your daughter? Or not?"

Laura sighed. "Yes and no."

He chuckled. "I see. Which is it?"

She took the note from her bag and handed it across the table. Laura watched his blue eyes scan the paper. He looked to her and quirked an eyebrow.

"As you can read, that paper says she is. I spoke to the sheriff this morning and he confirmed that she is mine, at least for the time being. He's searching for her parents, and when the judge arrives next month, well, he'll have the final say." Laura held out her hand for the note. The last thing she wanted to do was lose that piece of paper. It was the only thing that proved Hope had been given to her.

Clint handed it over. Pearl walked back to the table with her arms laden with plates. Laura waited until the other woman left and asked, "Does this make a difference in your job offer?"

"No, if Matt thinks you are fit to take care of one little girl and the school board has placed the care of all the children in the community to you, who am I to say you aren't fit to be a mother and a nanny?" He spooned potatoes onto Grace's plate.

Laura smiled. "Thank you." She prepared Hope's plate. She prayed the circuit judge thought the same way as Clint Shepard.

"Does that mean you will take the job?" He cut the sandwich into four pieces and handed one of them to Grace.

"Maybe, but I still want to pray about it this afternoon before I decide, Mr. Shepard. I'm sure I will have an answer for you tonight or first thing in the morning." Laura knew she needed to pray before making this important decision even though she felt comfortable with Clint Shepard and his daughter.

He nodded. "Speaking of prayer, how about I bless this food and let's eat?"

She smiled. "That would be very nice, thank you." Laura listened to his short blessing and knew that he was her answer from God. With the job Clint Shepard offered, she'd have enough money come summer to buy a small house for her and Hope to live in. If the judge let her keep Hope.

After lunch, Laura took Hope to the doctor. The little girl sat on Laura's lap while Dr. Stewart shone a light into her ears. He whispered into her ears, first the left, then her right. She responded as long as he stayed on the right side of her. Laura watched, fascinated with Dr. McAlester's manner of learning about the child's hearing.

He stood and looked at Laura. "This little girl doesn't hear with her left ear. Her right seems to be fine, but I think you'll need to make sure that you are on her right side, if you want her to hear you." He picked up a candle and tilted Hope's head to the right so that he could see into the left.

Concern filled Laura. Could Hope function like any other child, when she could only hear with one ear? "What can we do? Is this something we can fix?"

Dr. McAlester shook his head. "I'm just a country doctor, not one of those fancy city docs with lots of new equipment, but from what I can see…" He bent down and shone a light into the little girl's ear once more. "Her ear is grown up on the inside." His gaze met Laura's as he stood. "A city doctor might be willing to

try going in and cutting that layer of skin, but I'm not."
He set the candle on the table beside him and sighed.

"I see."

Dr. McAlester said, "She doesn't seem to be in any pain and isn't running a temperature. Mrs. Lee, I believe little Hope can have a long, good life with hearing in just one ear." He grinned at her. "Us old folks do it all the time." His light blue eyes and silver hair gave him a friendly look that set most of his patients at ease.

Shock at his words had Laura gasping, "You can't hear with both ears?"

"'Fraid not. Gun went off too close to my ear a few years back, and I still have a ringing in it, but no other sound can get through. Haven't you noticed I turn my head slightly to the left when I want to hear what you're saying?"

She shook her head. "No, sir. I hadn't."

Dr. McAlester put a gentle hand on her shoulder. "Little Hope will adapt, too. I believe this is a result of what we call a birth defect. She doesn't even realize she can't hear in one ear." He patted Hope on the head. "You can always take her to the big city and let one of those doctors look at her."

Laura stood. "Maybe when she's older." She didn't tell him that she couldn't make that decision right now. It wasn't hers to make, at least not until the judge came to town and gave her that right. So many decisions would need to be made when that happened.

Laura returned to the boardinghouse with a heavy heart. She and Hope both weren't complete. Hope couldn't hear, and Laura couldn't have children. Bitterly she thought, it was up to her to make a life for herself and the child. What man in his right mind would take her as a wife and Hope as a daughter?

Clint pulled the wagon to the front of the boarding-house. Relief washed over him at the sight of Laura standing at the door. She hadn't changed her mind. Several bags and a couple of large boxes rested about her feet, and if he wasn't mistaken, that was a writing desk on the porch.

The night before, shortly after dinner, Laura had expressed her desire to take the job of being a nanny to little Grace, with the understanding that she'd only do so until school resumed. He'd assured her that he'd begin looking for another nanny when it got closer to time for her to leave.

Hope's head rested on Laura's shoulder, and the little girl grinned sweetly at him. His gaze traveled downward to his own child. Grace held Laura's other hand tightly. The schoolteacher might be just what Grace needed in her life.

He leaped from the wagon. "Right on time, ladies." Clint winked at Grace.

"You did say to be ready by eight, didn't you?" Laura asked. Confusion laced her pretty features.

He picked up several of the bags. "I did. If you will get the girls in the wagon, I'll load up these bags." There weren't as many as he'd expected. His wife, Martha, had always taken everything with them, even for the short trip to town. Clint pushed thoughts of Martha away and carried the bags to the wagon.

"Very well. Come along, children." With her head held high, Laura led the girls to the wagon. She sat Hope on the seat, then bent down and picked up Grace.

Clint watched Grace touch Laura's hair. His little girl smiled at Laura and patted her cheek, much like she did his to show her affection. Clint forced himself to look away from the sweet scene. His heart ached that Grace would never know a mother's love. She deserved a mother, but he couldn't see himself ever taking another wife.

Grace's baby chatter filled the crisp morning air. He grinned as he set the bags into the already partially full wagon.

Laura answered as she set the child in the bed of the wagon. "Of course, Hope can sit with you, but you have to be a big girl and stay seated on the way home."

Grace babbled something and nodded.

"Good girl." She pulled Hope from the bench and set her beside Grace. Then she turned to him. "I hope you don't mind, but I packed a few of my school books, and I also brought along my writing desk." Her gaze moved to a wooden crate. "I plan to work on my schoolroom lessons, and there are a couple of new novels that I want to read during the break."

"I don't mind." Clint hurried to grab the last two carpetbags and the box that he assumed held the books. His surprise at the weight of the crate must have shown on his face.

Laura asked, "Do you think I might have overpacked the box?"

Clint grunted as he picked up the crate. He'd exaggerated a bit with the sound but not much. "Naw, it's not the least bit heavy."

To his surprise, Laura laughed. It sounded warm and low, not your typical giggle. He found himself grinning at her over the box.

She looked away first. "Would you like for me to ask Mrs. Potter for a lunch box to take on the trip while you load the desk?"

Clint shook his head. "No, if all goes well we should be arriving at the ranch around noon. Mrs. Murphy will have something for us to eat." At her doubt-filled look, he continued, "I'm sure."

Laura nodded. "Very well. I'll go inside and see if there is anything I've left behind." The door shut softly behind her.

He turned to look at the two little girls who were peeking between the slats in the wall of the wagon. "What are you two big-eyed calves looking at?" Clint asked as he pushed the book box into the wagon bed.

Grace giggled and Hope smiled broadly.

Clint finished loading the wagon and then dug under the bench for the blanket that he kept there. He laid it behind the seat and then put both the girls on top of it. His gaze moved to the house. What was taking her so long? Clint moved the bags and the boxes of purchases he'd made while in town to form a line to block the girls in between the bags and the back of the seat.

Then, Clint untied his horse from the back of the wagon and swung into the saddle. Laura Lee had said she was capable of driving the wagon to the ranch. He leaned against the saddle horn and waited.

His gaze moved to the boardinghouse. So far, everything was going well. Laura seemed to be the perfect nanny for Grace, and he could finally get back to work with no worries about Grace's care or his housekeeper leaving.

Chapter Four

A few hours later, Clint topped the hill that looked down on his home. For a brief moment, he stopped and enjoyed the view. The house was about a quarter mile from the river that ran across his property. The river supplied water for the fields, livestock and the family. A well had been built a few years earlier, closer to the house so that the women didn't have to go to the river every day.

Large fruit trees stood in the orchard at the back of the house. He grinned as his gaze moved to the front yard where he'd rigged up a small swing in the oak tree for Grace.

Laura's soft, stern voice drew his attention. "Grace, you need to sit down. We're not quite there yet."

With a frown, Grace did as she was told. She was two and a handful. After being cooped up in the wagon all morning, Grace was ready to get out and play. Hope lay curled in a ball beside her, sound asleep.

He led the way down the hill and home. A few minutes later, Laura pulled the wagon up in front of his ranch home. Clint had come to realize that unlike

Grace, Laura wasn't a big talker. She'd spoken softly to the girls during the trip and was very observant of her surroundings but didn't force a conversation between them.

What did the schoolteacher think of his home? He turned to look at her. She stared at the house but didn't say anything. Grace stood once more and began babbling with excitement.

Her gaze broke from the house. "Hold on, Grace. I know you want out of the wagon." She looked down at Hope.

Clint tried to envision his home from her perspective. The house was built in the typical farmhouse style. Long with windows positioned to catch the most sunlight during the day. He and his hired man, Richard, had whitewashed it a few weeks ago, so it looked fresh and clean.

The vegetable garden was off to the right, the barn and chicken coop to the left. A wide front porch offered shade in the afternoons along with the tall apple tree that grew a few yards away.

He expected that most women would be gushing and telling him what a beautiful home he had, but not Mrs. Lee. She simply tended to the little girls. Clint frowned. What did it matter what she thought? Laura Lee would only be here a few weeks, and then she'd be returning to her schoolhouse and town. Clint told himself it didn't matter, but for some odd reason, it did.

He leaped from his horse and tied it to the rail in front of the porch. Then he hurried to the wagon where he kissed the top of Grace's head before continuing around the wagon to help Laura down. "I hope you are happy here during your stay." Clint took her hand in his to help her down. The warmth and softness sent a spark of awareness up his arm.

Once her feet were securely on the ground, Laura gently pulled her hand from his. "I'm sure I will be." She turned to the wagon.

Grace jabbered excitedly as she waited for him to lift her out. Her impatience pulled Clint from the wonder of Laura's eyes and touch. He scooped his sweet daughter up and set her on the ground. She toddled toward the house, babbling happily.

Laura gently woke Hope and then helped her from the wagon. She hugged the little girl close and then sat her on the ground. A smile brightened Laura's face as she watched the little girl waddle after her new friend.

Grace stopped and waited for Hope. She took Hope's small hand in her own and then continued to the porch. Neither adult understood a word Grace said, but Hope nodded sleepily with a grin.

Laura turned to him. "They are so sweet together."

Clint gathered several of the bags from the wagon and followed the girls. His mind was on the connection he'd briefly felt while holding Laura's hand. Had she felt it, too? If she had, she hadn't shown it. Was he making too much of it? He hadn't felt that kind of connection since his wife. Clint swallowed hard.

He would ignore the feeling. His heart couldn't take another breaking like the one he'd felt the day Grace's mother had died. Clint silently vowed never to feel such pain again. Never.

Laura waited until Clint continued to the house. She released the pent-up breath in her lungs. Had he felt the electrical current between them? Or was she just being hypersensitive? So much had happened since the previous morning, Laura didn't know what to think of this newfound feeling.

She turned at the sound of Grace's excited squeal. "MumMum!"

A middle-aged woman with red hair and sparkling green eyes stepped through the front door. She smiled sweetly at Grace, who had grabbed her skirt and was hugging her legs. "Well, hello, wee one." She leaned over to hug the child close.

Hope stood beside Grace looking confused. She glanced back at Laura until Grace grabbed her hand and jerked her forward.

Grace babbled up at the redheaded woman and pointed at Hope.

She nodded. "I see. We have another wee one underfoot." A sprig of red hair mixed with gray at her temples escaped the thick braid that ran down her back. Her sharp green gaze seemed to pierce Clint Shepard.

Laura straightened her shoulders, scooped up two of her bags and walked to the porch. She sat her luggage down on the edge of the wood.

Before she could introduce herself and Hope, Clint said, "Mrs. Murphy, this is Laura Lee. She's Grace's new nanny."

Clint walked back to the wagon.

Mrs. Murphy's gaze moved over her, studying her, evaluating her. "Is the wee one yours?" She looked down at Hope, who had plopped down on the porch and was now trying to pick up a small insect.

Laura shook her head. "It's nice to meet you, Mrs. Murphy. Please feel free to call me Laura."

"Mrs. Lee, if the wee one isn't yours, whose is

she?" Confusion pulled at the skin between Mrs. Murphy's eyes.

Laura was very aware that Mrs. Murphy wasn't pleased with Clint's choice of nanny. The sharpness in her tone and the way her gaze moved over Laura as if evaluating her spoke volumes of her displeasure. What had the older woman expected?

"Mrs. Murphy, don't you think that is a bit personal?" Clint asked, walking back to them. He carried another bag and what appeared to be a box of kitchen supplies.

She huffed. "Not if she's going to be living here. She could have stolen the child for all I know."

Laura felt a rush of irritation at the woman's rude behavior. She pulled her shoulders back and held her head high. "No, I most certainly did not steal Hope. I have a letter stating she is in my care." She picked up Hope. The little girl snuggled her face into Laura's neck.

Clint walked around the women and continued inside. "I'll show Mrs. Lee and Hope to their rooms."

Laura set a wiggling Hope back down and picked up the bags she'd discarded earlier. Then she followed Mrs. Murphy and the girls inside.

Mrs. Murphy's voice stopped him. "You'll do no such thing."

He turned to face her. "Mrs. Murphy, she's staying."

"Perhaps so, but it isn't proper for you to be in her room." The Irishwoman's green eyes dared him to argue with her.

What kind of relationship did these two people have? Was Mrs. Murphy hired help? Or a part of the family? Laura watched as the two stared at each other. The muscles worked in Clint's jaw. His eyes never left

Mrs. Murphy's as he said, "Then you show her to her room, and I'll finish unloading the wagon."

Mrs. Murphy nodded curtly and then turned to Laura. "If you will follow me." She didn't wait for Laura to agree. Her skirt swished as she walked briskly down a hall. "Your rooms are behind the kitchen. I told Clint he didn't have to give up his room, but he insisted. It will be warm for the children come winter."

If he'd given up his room, where was Clint staying? Not that it should matter to her, but Laura couldn't help but wonder why he'd give up his room for the hired help.

"I don't intend to be here that long," Laura answered.

Mrs. Murphy stopped so fast that it took all Laura could do not to run over her. "What's this you say?"

"Hope and I will only be here a few months, then I'll be returning to my job in town." Laura shifted the bags in her arms.

"Your job in town?" She crossed her arms and waited for Laura to answer.

"Yes, ma'am. I'm the schoolteacher."

Mrs. Murphy nodded and then continued down the hall. She stopped in front of a closed door. "These are your rooms." Ice seemed to drip from her voice. She opened the door and took a step back.

Who was the woman angry at? Her? Or Clint for hiring someone who wasn't going to be permanent?

Laura followed Grace and Hope into the room. It was larger than she'd expected and felt warm and inviting. A large bed rested against the far wall. Other pieces of furniture filled the room. But it was obvious from the lack of lacy curtains, pretty rugs and of any type of feminine touch that this was a man's room.

"Lunch will be in a few minutes." Mrs. Murphy spun around and headed back down the hallway.

Grace and Hope toddled about the room. Hope seemed to take in each and every new item that Grace appeared to be showing her. Laura walked to the window and looked outside. A tall tree stood beside the window, offering shade and the potential of cool summer breezes. She turned back to the room and noticed another door to the side.

Hadn't Mrs. Murphy said "rooms?" Laura walked across the hardwood floor and opened the door. She was pleasantly surprised to find a small dressing room with a big chair and bookshelf inside. The room also contained a child-sized bed. A chest rested at the foot of the bed, and dolls and stuffed animals sat on its top. It was obvious that this was Grace's room.

Grace followed and babbled off something. Pretending as if she understood her, Laura answered, "I like your room, too, Grace. But I'm thinking it might be nice if Hope shared your room with you. Would that be all right with you?"

The little girl nodded and babbled away to Hope. She hurried across the room and picked up a small stuffed dog and brought it back to Hope.

Hope smiled at Grace and hugged the toy to her chest. Laura grinned. If Grace was a normal two-year-old, and Laura knew that she was, she'd be demanding her doggie back soon enough. While the girls played, Laura quickly unpacked the bags she'd brought inside. The top two drawers were empty, and her and Hope's few belongings fit nicely.

Just as she turned to gather the girls up to go get another bag and her box of books, Mrs. Murphy arrived with both. She set the crate of books inside the door and placed Hope's small bag on top, then turned without speaking and left. That book box was heavy, but evidently Mrs. Murphy was stronger than she'd first appeared.

As a schoolteacher, Laura occasionally dealt with unhappy parents and decided to treat Mrs. Murphy as one. The older woman made it more than obvious that she wasn't happy with Clint's choice in nannies. But what choice had he had? It wasn't like there were a slew of unmarried women about who needed a job out in the middle of nowhere. Laura put away the remaining few belongings she'd purchased earlier for Hope.

Taking a deep breath, she picked up Hope and grabbed Grace's hand. "Let's go have lunch, ladies."

Grace chattered as they walked back to the front of the house. Laura wished she could understand the little girl, but since she couldn't she simply smiled and nodded a lot. Hope giggled down at Grace.

The smell of frying ham greeted her as she rounded the corner to the kitchen. Mrs. Murphy stood at the stove, turning the meat over with a long fork. She frowned as Laura and the girls entered the room.

"Is there anything I can help you with?" Laura asked as she sat Hope down on one of the chairs that surrounded an oblong table.

Her Irish accent filled the kitchen with authority. "No, my job is to cook. Yours is to take care of Grace."

Laura nodded. "Yes, but I don't mind helping out."

Mrs. Murphy turned from the stove. She shook the

fork at her. "If you want to help, keep the children out of my kitchen until you are called."

So that was how it was going to be. Laura tilted her head to the side and studied the older woman. Why was she so unhappy? Had she hoped Clint couldn't find a nanny? If so, why not? Or, was she simply worried Laura would become even more important to Clint and Grace and she wouldn't be needed? Or, as she'd thought earlier, was she angry that Clint had hired a temporary nanny and not a full-time one?

Mrs. Murphy dropped her eyes and returned to the sizzling ham.

"Come along, girls." If Mrs. Murphy didn't want her in the kitchen, Laura vowed not to return until asked. As stubborn as the woman seemed, Laura had a feeling that would be the last time she saw the interior of the kitchen for the remainder of her stay.

Grace and Hope each took one of her hands and they left the warmth of the room. Laura hated that she wouldn't be allowed to cook or help out while she was here. It shouldn't matter to her. Her job was to care for Grace. But it did matter. For some reason, it mattered a lot.

Chapter Five

Clint sighed and ran his hand through his hair. After finishing his evening chores, he found Mrs. Murphy waiting on the porch for him. She sat in one of the two rockers. He greeted her kindly. "Good evening, Mrs. Murphy." He was bone-tired, and all he wanted was to crawl into his bed.

He'd stayed close to the house all day and tried to make the arrival of another woman easy on Mrs. Murphy. It didn't make sense that she was upset with the arrangement. She was the one who had insisted on him getting a nanny for Grace. But it was obvious that the Irishwoman wasn't happy.

"You have got to talk to that woman."

Clint blew air out of his lungs before asking, "About?"

"Leaving in the morning and getting another job."

Was the woman insane? They needed Laura, and from what he'd witnessed throughout the day, Grace liked her. "Look, Mrs. Murphy. I'm not firing Mrs. Lee. You said you didn't want to take care of Grace, so

I went to town and got a nanny. Now you are upset that I did as you asked. What is it that has you all riled up?"

Mrs. Murphy rocked the rocking chair even harder. "She brought another child in the house. I told you I didn't want children underfoot. I'm too old for such shenanigans."

"You aren't that old and they won't be underfoot. Mrs. Lee will be taking care of them." His frustration and tiredness was making him sound crankier than an old bull.

"She wanted to help in the kitchen at lunch, and you heard her after supper. She offered to clean off the table." Mrs. Murphy continued sewing on either an item of clothing or a quilt.

Clint wasn't sure which and he really didn't care. He grumbled, "I don't see the problem. Most women would be happy to have added help."

Her head came up so quickly, Clint feared she'd snap her neck. "I don't want help. I'm quite capable of running the household and cooking meals."

Clint pushed away from the porch post he'd been leaning on. "I'll talk to her and make sure she knows that you don't want or need her help. But I am not firing her. Grace likes Mrs. Lee. That's reason enough to keep her on."

Mrs. Murphy huffed. "I imagine it don't hurt that she's a pretty little thing, either."

He stopped at the door. "Mrs. Lee's looks have nothing to do with her taking care of Grace." Clint yawned and opened the door. He heard Mrs. Murphy muttering behind him but chose to ignore her.

Making his way across the room, Clint tried to figure out what the real reason was that Mrs. Murphy didn't like Laura. It couldn't be that she'd brought Hope. As far as he could tell, the schoolteacher only wanted to help. She'd taken care of both the little girls' plates during supper and offered to help Mrs. Murphy with the cleanup. It looked to him as though the two women should be getting along swimmingly.

He entered his room and pulled his boots off. It was times like these that he missed his wife and ma. Before his ma's death, the two women had gotten along like sisters. He'd guess that Mrs. Murphy and Mrs. Lee were about the same ages as his ma and wife. So why couldn't they get along as well?

Clint pulled on a fresh pair of socks and then walked the short distance to his old bedroom. Proper or not, he intended to say good-night to Grace. Just as he got to the door, it opened and Laura stepped out, holding Grace on her hip.

"Papa!" Grace held her arms out to him. His normally cheerful child had tearstains on her cheeks.

He took her in his arms and looked to Laura over the little girl's head. Clint stroked Grace's tiny back. "What's wrong, Gracie?"

Laura answered, "She is missing you. Is this the first time she's slept without you in the room next to her?"

Clint nodded. He pulled Grace back and looked into her sad eyes. "Gracie, did you think I wouldn't come say good-night?"

The little girl nodded, and fresh tears began silently flowing down her face once more. Grace tucked a tiny index finger between her lips and sucked on it, a sure sign she was distressed.

"Baby, I will always say good-night when I'm home." He cuddled his daughter against his chest. What was he going to do? It wasn't proper for him to enter Laura's room, but to put Grace back to bed, he'd need to do just that.

As if sensing his dilemma, Laura spoke. "Mr. Shepard, if I might make a suggestion." Laura laid a soft hand against his forearm.

He nodded, noticing for the first time that Laura's hair hung about her shoulders in what looked like a soft cloud. Her pretty eyes studied his face for several moments, and then she continued.

"Perhaps I should sleep in your room tonight and you return to your old room. That way you will be close to Grace. Hope and I will sleep in your new room tonight, and tomorrow we can make the switch. Since I'm not staying long, it's only fair to the child that we not disrupt her routine any more than necessary."

Clint frowned. If he understood correctly, she wanted him to take his room back, and she and Hope would take the guest room down the hall. The way she'd said it sounded confusing, but he thought he understood. "I don't know."

Laura's sweet soft laughter filled him. "Well, I do. I'll get Hope, and then you can show us our new quarters." She turned and left him standing in the hallway, hugging Grace and feeling perplexed. What was it with bossy women? Between Laura Lee and Mrs. Murphy, he had lost all control over his household.

The next morning, Clint felt like a million dollars as he walked down the hall toward breakfast. For the first time in several days he'd slept well. The sun hadn't made an appearance yet, and Grace slept soundly in her little bed. Life was good.

Laura had been right the night before when she'd told him both he and Grace would sleep better with him in his room. He'd shown her to the spare bedroom where she carried an already sleeping Hope and placed her on the bed. She'd assured him she'd sleep fine with the child, but his plans today were to make the child a bed of her own. It wouldn't take much, just a little wood and some nails, and he'd have a bed like Grace's ready before nightfall.

He entered the kitchen. The smell of bacon, eggs and fresh coffee filled the warm space. "Good morning, Mrs. Murphy."

She nodded in his direction. "Hope you slept well last night."

"I did." Clint contemplated telling her that he and Laura had exchanged bedrooms the night before, but then felt it wasn't something he wanted to discuss with her. It might seem cowardly to some, but he'd let Laura handle any questions the older woman might have.

"Well, I still think it was a bad idea to sleep away from our Grace. She probably didn't sleep nearly as soundly as you did."

He chuckled. "The child probably slept better than you think." Clint should correct her, but dab nab it, this was his home, and he didn't have to answer to his housekeeper.

A moment of remorse hit him like an old mule's kick. Mrs. Murphy wasn't just a housekeeper. During the last two years, she'd stuck with him, kept him and Grace fed and cleaned. First, she'd taken care of his late wife and then them. She deserved to know what had happened the night before. "You can rest your mind regarding the child. Mrs. Lee and I exchanged rooms last night. Grace wasn't taking to my not being there."

A grin formed on the older woman's face. "Good. That woman might have some sense after all."

"Well, that wasn't the nicest thing to say about Mrs. Lee. She's very intelligent, kind and thoughtful." He picked up his favorite cup and filled it with coffee.

She turned back to the stove and pulled out fresh biscuits. "You're right. I haven't been fair to the school-teacher. I'll do better."

"MumMum!"

How long had Laura been standing in the doorway with Grace and Hope? Had she heard his defense of her? Or Mrs. Murphy's declaration to treat her differently?

Nothing on her face gave away her thoughts or feelings. Laura asked, "Is breakfast served in here or the main room?"

Mrs. Murphy hugged Grace against her leg. "Breakfast is always in here."

Laura's eyes widened. Was she surprised that the other woman could speak in a nice, calm voice? Or that breakfast was always in the kitchen?

Clint shook his head and walked to the table. He placed his cup on the wood and knelt beside the table for his morning hug from his Gracie. It might look strange to Laura Lee, but he didn't care.

Grace saw him and quickly released Mrs. Murphy. Her little chubby legs carried her to Clint. He grabbed her close and hugged. This was his favorite time of the morning.

Hope watched.

Clint extended an arm out to the little girl. Like

Grace, her real mother was gone. Did the little girl understand? Or was she too young to realize that she'd been given away like a freshly made cake?

The little girl toddled over to him. She fell into his embrace and giggled along with Grace.

His gaze met Laura's. Her eyes seemed softer, as if cushioned with unshed tears. Were her thoughts on the fact that Hope's mother and father were missing?

From the looks of things, Hope needed a father figure, and Laura needed a friend. The silly thought came to him that he'd be here for both of them for as long as they needed him.

Clint gently released the girls and stood. The two girls looked up at him. He placed each of them on to a chair at the kitchen table, very aware that the two women watched his every move. He took a sip of coffee, and the bitterness coated his tongue. What had he gotten himself into, with four ladies in his house and not one man to help him muddle through the awkward times?

A couple of days later, Laura stood back and watched the girls splash water at each other. They both had smelled like hot little puppies when she'd decided they needed a good scrubbing. She glanced up to see Mrs. Murphy standing in the kitchen doorway.

Dread filled her. The other woman hadn't been mean, but she'd definitely been rude on more than one occasion. Laura put a smile on her face and said, "I hope you don't mind. The girls needed a good bath."

Mrs. Murphy returned her smile. "As long as you clean up after them, I'm fine with them taking a bath. My husband used to say, 'Cleanliness is next to godliness.'" She chuckled. "I think the dear soul really believed that one was in the Bible."

Laura couldn't help but grin at the familiar saying. "I'll have it cleaned up in a jiffy in here."

The other woman waved her hand. "There isn't any rush." She came farther into the kitchen. "I just came in to stir the beans and ham hock." She laid a worn Bible on the kitchen table.

It was good to see that the Irishwoman read from the book. Laura Lee held her own Bible study every morning before the children awoke. She didn't believe she would survive a day without reading the Word first thing.

The little girls played happily in the water. Their big eyes and smiles filled their tiny faces. This was the first time Clint had been gone from the house all day. Laura had worried Grace would fret, but the little girl hadn't.

The fragrance of ham filled the kitchen. Laura thought about mentioning that she could make a mean pan of cornbread to go with the beans and ham hock, but changed her mind. It had been a long time since she'd cooked, and over the last few days she'd learned that Mrs. Murphy wasn't the sort who would let another woman work in her kitchen.

Mrs. Murphy replaced the lid on the bean pot, sat down in one of the kitchen chairs and watched the girls. "Which do you think I should make? Biscuits or corn bread?" She didn't take her eyes off the children.

Was she trying to make up for her shortness of the last few days? Laura tilted her head to the side. "Whichever is easier for you."

The older woman laughed. "That's a very good answer, but which one do you have—" she tried to imitate a cowboy tone "—a hankerin' for?"

Laura laughed. The Irishwoman joined in, and the children splashed and giggled all the harder.

When everyone had settled down, Laura answered, "That was the funniest imitation I have ever heard. I think corn bread would be a good choice, if you don't mind."

"No, I don't mind. Corn bread was what I was thinking, too."

"Good. I…" Laura stopped. She'd almost offered to help again, but decided against it. Mrs. Murphy seemed to be in a pleasant mood, and there was no reason to spoil it.

She helped Grace from the tub of lukewarm water. "Come on, pumpkin. Let's get you dressed."

Grace giggled and kicked her feet as Laura wrapped a clean towel around her. Mrs. Murphy scooped Hope from the bathwater and proceeded to towel her dry, as well.

"You really don't have to do that, Mrs. Murphy. I don't want the girls to be a bother to you, at all."

She towel-dried Hope's curly hair. "It's no bother. And please, call me Camelia."

Laura sat back on her heels. "So now you want to help with the girls?"

Camelia sat back also. Her gaze met Laura's, and honesty shone through her words. "I'm sorry. I haven't behaved in a very Christian manner since you've been here. I'm new to this Christian life and don't always act correctly. I love Gracie, but I just don't have the patience I used to with children. Or adults, for that matter, but I'm trying to do better." Her gaze moved to the Bible on the table.

Laura continued drying Grace's little arms. "I know what you mean. I'm not always good with adults, either. I love children, but oftentimes their parents set my teeth on edge." The two women shared knowing grins. Then Laura pressed on. "Maybe we can work together and learn from each other."

Laura held her breath while she pulled Grace's little dress over her head. What would Camelia think of her suggestion? Laura wanted to befriend the woman. Honestly, she'd never had a woman friend that she could talk and work with. Most women didn't have time for a widow or friendship. Would Camelia?

Chapter Six

Clint's back ached, his hips hurt and his legs felt full of lead. He'd started the day checking on his herd of cows and the two bulls in the west pasture. Then in the afternoon, he'd plowed the east field and ended the work day with feeding the cows and calves again and checking on the ones that would have calves soon.

His thoughts had been preoccupied during the day with Laura and Grace. What were they doing? The schoolteacher had brought lots of books, and even though Grace was only two, Laura had started showing her the books and asking her questions such as "What color is this?" And pointing to pictures of fruit trees and asking questions like, "How many apples are in the tree?" And other stuff like that. Mrs. Murphy had criticized Laura's attempts at educating the little girls. Personally, he'd found it interesting.

Clint hated that the two women didn't seem to get along. He'd tried to soften the verbal blows that Mrs. Murphy had rained upon Laura. He felt the tension in the air and wondered if the little girls could feel it, too. Laura had said she didn't mind Mrs. Murphy's rude behavior, but he could tell it was wearing on her.

He both dreaded and looked forward to going to the house. A hot meal and soft bed were welcomed, but what would the atmosphere with the ladies in the house be like? He'd gone from having two females in the house to having four, not an easy transition. Clint knew he'd have to have another talk with his house-keeper and he dreaded it.

Richard met him outside the barn. "I'll take your horse, Clint."

"Thanks." He swung from the saddle with a groan. His gaze moved to the front of the house. "How have things been here today?"

"Pretty quiet. The ladies have been inside most of the day. Mrs. Murphy threw bathwater out the back door earlier."

"Bathwater?" A grin split his face.

Richard nodded. "Yep."

Just as he'd thought, Laura Lee was a woman who believed in cleanliness. Thank the Lord! He had no-ticed that Grace had begun to smell a little ripe but hadn't wanted to be the one to give her a bath. He didn't know how the little girl could manage it, but every time he'd given her a good scrubbing, he'd come out of the ordeal almost as wet as she did.

With a lighter step, he turned toward the house. "Thanks, Richard. I'll see that you get a piece of Mrs. Murphy's dessert tonight."

"Don't know what I did to deserve that, but I'll take it. Thanks, boss." Richard whistled as he disappeared into the barn.

Clint was happy Grace had received her bath but

wasn't sure it was time for him to start whistling just yet. He'd skipped lunch, and his belly gave a growl of displeasure at the missed meal. Thankfully, Mrs. Murphy hadn't stopped cooking good meals, but after their meeting tonight, she might. He couldn't let her continue to treat Laura badly. The young woman had done nothing to warrant the older woman's mean spiritedness.

Laura's soft laughter drifted through the open window as he approached the house. The little girls squealed their pleasure and then he heard the Irishwoman. Was she telling them a story?

Clint opened the door and entered the house.

Mrs. Murphy chased the little girls about the sitting room, saying in her thick Irish accent, "I'm gonna get you!"

Hope's little legs toddled, and a big grin filled her face. Grace squealed and ran for her father's legs. His daughter grabbed him and turned to Mrs. Murphy with a squeal. Hope grabbed the other leg and plopped down on his boot.

The Irishwoman stopped and looked at him, confused. She then turned to Laura. "Goodness, we've let the time escape us. Come help me get supper on the table, Laura. Clint, you take care of these squealing children." With her head held high, Mrs. Murphy hurried from the room.

Since when had Mrs. Murphy started asking for Laura's help? His gaze moved to the schoolteacher. She shrugged her shoulders at him and followed his housekeeper to the kitchen.

Grace babbled against his leg. He scooped her up and gave her a quick squeeze. In a very low voice he confided in her, "Well, seems a lot has changed since I left this morning."

The child took his face in her little hands and babbled seriously.

Clint couldn't help but laugh. "Child, I'm looking forward to the day when I can understand you."

His gaze moved to the silent Hope. She stood rested against his jean-clad leg, watching them with big eyes. Where was her pa, and why had he and Hope's ma left her on Laura's porch?

Grace pushed against his shoulder, a clear indication that she wanted to be released. He lowered her to the ground and gently picked up Hope. "Hey, sweetie. How are you doing?"

Her finger went straight into her mouth. Hope's eyes widened, but she didn't push away.

He gave her a squeeze much like the one he'd shared with Grace. Hope grinned around her finger and then laid her head on his shoulder.

Clint lost his heart. Now what was he going to do?

Laura stuck her head around the door to the kitchen and called, "Supper's ready. Send the girls in here and go wash up." Her head disappeared around the corner.

Hope raised her head and pushed away from him much like Grace had done moments earlier. He sat her down beside Grace, who had been leaning against his leg.

With his heart in his throat, Clint watched as Grace took Hope's hand in hers and walked toward the kitchen. Just as she got to the door, Grace turned, looked to him and babbled something before going into the kitchen where the other ladies waited.

Once more he felt the pressure of living with four

females. They had begun to boss him around and steal his heart. This wasn't good. Not good at all. If Hope could get into his heart so quickly, Clint knew he needed to stay away from Laura. He'd vowed not to fall in love again after his wife's death. That was one promise Clint intended to keep. No matter how pretty the nanny looked tonight.

They'd been on the ranch now for a week and still no news about Hope's family from the sheriff. Laura couldn't get the image of Clint cuddling Hope close to his shoulder out of her mind. He'd looked genuinely happy to be holding the little girl, and Hope's expression had been one of pure bliss. They seemed to just go together. She'd been trying to push the image out of her mind for days.

Even now, Laura tried to think of something else. But when she did that, her mind would turn to Hope's future. What was going to become of the little girl?

Where were Hope's parents? How could they stand to be away from her for so long? She was a sweet child. Thanks to Grace and her chattiness, Hope now whispered what Laura knew were the beginnings of words.

It was time for Laura to take a trip into town and see if he'd learned anything. She dreaded the thought that Hope's parents could be there, waiting for her to return the child.

"You seem deep in thought."

Laura looked up at Clint. She'd not heard him come up onto the porch. "I was thinking about Hope and the sheriff."

He sat down on the step and leaned his back against the railing. "I've been thinking about them, too."

She looked down at the bowl of potatoes she'd been peeling before her mind had wandered. "You have?"

Clint took his hat off and rested it over his bent knee. He nodded. "Seems to me, you should have heard something from the sheriff."

A slight breeze lifted the hair from his brow. Laura looked away once more. She stared out at the three horses that had been put in the corral closest to the barn. "I think so, too."

He cleared his throat, then said, "If the sheriff doesn't come out soon, would you like to take a trip into town?" He played with the brim of his hat.

"Honestly, I'd rather hide out here, but I suppose I'll need to go talk to him sooner or later." She peeled the potato in her hand and sighed. "I never knew I was such a coward, but where that little girl is concerned, I am."

"What are you afraid of?"

Laura tried to smile at him but failed miserably. She swallowed before answering. "I'm afraid that he'll tell me her ma and pa have been looking for her, and I'll lose her. If only we could stay out here forever and I'd never have to give her up."

"I wish that were possible, too, but the sheriff knows you are out here." He shook his head. "By now, the whole town knows you are out here."

"True." She dropped the last peeled potato into her bowl and stood. "So, I'll face the inevitable." Laura realized he must have had a reason for coming to the house midafternoon. "Did you want to talk to me?"

Clint grinned up at her. He stood also. "I am headed out to the west pasture and thought maybe the girls would like to take a swim in the stream while I check on the fence line."

His grin and the sparkle in his eyes set her heart to doing flip-flops. What was it about this man? Her breath quickened, and she nodded. Thanks to an overly hot spring this year, the water should be perfect for the girls to splash about in. "I'll need to get them up from their afternoon nap. Can you give us a few minutes?"

At his nod, she turned to enter the house.

"Laura?"

She turned back to look at him. "Yes?"

"If you don't want to go, I'll understand. Not all women like roaming around a ranch." A frown replaced the smile. Was he thinking of Grace's mother?

She smiled to ease his concern. "Good thing I'm not one of those women."

He tipped his hat at her. "Then I'll go ask Richard to help me hitch up the wagon."

"Why in the world would you hitch up the wagon for a trip across the pasture?"

Clint tilted his head to the side. "I just thought…"

The frown was back. "I know you did. But honestly, if you don't mind holding Grace in front of you, I'd rather ride out on one of the mares." Laura smiled sweetly. "I've missed riding."

He laughed. Not a soft gentlemanly laugh but a flat-out laugh. It warmed her toes to hear the sound, and lightning bugs started fluttering in the pit of her belly. "Then I'll go saddle the lady a horse." Clint started whistling as he left the porch.

Chapter Seven

Clint gasped at the sight of Laura Lee in a pair of his old trousers as she marched toward him holding each of the girls' hands. She wore a pair of girly boots and the big, floppy sombrero-type hat that Mrs. Murphy wore while gardening. The pants were sagging about her waist and looked as if they would fall to the ground at any moment.

When she came within talking distance, Laura announced, as she looked down at the girls, "If we are going to make a habit of this, I'll need to make Grace and Hope a pair of pants, too. I hope you don't mind, but Mrs. Murphy said that you never wear these anymore and that I could borrow them. I know they are too big, but it will be much easier to ride on the horse and I'll be able to play with the girls in the water without fear of my skirts weighing me down when they get wet."

Her words came out faster than he'd ever heard her speak. Even Grace looked up at her with wide, amazed eyes. Laura's cheeks were pink when she finally raised her gaze to look at him. Was she embarrassed to be wearing men's pants? Or did she think he'd be angry at her for doing so? His wife, Martha, would have fainted if anyone had even suggested she wear pants.

He couldn't stop the grin that spread across his face. Clint walked about her and clicked his tongue. "Seems to me, while you're making the girls pants, you might oughta take those up a mite, too. They are falling right off of you."

Laura released Hope's little hand. "There's no chance of that happening." She held up the end of her shirt just enough for him to see the dark brown drapery cord that held the pants up around her waist. Laura's smile and her look of triumph caused the breath to quicken in his throat. She really was quite a woman.

Hope toddled over to him and clutched his leg. He bent down and asked, "Want to ride with me? Or—?" Clint was at a loss for words. He'd never heard what Laura called herself to the little girl. His gaze searched hers.

"Laura," she answered softly.

His gaze returned to the little girls. "Or Laura?"

The softest of whispers answered, "Ewwww."

He swung Hope up into the air and was rewarded with a sweet giggle. Clint looked to Laura and Grace. "You don't mind riding with Laura, do you, Gracie?"

The little girl tugged Laura's hand and tried to walk toward the mare Clint had saddled for her earlier. Her little voice chattered as she tugged.

"I'll take that as a no." He chuckled.

"Hold up, Grace. I need to get our bag from the porch."

Grace dropped Laura's hand and started walking to the porch. While they retrieved the bag, Clint put Hope on his shoulders.

Laura returned with the bag and Grace. She tied the bag to her saddle horn and then swung into the saddle as if it were an everyday occurrence. Her lips twitched as she looked down at him and said, "Would you mind handing Grace up to me?"

Clint balanced Hope on his shoulders and scooped Grace up. He handed the child to Laura and grinned. "Why, Mrs. Lee, I believe you have some explaining to do. I've never met a prim and proper schoolteacher who can swing into a saddle like you just did."

Laura adjusted Grace in front of her. "It's been a while, but I'll be honest. It felt good."

Once Hope was off his shoulders and sitting in front of him, Clint urged his horse toward the west pasture. "Do you mind if I ask where you learned to mount a horse like that?"

She guided the little mare he'd chosen for her up beside him. "Not at all. I grew up on a small farm. Daddy only had me and my younger sister to help out. We learned to ride at a young age." Her blue eyes met his. "If you need help with the fence line, I can do that, too." She raised her head high. "I'm not ashamed that I can ride and work a farm, Mr. Shepard."

"You shouldn't be, Mrs. Lee." He pressed Hope's back closer to his stomach as the little girl seemed to want to slide to the left. "I'm hoping Gracie will want to ride and fix fences someday, too."

"I never said I wanted to fix fences." She wrinkled her nose at him.

He laughed. "I'm not sure anyone wants to fix fences. I know that I usually take on that job. My men would rather be herding cattle or feeding. Can't blame them for that. It's a hot job."

The little girls babbled to each other as they rode along. Laura nodded her head. Her floppy hat had fallen to her back, held by the string that she'd tied under her chin. The sun caught the reddish highlights in her hair.

"It gets pretty cold during the winter, too. I remember one year the snow was up to our horses' bellies. We had an old bull that had kicked through the fence and headed to the barn. Pa and I spent half a day just fixing it enough to keep the other cows in, but come spring we had to fix it proper." She shuddered. "I don't believe I had ever been that cold before."

"You grew up here in Texas?" Clint heard the sound of running water ahead.

The horses heard it, too, and picked up the pace.

"No, I grew up in Kansas." Laura gave her horse its head, and it galloped across the pasture where the stream, grass and trees awaited.

Clint followed at a slower pace. The sound of Grace's squeals of happiness touched a part of his heart that had lain dormant for the past couple of years. Grace was his pride and joy, but very seldom had he heard the child laugh with such abandon.

It seemed Laura brought out the joy in the little girl. She'd had that effect on him earlier, too. Was it because she was a woman? Or was it because she belonged on the Shepard Ranch? The unbidden question entered his mind. Was it possible she belonged with them?

He squished the thought of her belonging on the ranch and with them. Clint mentally reminded himself that Laura was only going to be with them a few months and that he had no business thinking of her staying any longer.

Laura tucked the children into their beds. It had been a fun afternoon with the girls. They'd giggled and splashed in the water while Clint worked on the fence. She'd watched him and wondered why he'd suddenly gone from chatty to quiet. It didn't matter. For a few moments she'd allowed herself to become too friendly with her boss. Thanks to his response to her being from Kansas—at least that's what she figured had turned him into a quiet cattleman—she'd come to her senses and become the nanny she was supposed to be and focused on the girls.

Still, she couldn't help but think of Clint's change in behavior. He'd gone from teasing and laughing to quiet, almost somber. Laura shook her head. If she went to bed thinking like this she'd never get any sleep. She walked to the kitchen to make a warm glass of milk. Warm milk always helped her to sleep better.

Clint was still out in the barn. He hadn't come in for dinner. Mrs. Murphy had sent plates out to the barn for him and Richard. They had a cow out there that seemed to be having difficulty birthing her calf. Laura made a mental note to check on Grace again before heading to bed.

Camelia sat at the kitchen table sorting brown beans. She looked up when Laura entered. "Can't sleep?"

Laura smiled. "I haven't tried, yet. Thought I'd have a little warm milk before bed."

She nodded. "I wouldn't mind having a mug of warm milk, too. If you don't mind."

"Not at all." Laura pulled out a pot to heat the milk. "Any word on how Bessy is doing?"

"Bessy?" Camelia frowned.

"The cow." Laura poured the milk into the pan and looked over her shoulder at the older woman with a grin.

"You named the cow?"

Laura shrugged. "Sure. Why not?"

The other woman chuckled. "Bessy—" she paused in her bean sorting "—is still laboring away."

Stirring the milk with a wooden spoon, Laura sympathized with the cow. "Poor thing."

"Having three children myself, I feel her pain." Camelia slid the remaining beans into her pot and stood.

"You have three children?"

Camelia laughed. "Don't look so shocked. I had a life before we moved here, ya know."

"I suppose you did." Laura didn't want the milk to stick and so continued to stir.

"We both did." She washed the beans. "I know we didn't get off to a good start. How about we share how we both ended up here?" Her hand sloshed the beans and water about.

Laura poured the warm milk into two mugs. "My story is rather boring." Did she want to tell the Irishwoman of her past? Would the older woman think less of her?

"Mayhaps, but from where I come from, storytelling, whether good or bad, is always interesting. Of course, if it is painful or you wish to keep your privacy, that is all right, too."

Laura searched the older woman's green eyes. She wanted a friend. Not having opened up to another woman before had always left her feeling empty. "It will be painful, but perhaps it will be worth the pain, if I share it."

Camelia nodded. "How about a cookie?"

"I'd love two."

"Aye, so you are a two-cookie eater. See? I am learning new things about you already." She pulled a small plate from the cabinet and opened the cookie jar.

Laura carried the milk to the table and waited. Where would she begin? How much sharing did Camelia want to do? "Would you mind telling me your story first?"

Camelia carried the plate of cookies to the table and sat down. "Not at all. Let's see." She paused and placed two cookies in front of Laura. "My beginning years were in Ireland. When I was six years old my parents thought it wise to move to America. They'd heard of work and wanted a new start for their wee one." She looked up and grinned. "That was me."

So, they were starting at the beginning. This might turn out to be a long night. Laura smiled. "Did you have any brothers or sisters?"

"No, my mother said that God had blessed her with one child, and if that's all He saw fit to bless her with, she would be content. Do you have brothers or sisters?"

"I had one sister."

Camelia sighed. "I take it she is with the good Lord now."

Tears pricked the backs of Laura's eyes. "Yes, the good Lord took her, my mother and father."

The older woman reached out and covered her hand. "I am sorry, lass. I take it you are alone now?"

Laura swallowed. "Yes, but their deaths took place several years ago." She pulled her hand out from under

Camelia's and sipped at her warm milk. "Please, continue with your story."

"My sweet mother died on the journey. She couldn't take the sickness that consumed the ship. When we'd first boarded the ship, I thought it was wonderful but soon learned it was to be a place of sorrow and sickness. My father arrived with me in America, but he was sick and without money. I often wonder if his illness was due more to the loss of my mother, than actual sickness." Her eyes took on a faraway look.

Laura sat quietly thinking of her own parents. After a few moments, she spoke. "My mother died when I was young, too. Papa had myself and Ellen. Ellen died shortly after Ma. They both had caught the same horrible sickness. Papa and I continued taking care of our farm, cows and land, but after a year without Ma and Ellen, he decided to sell the farm and move to town." A bitter sweetness filled her. "He said I was going to need a husband soon, and living on a farm was only hiding me away."

"Did you find your young man in town?" Camelia asked. She nibbled around the edges of the sugar cookie.

"Yes, I got married shortly after we moved. Pa took a job at the sawmill where Charles worked. I volunteered at the school and helped Mr. Peters with the younger children." Laura looked at Camelia. She wasn't ready to talk about her marriage to Charles just yet and asked, "What about you? Did you marry a nice Irish boy?"

She sat her cookie down and wiped her hand on her apron. "No, after Father died I went to work at the orphanage there in New York."

Laura had heard of the orphanages in New York. "How old were you?"

"Ten." Her tired gaze met Laura's. "My story is a bit sad in this part of it."

This time Laura reached out. She laid her hand on Camelia's and said, "You can skip this part if it is too sad."

"No, I'll press onward." Camelia took a deep breath. "I was fifteen when I ran away from that horrible place. I'd washed enough clothes and saved enough money to hire a ride on a wagon to get out of the city, and I did just that." Pride filled her eyes now. "I got out."

Laura smiled. "You did well." She released the older woman's hand. "What happened next?"

They continued talking until well into the night. Laura learned that Camelia had married an older man who died a few months later. She'd married two other times and had three children. All had died at various stages in their lives, leaving Camelia sad and alone in life.

Laura realized that none of Camelia's children had lived past the age of three. She'd wanted to ask the older woman if that was why when Grace had turned two, she'd insisted on having a nanny for the child. But it was too sensitive of a subject, and Camelia had wanted to hear her story.

As she climbed into bed, Laura felt a little better about her past. Camelia had been furious when she heard how Charles had belittled her with words. She'd insisted that it was not Laura's fault that she was barren. Camelia voiced her concern that all men seemed to want was a legacy.

Laura felt a trickle of warmth run from her eyes as she agreed. Men wanted someone to carry on their name. It didn't matter that they loved you. They wanted that namesake, and when they realized it would never come…well, she knew firsthand just how hurtful a man could become to the woman he loved because of his disappointment.

Her thoughts turned to Clint. As far as she knew, the cow still labored on, and he remained at her side. She admitted to herself that she was attracted to the cowboy. But it was wise to keep distance between them. Even if she could learn to love him, she couldn't tolerate resentment and hurt appearing in those big brown eyes when he discovered she wouldn't be helping him carry on the Shepard name.

Chapter Eight

Clint curled up on the pile of hay in the farthest corner of the barn. Sunlight would be making an appearance soon. He'd much rather curl up in his own bed but knew Grace would be waking in a couple of hours, and he'd have to take her to Laura. It was far easier to fall into the hay and sleep than it was to go to his room, sleep two hours and have to get right back up.

The mother cow had labored all night but had finally produced a fine-looking little bull. He'd sent Richard to his bed in the bunkhouse, then made his own little nest in the hay. If all went well, he'd get at least four hours of sleep before the ranch began waking up.

Clint shoved the hay about, trying to get a comfortable spot. He'd slept in barns as a child, a teenager and even as a man. It felt foolish to sleep in one now, with a nice bed inside. He sighed and stood.

A few hours of good sleep would be better than hayloft sleeping any time. Clint made his way to the house. A light shone in the kitchen window. Was Mrs. Murphy waiting up for him? If so, why? Maybe Grace was sick. His footsteps quickened. He entered the house through the kitchen door and looked about.

Mrs. Murphy turned from the sink. "Did she have the calf?"

"Yep, a healthy bull." His eyes searched the room. "What are you doing up so late? Surely not waiting up for me."

She shook her head. "No. Laura and I had a late-night chat. I was about to turn in. Are you hungry?"

Clint shook his head. "No, I'm going to hit the hay." He grinned at his private joke.

"Good. If you can, you should sleep in tomorrow. Laura took Grace to her room for tonight. She thought you might want the added sleep." Mrs. Murphy yawned, her Irish accent thickened as she said, "I'd best be getting my sleep also. Good night."

Clint bid his housekeeper good-night and walked to his room, where he pulled off his boots and flopped across the bed. His tired body wanted to rest, but his thoughts turned to Laura. She really was a kind woman. She could have left Grace in his room, but instead had taken the child to hers so that he could get the rest he needed. It still surprised him that she was a country girl at heart.

Clint pushed himself off the bed and dressed for the night. His thoughts moved to his wife, and he couldn't help but remember that Martha hadn't liked living out on the ranch. She'd often asked him if they could get a house in town, and he'd always refused. He sat back down on the edge of his bed. If only he'd known that she'd get sick after having Grace, he would have moved to town. But he hadn't.

With a sigh, he crawled under the bedsheet. Laura

seemed to like the ranch, but like Martha, her place was in town. Even though they'd only known each other for a week, Clint knew if he allowed himself, he could easily—he pushed the thought aside.

"Get some sleep, Shepard. Your mind is muddled." He curled into a ball and pulled his pillow to him. The thought refused to go away, and he questioned it. He could easily what? Fall in love with her? Get used to having her around?

He awoke with a start. The sun streamed through the window. Normally his mornings started before the sun came up. Clint tossed the covers back and quickly dressed. He'd slept way too long.

The smell of fresh coffee pulled him to the kitchen. He expected to see Mrs. Murphy or Laura, but instead found an empty room. Clint poured himself a cup of coffee and snatched up a piece of fried bacon.

He chewed slowly and listened. Where was everyone? The house seemed too quiet. There were no sounds of women talking or working, no sweet giggles and babbles from the little girls. They were probably outside.

Clint noticed the biscuits sitting on the back of the stove. He grabbed one, pulled it apart, stuffed it with more bacon and headed out to the barn to check on his new bull.

As he approached, he heard Grace's sweet laughter and saw her standing on a ladder looking into the stall where he'd left the cow and calf. Laura stood beside her, pressing a hand against the little girl's back to keep her from falling backwards.

Laura turned as he approached. She held Hope on her hip. Laura's hair hung down her back in a braid.

Strands had escaped about her face. She smiled at him. "Good morning."

"Morning." His voice sounded deeper and full of sleep. Clint cleared his throat to get the frog sounds out.

Grace scrambled down the short ladder and ran to meet him. She grabbed his leg, then sat on his boot.

"You little tadpole. What are you doing on my boot?" He knew that she wanted him to walk with her sitting there. If she got much bigger, they'd have to stop playing this game and move on to something that didn't take quite as much leg muscle.

She babbled up at him with a grin.

He swung his child-laden boot forward and walked toward the stall. "How is he this morning?" Clint asked Laura. He pulled Grace from his foot and swung her up on to his shoulders. Only then did he realize he'd left his hat at the house.

"He's beautiful. I love that splash of black around his right eye. What are you going to call him?" Her eyes sparkled, and she carried the sweet scent of lavender water.

Clint focused on the calf, trying to ignore the fact that he enjoyed spending time with Laura. "I was thinking I'd call him Target."

Laura laughed. "And here I thought you might name him Bull's Eye."

Her sense of humor and joy were contagious, and he found himself laughing, too. Once he'd regained his composure, Clint focused on the calf and mother. Both seemed to be doing well. The baby had a healthy appetite as it nursed.

Laura pushed away from the fence. "Would it be all right with you if I took Grace into town today?"

His gaze moved to her face. Worry filled her eyes. Or was it anxiety? "I'd rather you not go alone."

"I could ask Camelia if she'd like to go with us." She nibbled on the corner of her bottom lip. "She might need a few supplies."

Clint knew that Mrs. Murphy preferred to stay on the ranch and let others do her shopping for her. He doubted the older woman would want to go to town. "If you could put your trip off until tomorrow, I will go with you."

"I don't want to pull you from the ranch." She shifted Hope's weight, then set her down on the ground. "I know you have things to do here."

Grace began wiggling on his shoulders. She patted his head and babbled. "Down, down, down…"

Clint pulled her from his shoulders and sat her beside Hope, who happily dug through the hay with her small hands. He faced Laura. "Is it important that you go today?"

Her gaze moved to Hope. "I thought I'd go visit the sheriff."

He looked to the child, too. "I see. Well, give me a couple of hours and I'll go with you."

"Today?"

Clint nodded. "Yep. You won't be happy until you hear what the sheriff has found out." He offered what he hoped was a reassuring smile. "Besides, I don't mind putting off branding for a day."

Richard entered the barn. "We aren't branding today, boss?"

"No, Mrs. Lee has some business in town so I'm going to escort her and the girls."

Richard smiled confidently at Laura, but his words

were for Clint. "If you need to brand, I'll escort her to town for you." He winked at Laura, who blushed and looked away.

Clint frowned. Was his foreman sweet on Laura? Had they started a relationship he didn't know about? That was ridiculous. Laura hadn't been to the barn before, and Richard seldom went up to the house. He shook his head at the foolishness of his thoughts.

"That's very kind of you, Richard, but I think we'll do it tomorrow, and I'll let you do the actual branding." Clint laughed at the mock look of horror on his friend's face.

Laura bent down and picked up Hope. "We'll head to the house and get ready."

Clint realized that his banter with Richard had embarrassed her further. "I'll get the wagon ready."

She nodded and then hurried with the girls back to the house.

Richard watched her go and then turned to grin at him. "She is a pretty little thing."

Clint grunted as if he hadn't noticed. He pulled the wagon from beside the barn and proceeded to hitch up the horse, aware that Richard stood close by, watching.

"You trying to convince me that you hadn't noticed?" he asked, crossing his ankles and leaning against the side of the barn.

Clint grinned. "I noticed, but a true gentleman doesn't embarrass a lady to get her attention."

Richard laughed. "Oh, so now we're gentlemen. Here I thought we were simple cowboys working a ranch." He turned and walked away, calling over his shoulder. "I'm heading to the south pasture to see if we've had any more calves overnight. Have fun in town."

Clint wondered just how much fun he and Laura would have. He knew she was concerned about Hope's parents. If she had to turn the girl over to them, her heart would be broken. It didn't take a genius to realize that Laura loved Hope.

Laura sighed with relief as the sheriff shook his head no and said, "I can't find hide nor hair of this little one's mama and papa."

Clint laid a hand on her shoulder. "Does that mean you'll keep looking?"

The sheriff nodded. "I have to. At least until the judge gets here and can decide what to do." He tucked a curl behind Hope's small ear. "But until then, she's to stay in your care, Mrs. Lee. Unless you've decided to give her up."

Laura hugged the little girl closer. "No, if anything, I want her even more." She looked deeply into Hope's eyes. "I love her."

Clint squeezed her shoulder. His warm hand assured her he'd stand beside her, even if he hadn't said the words. Laura looked up at him and saw that he too cared for the little girl. Grace babbled as if to say she loved Hope, as well.

"I can see she's in good hands." The sheriff walked to his desk and picked up a wanted poster. "Mrs. Lee, you don't need to come check with me about Hope's parents. If I find them, I'll come to you." He looked up and grinned at her. "We miss you at the boarding-house."

She turned her gaze back on him. "Thank you." Laura didn't elaborate on what she was thanking him for. It was nice to be missed, but the truth was, she enjoyed living out at the ranch. And now that she and Camelia had spent an evening getting to know one another, Laura felt like she had a real friend.

"If you don't have any more questions for the sheriff, I suppose we should be heading back to the ranch." Clint bent over and picked up Grace. "Thanks again, Sheriff." He turned and opened the door.

Laura exited, feeling both happy and sad. She still had Hope, but Hope's future with her wasn't secure. "I'm sorry. I've wasted the whole day for you."

He yawned. "No need to apologize. It wasn't a waste of time. We found out that Hope's parents haven't been found." Clint put Grace into the wagon.

"Thank you." Laura set Hope up on the seat beside Grace. She took Clint's extended hand and climbed into the wagon. "Do you mind stopping at the school? I'd like to make sure everything is all right."

He walked around the wagon and climbed aboard. "That would be fine. Maybe we can have that picnic you packed while we're there."

"That's a great idea. We can eat under the big oak tree." Laura noticed several people watching them as they drove through town to the schoolhouse.

Clint appeared to be ignoring the curious stares. "You and Mrs. Murphy seem to be getting along better today." He turned the wagon up the small incline to the school.

Laura grinned. "Yes, we are."

"Any idea what brought about the change?" He set the brake and turned to face her.

What could she say? She really didn't know for sure. Laura suspected it was something Camelia had read in the Bible, but since the other woman hadn't said that, she couldn't be positive that was the reason for the change. Laura shrugged. "I suppose she simply decided to be friends."

Clint nodded. He stopped the little mare and set the brake. Laura stood to get down from the wagon.

Grace did the same.

Clint put his hand out and stopped his daughter. "You sit tight. I'm going to help Laura down first."

"I can get off the wagon by myself." Laura started to do just that. She was surprised when she felt warm hands around her waist.

He pulled her from the wagon and gently set her feet on to the ground.

Laura turned and looked up at him. "Thank you, but I was doing fine by myself."

"True, but it wouldn't have been right for me not to at least assist you." Clint walked back to the other side of the wagon and helped Grace over the side and then Hope.

Laura reached for the picnic basket. She didn't want to admit that she enjoyed him helping her. Clint Shepard was turning out to be quite the gentleman. If she wasn't careful, she could learn to lean on him, and that wasn't something she planned on doing.

Chapter Nine

Clint took a big bite out of the apple Laura handed to him. A picnic beside the schoolhouse was just what he needed. Yes, for the first time in days, he could forget about the ranch and simply enjoy the quietness of the schoolyard.

Both little girls were curled up like puppies after playing hard together. Hope's head rested on Grace's little tummy while they napped. Hope sucked on her index finger, and soft contented sounds came from Grace as she too slept. They were sweeter than peppermint sticks.

Laura smiled across at him. "Thank you for today."

"It was my pleasure." Clint yawned. He envied the little girls and the way they could just curl up and sleep. As the owner of the Shepard Ranch he had many a night where he couldn't sleep at all. Ah, to be young and worry free.

She spread her skirts about her legs. Then she brushed the hair off Hope's forehead. "She is a real sweetheart. I can't begin to imagine why her parents left her with me."

He wasn't sure if she was talking to herself or him.

Clint tossed the apple core toward a tree a little distance away where he'd seen a squirrel scavenging about for nuts earlier. "They knew she'd be in good hands with you, that's why."

That beautiful smile filled her face. "Thank you. It's sweet of you to say that."

Clint could sit here all day looking at her. From what he'd seen, she was beautiful both inside and out. He shouldn't be thinking like this. They'd only known each other for a short time. If he continued on with this line of thinking, he'd be falling in love with her and that wouldn't do. No, he would be her friend and admire her beauty, but Clint made a mental effort to block all feelings of love. The only question that remained was, could he keep that block in place?

Over the next few days, Laura established a routine for herself and the little girls. She liked order in her life and felt that children should know what was expected of them. They rose at the same time each morning and had breakfast. They played most of the morning in the house, had lunch, a nap and then in the afternoons spent a couple of hours outside playing. Before dinner, Laura got her books down and shared them with the girls. She loved watching their gazes scan the pages. Grace pointed at pictures and babbled excitedly. Hope simply watched and tilted her head from side to side.

After dinner, Laura and the girls helped clean up the kitchen, and then everyone retired to the sitting room where the girls played with their toys and the adults read or sewed. She loved the evenings the best. Clint often joined them and studied several ranch catalogs. Then before bed, he'd read a Bible story to them from the big family Bible that sat on the table in front of the settee.

Laura peeked in on the girls. They were curled up on their little beds taking an afternoon nap. She returned to her side of the room and looked at the trunk she'd pulled out from under the bed a few moments earlier. Her foot had caught the corner of it more times than she cared to admit. Laura studied the chest. It was old and the paint was chipping.

Curiosity nibbled at her. Should she open it? Clint had assured her she could use anything in the room. Giving in to the nosiness, she opened the chest.

Folded neatly were lots of dresses and a few men's shirts. She pulled them out and studied the material. Holes could be seen in the fabric, but maybe she could salvage part of the cloth and use it to make quilts for the little girls' beds.

Did the dresses belong to Clint's wife? His mother? The shirts were probably his or perhaps his father's. Laura realized she knew nothing about Clint's family.

She refolded the clothes and made a mental note to ask Clint if she could use the fabric from them. It would be fun to sew something for Grace. After she and Hope were gone, the little girl would have something to remember her by.

Laura moved to the writing desk that Clint had placed in her room. It sat under the window where natural light would make it easy for her to study and read. School would be starting in a few weeks, and she wanted to be prepared.

As she sat down, her thoughts moved to Clint. What was he doing today? Riding the range? Branding cattle? Fixing fences? The jobs were endless for a rancher. Many a night he came home tired but happy.

It hadn't taken long for Laura to learn that Clint expressed happiness by whistling. She wondered if he was even aware of it. How many evenings had he come into the kitchen whistling a happy tune? Many.

Laura leaned her elbows on the desk, rested her chin on her hands and remembered how Grace often heard him coming before everyone else. The little girl clapped her hands and babbled happily at the sound of his arrival. Grace delighted in her papa. Her face and eyes lit up when he entered a room.

Aware she was neither reading nor studying, Laura sighed and stood. She shouldn't be daydreaming about Clint Shepard and his daughter. Checking on the girls one last time, Laura left the bedroom in search of Camelia.

The older woman always had work that needed to be done, and today, Laura thought she would offer to help. Camelia still refused her assistance most of the time, but every so often a job was just too big for one woman.

She found Camelia in the small garden beside the back door. "The girls are sleeping. I was wondering if there is anything I can help you with."

Camelia looked up from her kneeling position on the ground. "Not today, dear. I'm planting beans and it's a one-woman job."

Laura smiled. "Only because you enjoy doing it by yourself."

"That's right. Now go along and let me to get on with me fun." She bent back to the beans and dirt.

"Camelia?"

A heavy sigh was her answer.

Laura chose to ignore it and pressed on. "Would you

mind keeping an ear out for the girls? I'd like to take a walk along the river bank and gather my thoughts."

The older woman looked up at her and grinned. "Sure, I'll keep me ear open for them. I forget that you might like a few moments away from the house. Go on with you. I'll be here should they need anything."

"Thank you." Laura hurried to the house and slipped into her boots. One never knew if a snake might be lurking about in the grass. It was all she could do not to giggle at the prospect of taking her boots off once she got to the water and wading on the edges of it.

Once Laura had her boots on, she hurried past Camelia. "Thanks again. I won't be long."

Camelia ignored her and continued planting.

Laura sighed with happiness as she walked to the river. A cool breeze teased the hair at her temples. She'd not realized how much she missed having a few minutes alone.

She loved being with the girls, but it felt nice just to be outside and enjoying God's creations. A bird sang happily in the limbs above her as she followed the wooded path to the river. Laura heard it gurgling long before she arrived at its banks.

The water looked clear and cool. She walked to the edge and sat down on the rocky shore. Thankfully the rocks weren't so big that she couldn't see snakes if one should be cooling in their shade. She yanked off first one boot and then the other.

They were brown and looked much like men's cowboy boots. No buttons to mess with and no ribbons to worry about getting soiled. They were perfect for a schoolteacher who oftentimes walked through snow and mud to get to work.

She wiggled her sock-free toes in the cool air and then stood. The warm rocks under her feet felt nice and smooth. Laura giggled as she dipped a toe into the water. She was going to take this time and simply enjoy it.

Clint sat on top of his horse watching the schoolteacher splash around at the water's edge like a child. If Laura knew he was there, she would be mortified. Especially since she was showing quite a bit of her ankles with each kick and splash.

He'd heard her coming down the path and was curious what she planned on doing. A grin teased his lips. Now he knew.

It was good to see her having fun. She stopped and looked down into the clear water. What was she looking at? He wanted to inch forward and get closer. But he knew he couldn't conceal himself or his horse if he left the shadows of the trees.

Clint shifted in the saddle. His gaze scanned the riverbanks on both sides. With the amount of splashing noises Laura was making, he doubted that an animal would disturb her fun, but that wasn't always true of man.

He shook his head. Maybe he was being a bit overprotective. They hadn't seen Indians or trappers in the area in quite some time. Still, he'd wait until she'd finished playing in the water before heading back.

His stomach growled. Clint pulled a small package of beef jerky from his saddlebag and proceeded to chew on the dry meat. Thankfully branding was over. It was a hot job that he didn't enjoy doing but knew was a necessity.

Bull's Eye hadn't cared for the experience, either. The little animal had snorted his discomfort before running back to his mama and the comfort she offered.

His thoughts went to Gracie and her lack of a mother. Just this morning Mrs. Murphy had hinted that the little girl needed a real mother's attentions, not just a hired hand. Clint looked back to Laura.

She'd settled down and was now sitting on the riverbank. Her boots rested beside her, and her toes were still in the water. Gracie grew fonder of the woman every day. Had it been a mistake to hire Laura? Should he have found a woman to marry so that the child could have a mother in her life?

Laura used her apron to dry her bare feet and then began to pull on her stockings. With a frown she picked up her boot and shook it out before putting her foot inside. She was a smart woman and knew that snakes and insects liked climbing in nice, dark spaces. Since she had some experience living on a farm, Laura would be a suitable candidate for a wife and mother. Of course, he didn't want a wife in the biblical sense. No, he only wanted someone who could guide Gracie as she grew into a woman.

But Laura wasn't the woman for them. She'd already expressed her desire to continue teaching. The thought of looking for a suitable mother for Grace had him avoiding such thoughts by gently urging his horse toward the bank where Laura now stood.

She looked up at his approach. A smile tilted her lips. "Looks like you caught me off playing, Mr. Shepard."

Clint stopped a few feet away from her and grinned. "Mrs. Lee, do you think it would be all right if we called each other by our first names?"

She surprised him by asking, "Why?"

"Well," he leaned forward on to his saddle horn, "I just thought since we live in the same house and take our meals together, we might as well be a little more friendly." Clint waited for her answer.

She never ceased to amaze him. Her shoulders straightened, the smile left her pretty face, and her chin came up a tad higher. "Mr. Shepard, at this time this is as friendly as I get. I'm not sure what you have in mind, but I want you to know I am not interested in becoming overly friendly with any man."

Clint couldn't help himself. Laughter, loud and robust, filled the quietness. Once composure had finally settled about him, he answered her. "Trust me, Mrs. Lee. Friendship was all that I was offering. I'm not interested in romance. I just wanted things to be a little more comfortable between us."

Her shoulders visibly relaxed. A soft grin and pink cheeks appeared on her face. "I'm sorry. I didn't mean to sound so stuffy. In my profession, I've met several single fathers who thought that addressing me by my given name meant they could call on me after school. I've sort of built a wall to prevent those types of misunderstandings from happening."

He nodded. As a schoolteacher, Clint was sure she'd surely had her fair share of proposals from unmarried men. "I can assure you, there are no misunderstandings going to happen here."

She tilted her head to the side and looked up at him. Her eyes searched his face. Then she straightened her head. "Then I don't see why you can't call me Laura."

"Good. Now that that's settled I should get back to work." He turned his horse around.

"Wait!"

The urgency in her voice had him twisting about in the saddle. His eyes searched the area for any indication that they were in danger. Seeing none, he asked, "What?"

Laura pulled her skirts up and hurried to stand beside the horse. "I found a trunk under the bed earlier, and it has some older dresses and things inside it." She paused as if waiting for him to acknowledge that he knew which chest she spoke of.

Clint did. He'd forgotten that he'd placed it there, but without having to look at it, he knew its contents: Martha's old dresses. She'd planned to either repair them or make something else with them and had never had the time to do so. He swallowed hard at the memory and then nodded at Laura, who watched him.

"I was wondering if you'd mind if I cut them up and made a small quilt for each of the girls." She pressed on. "Winter will be here again before we know it."

"You are going to make a quilt for Grace?"

Laura laughed. "I said the girls, and Grace is a girl."

Grace would have something of her mother's, if Laura followed through with her plans and made the little girl a quilt. He liked the idea and smiled. "That is very thoughtful of you. I don't mind at all. Someday Grace will cherish a quilt made from her mother's clothes."

She returned his grin. "Good. I'll get started on them this afternoon, if the girls are still sleeping when I get back to the house." Laura began walking up the path.

Clint dismounted and walked along beside her. "Laura?"

Her eyes met his. "Yes?"

"Would you mind telling me what happened to your husband?" Clint wasn't sure why he'd asked but found that after the question had crossed his lips that he truly hoped she'd tell him.

Laura looked away. "His heart gave out on him."

"I'm sorry to hear that." Clint tugged on the horse's reins. He really was sorry to hear that Laura's husband had died. The sorrow in her voice pulled at his heart.

"What happened to your wife?" Laura looked at him through lowered lashes. Did she fear he wouldn't answer her?

Clint looked toward the house. He cleared his throat and then answered, "Shortly after she gave birth to Gracie, she caught an infection."

"I'm surprised the doctor didn't catch that in time." Laura's brow was knitted as she looked at him fully now.

What would she think of him, once she learned he hadn't taken the time to get Martha to the doctor? Would she be disappointed in him? Blame him for Martha's death?

Chapter Ten

When he didn't answer her immediately, Laura's frown deepened. "Don't tell me you blame yourself?"

"Don't you?"

Confusion fought its way to the surface of her emotions. "Don't I what?"

"Blame me for Martha's death?"

Laura shook her head. "No, why would I? Things like that happen all the time after a woman gives birth."

"Maybe, but if I had gotten her to the doctor sooner, she might have lived." He looked back at his horse, avoiding her eyes.

She stopped. "She might not have, either." Laura sighed and prayed Clint wouldn't take her words the wrong way. She placed her hand on his arm. "Clint, God decides when it is time for us to leave this world. We are not in control of such things. Your Martha would have died, whether you had gotten her to the doctor or not. So please, if you are blaming yourself, don't."

He looked deeply into her eyes. Laura saw the hurt

and loss in his. Clint reached up and touched her cheek. "Thank you, but I can't blame God for her loss, either."

"No, and you shouldn't blame Him. God knows so much more than we do. Worse things could have happened to your wife. Maybe He was saving her from something far worse." Laura removed her hand from his arm and stepped away from his touch.

Clint nodded. "I'll keep that in mind." His gaze moved to the house. "Looks like you are back. I'll see you later." He mounted his horse and gave her a sad grin before turning the horse and trotting off across the pasture.

Laura watched him sway in the saddle until he was no longer in sight. She felt sad for him. It was obvious that he loved his wife very much. Would she have felt differently if Charles had loved her as much?

Taking her mind off Charles, Clint and Martha, Laura returned to the house. She stopped by the garden where Camelia still toiled. "I'm back."

Camelia leaned on her heels and looked up at her. "I've about got these wee plants in the ground." Satisfaction at a job well done shone on her face.

Laura knew she'd not get to sample any of Camelia's vegetables. She'd be back in town when the garden would finally be ready for harvest. "They look wonderful." Sadness entered her heart at the knowledge that she wouldn't be staying on at the ranch.

Camelia pushed up from the ground. "I should go check on my bean pot." Her gaze moved to the newly planted seedlings.

"I'll check on them, if you like. I'm headed back into the house anyway." Laura wondered if Camelia would let her, or if she would insist on doing it herself.

"If it isn't any bother…"

Laura didn't give her the chance to finish. She spun toward the kitchen door. "No bother at all." Laura grinned as she entered the house.

Once the beans were stirred and more water added, Laura returned to the bedroom where the girls still napped. She pulled the chest from under the bed once more. Now that she knew for certain that the dresses had belonged to Clint's wife and Grace's mother, she studied the material more closely.

Martha Shepard had good taste in fabric. The material felt sturdy yet delicate in Laura's hands. Thankfully, Martha also enjoyed a variety of colors. The dresses had been store-bought and still had pretty buttons down the fronts. Laura's mind raced with ideas of how to mix and match the colors, creating a nine-patch quilt that Grace could keep forever.

She decided the fabric would need a good washing. Once again she checked on the little girls. Grace stirred in her slumber but continued sleeping.

Laura knew she didn't have much time. Maybe a quick rinse in cold water would be enough to get the stored, musty scent out of the clothes. She gathered the clothes up in her arms and started toward the door.

A sleepy voice whispered. "Warwa?"

She turned to find Grace sitting on the edge of her small bed. Her light brown hair stood straight up with static electricity. Laura grinned at the child. She placed a finger over her lips and motioned for Grace to follow her.

When they got to the hallway and closed the bedroom door behind them, Grace asked, "Waaaaahhhh rrrrrr ooooo ddddddd, Warwa?"

Laura held out the clothes for her to look at. She assumed the child meant, "What are you doing, Laura?" She answered, "I'm going to rinse these out and hang them on the clothesline to dry. Want to help?"

Grace took a sniff and shook her head. "Ick."

She laughed. "I know, they smell musty now, but maybe we can get the stench out with a little water."

Camelia came out of the bedroom across the hall. "It's going to take more than just a little water to get that smell out."

Laura sighed. She'd really wanted to simply rinse them out, not do a full wash. "What did you have in mind?" She prayed it was something other than pulling out the washtub and filling it with hot water and lye.

"Putting them in a tub of water with vinegar and lavender oil. That should cut the smell and add a soft fragrance you can stand." Camelia carried the sheets she'd just taken from her bed toward the kitchen.

Grace toddled after Camelia. Laura followed, glad that she wouldn't need to break out the large tub for clothes washing.

Camelia led them to the kitchen where she pulled out a small washtub. She dropped her sheets to the floor and smiled at Laura. "Go ahead and toss those in, I'll get one of the men to bring in the water from the well." She walked out the kitchen door and toward the small bunkhouse beside the barn.

Laura returned her grin. She did as told and then helped Grace up to the table. "How about we have an afternoon snack?"

Grace babbled happily.

"Good." She buttered a slice of bread and handed

it to Grace. "Here, I'm going to go get Miss Hope up. She wouldn't want to miss snack time."

The little girl smiled around with butter-coated lips.

Laura hurried to the bedroom. Hope still rested, curled up on her side, sucking her index finger. She grinned at the sweet face surrounded by blond curls.

One little blue eye opened, then Hope grinned around her finger. She raised her arms, silently asking Laura to pick her up.

"Did you sleep well, little one?" Laura scooped her up and carried her from the room.

Hope nodded. She shifted until her little head could rest on Laura's shoulder. The finger retreated between her lips once more.

"Good. Grace is having a snack in the kitchen. Would you like a snack, too?"

Again Hope nodded.

Laura longed for the day when the child would open her lips and speak. She didn't press the issue because Hope had been through enough already, and even if she never talked, Laura knew she'd love the girl forever.

Worry ate at her. Even though the sheriff had said she could keep Hope, what would the judge say when he returned to town? Would she be allowed to keep the child then?

As he drew near the house, Clint noticed movement to his left. He squinted his eyes to see better against the glare of the sun. From his vantage point it looked as if Laura and the girls were playing in the pasture.

Clint turned the horse to see what they were doing. He heard giggles and laughter as he approached. Stopping a few feet away, he could see that the girls had gathered wildflowers, and Laura was making flower wreaths for their little heads.

Grace saw him and squealed. She ran on her short legs to where he was dismounting from his horse. Her babbles were filled with joy.

He scooped her up and swung her around. His gaze landed on Hope, who stood a few feet away. Clint hugged Grace. "Are you being a good girl today, Gracie?"

She bobbed her little head and then began pushing away from him.

Hope watched with a little crown of flowers in her hair. She smiled sweetly up at him.

Clint grabbed her up and swung her around, as well. He laughed at her sweet giggle, then put her back on to the ground beside Grace.

Laura stood off to the side watching them. He was tempted to grab her around the waist and swing her around, too but something told him the prim and proper schoolteacher would not approve of such behavior. "Hello, Laura."

She placed the wreath of flowers on Grace's head. "Hello. The girls and I were about to have a picnic lunch. Would you like to join us?"

His stomach chose that moment to growl loudly. "Do you have enough food?"

"Yes, I packed enough bread, meat, cheese, apples and cookies to feed a small army." She led the way back to a blanket spread on the ground under one of the many oak trees. "But if you'd rather have leftover ham and beans from last night, I'm sure Camelia will be happy to dish you up a batch."

Clint laughed. "No, I think I'll go with a lighter meal."

He eased down on to her picnic blanket and sighed.

"Girls! Come over here and play with your dolls." Laura pulled bread, cheese and ham from the basket and began to make sandwiches. "Rough morning?"

He watched the way her hands speedily and efficiently created a large sandwich for himself and three half-sandwiches for herself and the girls. "It wasn't too bad. Just hot and sweaty."

"That's what Papa used to say." She handed him the sandwich and then looked to the little girls who were trying to sneak cookies out of the basket. "No, ladies. You don't get cookies until after you finish all your sandwich and a slice of apple each." They plopped down on their bottoms and reached for the half-sandwiches.

Clint laughed. Those two were a mess together. He'd noticed that they liked to be sneaky. It was a good thing Laura knew how to handle children. He took a large bite from his sandwich and chewed as he watched Laura interact with the children.

His heart seemed to melt a little at her motherly ways. He wondered why she hadn't remarried and had children of her own. She was pretty and good with kids. She should be married and have a whole houseful of children.

Grace played with the flowers on her head and giggled at Hope. His little girl needed a mother to guide her and other children around to play with. What was going to happen when Laura and Hope left? Would Grace be lonely? Sad? Probably both. The bread turned to dust in his mouth, and he set the sandwich aside.

"Oh, I'm sorry. Here." Laura handed him a mason jar filled with milk. His gaze moved to the girls, who each had a smaller jar of milk beside them. Clint assumed Laura had only packed one more jar of milk, and it was for her.

He stood and smiled. "Thanks, but if you don't mind, I think I'll drink the water from my canteen. I'm not much for drinking milk at lunch." He turned and looked down at her. "Unless you have a nice cake in that basket. Then I'll drink the milk."

The little girls' heads popped up at the word *cake*. They reminded him of prairie dogs. Their mouths turned down when Laura shook her head no.

"Not today, but if you'll tell me what kind you like, I'll see if Camelia will let me bake you one." Laura handed each of the girls an apple slice.

Clint walked to his horse and got the canteen. "In that case, I'll just drink water." He wasn't really much of a cake eater and had been teasing with her. Truth be told, of all the cakes he'd eaten, a simple white cake was his favorite. He returned to the blanket. "I prefer peach cobbler, but if I must eat cake, let's make it a white one."

Laura laughed. "I like peach cobbler, too. Maybe when the peach trees ripen, I'll bake you a cobbler." She nibbled at the crust of her half-sandwich. "Maybe by then, Camelia will let me bake and cook."

Clint frowned. "She still won't let you bake or cook?"

She unscrewed the lid of the milk jar and sipped at the creamy beverage. A white line coated her top lip. "No, but I understand. She's been the woman of the house for so long that she doesn't like anyone else in her kitchen."

Maybe Laura understood, but he didn't. First thing

this evening, he'd have a talk with the little Irish-woman.

As if reading his thoughts, Laura said, "I wouldn't interfere if I were you, Clint. She's a little older than I am, and I have to respect her boundaries and wishes."

He shook his head. "Have you always been this—?" Unsure of where he was going with that line of questioning, he stopped.

"Considerate of others? Respectful to those older than myself?" She grinned across at him, obviously enjoying his discomfort.

"Yes and yes." He answered with a wink.

She lowered her head. Pink colored her cheeks. "Yes. I believe so."

Grace interrupted them. "Cookie?"

Hope nodded happily around a mouthful of apple.

Laura reached into the basket and pulled out two cookies. She handed them to the girls. Grace broke hers in two and grinned before eating one half. Hope simply chewed on the apple still in her mouth.

Clint smiled. Laura and the girls were becoming more and more important to him. Was this normal? Was it because they all lived in the same house? Or was he starting to like the idea of them becoming a family more than he cared to think? He sure didn't like that line of thinking.

Chapter Eleven

Laura sensed more than saw his mood swing. He'd gone from a teasing, sweet man to a serious one. She searched his face, waiting to hear whatever it was that had changed his temperament.

"Laura, would you and the girls like to go to town with me tomorrow?"

It had been about two weeks since their last trip to town, and she would love to go to the general store for more thread. But had he just decided to go? Or had he been planning to ask her since the moment he'd arrived at their picnic? "Why are you going?" she asked, knowing full well it wasn't any of her business.

"Well, I've been thinking." He took a deep breath and blurted, "It's time I place an ad in the paper for a new nanny. You'll be wanting to return to town soon. Who knows how long it will take to replace you."

His words, "replace you," hit her hard. She'd enjoyed being on the ranch, she and Camelia were becoming good friends, and she loved Grace dearly. How had a month passed so quickly? And how had she allowed herself to get so comfortable here? She looked across at him. "Yes, you're right. It's time."

Both girls sat quietly watching them and eating their cookies. How much did they understand of the adult conversation?

Laura began gathering their picnic scraps and placing them in the basket.

"Then I will see you at supper. I'd best get back to work." He walked over to his horse and mounted. "Thanks for lunch."

Laura nodded, afraid to speak. She hadn't realized how comfortable she'd gotten on the ranch. Her gaze moved to Grace, who waved goodbye to her daddy.

It wasn't until she heard his horse galloping back across the pasture that Laura was able to look in his direction. Clint's shoulders swayed in the saddle as he rode. She knew, without thinking too hard on it, that she would miss Clint and his sweet daughter.

Laura climbed down from the wagon. The trip into town had been quiet. Clint seemed to want to keep to his own thoughts, the girls were both tired from a restless night, and Laura just felt sad. "The girls and I will walk to the general store," she told Clint as he released her waist.

"I'll be at the newspaper office, if you need me." He set Grace on the ground beside Laura and then gently lifted a sleeping Hope out of the wagon.

He looked into the baby's face and smiled. "I'd keep her with me, but I'm afraid she might wake up and want you." Clint passed Hope over to Laura.

She rested the little girl against her shoulder and

then took Grace's hand in her own. "We'll be fine. She's used to sleeping like this."

Clint nodded. He knelt in front of Grace. "You be good for Laura and don't wake up Hope."

"Awwhite." Grace squeezed Laura's hand and leaned against her skirt.

"Good girl." He stood. "I'll meet you at the store."

Laura smiled. "All right." She turned and walked up the block and then started down Main Street.

Town seemed quiet this morning. Most people were probably home. Now that summer had arrived, folks tended to stay home in the mornings and do their chores before it got too hot.

Laura felt a stillness in the air that troubled her. Usually when she felt like this, it meant one of the boy students in her classroom had done something that would or could cause her class to erupt at any moment. It was almost as if she were being followed or watched closely. She turned her head and looked behind them. Seeing no one, Laura decided to hurry Grace along.

As soon as she arrived at the general store, Laura breathed a sigh of relief. She pushed the door open and hurried inside. The scents of leather and spices filled her nostrils. Laura hurried to the fabric table and turned to face the door. If someone was following her, she felt sure they'd come inside.

"Can I help you find anything, Mrs. Lee?"

She glanced at the storekeeper. "No, thanks. I'm just looking at the thread."

"It's behind you dear, on the wall."

The bell over the door jingled. Laura turned to see Priscilla Maxwell, the banker's only daughter, enter the store. Flabbergasted, Laura stared at the young woman. She'd moved to Denver, Colorado two years earlier in pursuit of an art degree. Surely she hadn't been the one following them.

Priscilla's face seemed gaunt and pale. She'd always been a pretty girl with rosy cheeks and a little on the plump side. Laura couldn't help but wonder what had happened to her in the last two years.

Grace pulled at her hand. She motioned toward the candy case and babbled several words.

"In a minute, Grace." Laura picked out two spools of thread, one dark blue and the other a soft yellow. Even as she studied the thread, she listened to Priscilla and the storekeeper.

"I would like to get a bottle of cough medicine, please." Priscilla's voice still sounded as sweet as it had two years ago.

"You need to slow down on this stuff, Prissy."

Laura turned to face them again. She allowed Grace to pull her toward them. Priscilla had hated the name Prissy in the past, but to look at her now, she didn't seem to notice. As a matter of fact, the young woman acted as if she didn't want to look around. She kept her head down and her eyes on the counter top.

Why?

When Grace got to the glass counter, she pressed her face against it and babbled away. Laura feared her loud chatter might wake Hope and shushed her. Then she turned to her former student. "Priscilla Maxwell?"

A sigh issued from the young woman. Then she turned. "Hello, Mrs. Lee."

"I thought that was you." Laura smiled her sweetest smile at the girl.

Dark circles rested under Priscilla's blue eyes. Her

eyes reflected sadness as she gazed upon Hope. Priscilla reached out and touched the little girl's fingers. A soft smile filled her face as tears threatened to spill over her lashes. "She is beautiful."

Laura nodded. "She resembles her mother." She knew it was true. Priscilla and Hope each had blue eyes, a soft bow-shaped mouth and blond curls. Priscilla had learned how to tame hers over the years but they were noticeable nonetheless.

Priscilla looked up sharply at her. She jerked her hand from Hope. Fear and sorrow filled her young eyes.

The storekeeper returned with a brown bag for Priscilla. "That will be five cents, please."

The young woman nodded and pulled the money from her apron pocket. She handed the money over and took the bag. "Thank you."

Laura wasn't sure if Priscilla was thanking the storekeeper or her. She wanted to talk to the young woman. So many questions raced through her mind that she wanted answers to now. "How about we visit for a few minutes? I'd love to hear about your life in Denver."

Priscilla nodded.

"Warwa?" Grace tugged at her hand. "Want." She pointed up at the peppermint stick jar.

Laura smiled at her and looked to the storekeeper. "We would like six of your penny peppermint sticks, please."

Grace clapped her little hands. She grinned broadly in anticipation of eating the sweet treat.

Laura paid for the candy and her thread, then turned to Priscilla once more. The young woman only had eyes for Hope.

"How about we move to the back of the store, out of everyone's way?" She didn't give Priscilla time to answer but led the way.

Grace hurried along beside her while Priscilla followed a little more slowly.

When she got to the table that normally housed a checker game, Laura sat down. Thankfully, Hope still slept peacefully against her shoulder. What would the child do, if she woke up and her mother was sitting there? She'd not once asked for Priscilla or cried from being separated from her. It seemed odd, but Laura had always been thankful.

She broke the peppermint stick in half and gave it to Grace. "Sit down here." She pointed at a spot beside her chair on the floor.

Grace plopped down happily and began sucking on the candy. Her eyes danced with happiness.

Then Laura looked up at Priscilla. She indicated the chair across the table. "Please, have a seat and let's visit."

Priscilla eased into the chair. Her blue eyes searched Laura's. "What would you like to know?"

"Well, first I'd like to know why you left this sweet baby on my doorstep." Laura patted Hope's back softly.

Blue eyes pleaded with her to understand. "I'm sick and have no husband to leave the child with. You were a wonderful, caring teacher, and I knew you'd be the perfect mother for her."

Laura sighed. "What about your parents?" Deep down she knew they had no idea that they were grandparents.

Fear filled Priscilla's face. She reached out and

grabbed Laura's hand. "Please don't tell them about Hope!"

Hope stirred but didn't wake. Laura gently removed her hand from Priscilla's and patted the little girl's back. "Priscilla, they already know someone left her on my porch. The whole town knows."

She folded her hands on top of the table. "Yes, but they don't know she's mine."

"Maybe you should tell me the whole story. I can't imagine your parents not wanting to know about their grandchild, and now that I know, I feel you should tell them."

Tears ran down Priscilla's cheeks when she looked up. "When I left here, I thought I knew everything, but I was wrong. Art school is fun but not everyone that attends is nice." She coughed.

Laura wanted to comfort her but knew she couldn't, at least not until she'd heard the whole story.

Priscilla pulled a white handkerchief from her sleeve and coughed again. "I fell in love with a man named Jerry Roberts. He swept me off my feet and married me within a month. Only after Hope was born, he turned mean. He wanted me to write my folks and tell them they couldn't see her without paying him to do so." She coughed again.

Laura saw specks of red in the handkerchief before Priscilla folded it up. The young woman wasn't simply sick, she was very sick from a lung disease called tuberculosis. She'd read about it in one of her science books. As far as she knew, there was no cure.

"I couldn't do that. I hadn't even told them I was married or that I'd had a baby," Priscilla continued. She wiped her mouth. "Jerry abandoned us. He told me I was of no use to him, if I wouldn't contact my parents." She wiped the tears from her eyes. "I waited for him to come home, but he didn't. And when I got sick and the money started running low, I knew I had to come back." She stared at Hope for several long minutes, then continued. "I left Denver and returned here. You are the only person I trust with my child."

Fear touched Laura's heart as she realized that Hope's father could claim her. She tightened her grip on the little girl. "What if Jerry comes looking for her? He'll be able to take her from me."

Priscilla shook her head. Bitterness dripped from her tongue. "He won't come for her. Jerry made it clear he had no desire to be a part of Hope's life. He wanted to use us to get money from my parents. I don't believe he will ever come looking for her." Coughing racked her body once more.

How Hope could sleep was beyond Laura's comprehension, but she was grateful that the child slept on. The little girl was unaware that her mother sat less than two feet from her.

"I don't know, Priscilla. You need to at least tell the sheriff that you left Hope with me. He's been trying to find out who left her on the school porch." She continued rubbing Hope's back in slow circles. Her gaze moved to Grace. Sticky fingers played in the dirt on the floor.

"Will he put me in jail?" Fear laced Priscilla's voice.

Laura shook her head. "No, and I imagine he'll keep your secret from your parents. But I still think you should tell them."

Priscilla shook her head. "No, they are too old to raise a child. Ma isn't well and Papa is too busy at the bank. She is better off with you." A new cough shook her body. "I'll go to the sheriff's office and tell him I want you to have Hope. You do want her, don't you?" Fresh tears filled her eyes.

"I do, but maybe you should take her home and explain to your parents what you've told me." Laura didn't want to give Hope up. Her heart broke even as she said the words, but Hope should be with her family.

"No, I'm dying. She's better off with you. I'll tell my parents someday but not today. It will be hard enough telling the sheriff. I'm so ashamed." Priscilla stood. "Thank you for taking care of Hope." She reached down and touched the child's soft curls. "Maybe someday you can tell her that I love her and only gave her up because I knew I couldn't keep her." She covered her mouth and hurried out of the store before Laura could answer.

Grace grabbed a handful of Laura's skirt and pulled herself up. "Warwa?" Her little brown eyes searched Laura's face.

Laura reached out and pulled Grace closer to her. "It's all right, Grace." She hugged the child close.

Would Priscilla keep her word and talk to the sheriff? Should she go see him and tell him what she'd learned? Or give Priscilla time? The young woman might change her mind and want Hope back. Then what?

Chapter Twelve

Clint stepped away from the general store door to avoid running into a young woman who hurried past him. Her blond head was down, and her shoulders shook as if she were crying. He watched her hurry toward the sheriff's office. Fear immediately jumped into his throat.

He opened the door to the general store and saw Laura standing at the back. She held Grace's hand, and Hope still rested against her shoulder. Laura clutched a brown bag in the hand that held Hope.

His gaze moved about the rest of the store, but all seemed calm. He couldn't help but wonder about the young woman. She'd seemed very upset.

Laura looked up at him with troubled eyes.

Clint hurried forward. He scooped Grace up and asked, "Ready to go home?"

Grace babbled happily. Sticky fingers touched Clint's arm.

"You are a mess," he told her, tickling her tummy.

The little girl squealed with happiness, waking

Hope. Hope looked about, wide-eyed until she saw that Grace was happy and laughing.

Laura hugged Hope to her. "We're ready." She led the way to the door.

Clint followed, unsure why Laura seemed so unhappy. She held on to Hope as if afraid the child would leave. When they got to the wagon, he helped Grace into the bed of the wagon, then turned to assist Laura up.

Laura reluctantly put Hope in the bed of the wagon with Grace. The two little girls chattered happily as if sharing some great adventure. She accepted his hand and pulled herself on to the wagon seat without speaking a word.

Was she upset that he'd placed the advertisement? Was that the reason for her silence? Martha had often grown quiet when she was angry or scared. He couldn't help but wonder if Laura was the same.

His gaze moved to the sheriff's office where the young woman he'd seen earlier exited. She seemed a little more composed as she looked directly at him. A brief nod of her head indicated that she was trying to tell him something. Clint looked to Laura to see if she'd noticed. He was shocked to see her return the young woman's nod.

Feeling foolish, Clint pulled himself up on to the wagon seat and released the brake. Laura didn't comment on either the woman or her strange behavior. She looked straight ahead as if in deep thought.

Clint slapped the reins over the horse's back and steered her toward home. If he lived to be a hundred, he doubted he'd ever understand women.

By the time he'd pulled up into the yard, Clint felt as wound up as a cowboy herding cattle during a thunderstorm. Laura hadn't spoken to him since leaving town and seemed to be in deep thought. Her gaze had darted back to the girls several times during the trip home. Other than to tell Grace to stay seated, Laura hadn't spoken to any of them.

Maybe she was angry with him. Or maybe she was simply worried about something. If he knew her, she was worried about losing Hope. Had the young woman in town threatened to take the child from her? Was she the little girl's mother? Was that why she'd run to the sheriff's office?

He pulled the wagon up to the front porch and climbed down. Clint reached up and helped Laura from the wagon. Slowly lowering her to the ground, he asked, "Are you all right? You've been mighty quiet."

She stepped from his arms. "I'm fine. I just have a lot on my mind."

Clint reached up and brushed a strand of hair away from her mouth. "Anything I can help you with?"

Her gaze darted to Hope and Grace. "No."

He knew it had something to do with Hope. Clint also knew that he'd fight by her side to keep the child. He'd been thinking about the judge and his decision as to if Laura could keep Hope or not. If the judge said no, because she was a single woman, Clint knew he'd marry her so that she wouldn't lose Hope.

His mind worked through the thought that he'd just decided he'd marry again to protect Laura from pain. Clint watched as she reached up and lowered the girls to the ground. Her eyes locked with Hope's, and she hugged the child tightly.

"I'll let Camelia know we are back." Laura followed a running Grace inside the house.

Clint moved to the head of the horse and gently tugged her toward the barn. He asked himself, would he really marry Laura to save her from the pain of losing a child? A resounding yes bounced about his brain.

The sound of a trotting horse caught his attention. He looked toward the main entrance of the ranch and saw the sheriff riding toward him. His heart sank. Laura had known the sheriff would soon be visiting. That explained why she had been so quiet and why she'd clung to Hope on the way home.

He waited until the sheriff was close and asked, "What brings you out here, Matt?"

The sheriff stopped his horse a few feet away from Clint and swung from the saddle. "I've come to see Mrs. Lee." His gaze moved toward the house.

"Mind if I ask why?"

"Nope."

Clint waited for a few moments for the sheriff to continue. "Well?"

Matt grinned at him. "You didn't ask why."

He felt like groaning. Matt always did have a warped sense of humor, but if he wanted an answer, he'd have to ask the question. "Why?"

The sheriff slapped him on the back. "Let's get your horse and wagon put away, and I'll tell you both at the same time."

Clint nodded. "How's the sheriff business been?" He led the horse to the barn and guided her as he positioned the wagon on the right side of the barn.

Matt had followed. He tied his horse to one of the two hitching posts as he answered. "Quiet. Which I'm grateful for."

"Maybe time for you to settle down then. Find a respectable woman and start a family." Clint glanced at his friend as he unhitched the horse from the wagon.

"Not on your life. Just because it's quiet now doesn't mean it will stay that way." He leaned against the barn and crossed his arms over his chest.

Clint patted the horse's velvety nose. "That's true enough."

"What about you? Think you'll ever remarry?"

Marriage required loving deeply and opened the door for hurt and mistakes. His thoughts went to Laura. He could see himself marrying her, not for love but because she was a kind person who felt deeply and cared about his daughter. But no, if he married her it would have to be in name only, and Laura didn't strike him as a woman who would want a marriage like that. "No, I don't think I could stand to lose another woman." Clint tied the horse's reins to the hitching post beside Matt's horse.

The sheriff pushed away from the barn "I'd best get on with my business with Laura and then head back to town."

His voice sounded as depressed as Clint now felt. He and the sheriff walked side by side to the house.

Laura stepped out onto the porch with a tray of cookies and a couple of mugs of coffee. Her face revealed nothing of her thoughts. Clint recognized the no-nonsense teacher. Gone was the relaxed woman of yesterday. "I thought I'd bring refreshments." She sat the plate on the small table that rested between two rocking chairs.

"That was very thoughtful of you," Matt said as he climbed the porch steps.

Clint followed but instead of sitting down, he stood

at the top of the steps. He wondered briefly if Laura had turned the girls over to Camelia or if she'd laid them down for a nap. Either way, he knew she would have seen to their needs before coming out onto the porch.

Matt took one of the coffee mugs and handed him the other.

"I gather you came to see me, Sheriff?" Laura's normally steady voice shook slightly.

Matt nodded. "Hope's ma came to see me today."

"Was she a short woman with blond hair and seemed to be crying?" Clint asked.

"She was." He pushed his hat back and asked a question of his own. "Besides the fact that Hope is blonde, how did you know her mother was blonde and upset?"

"I saw her leave the general store, where Laura and Hope had been and saw her at your office."

Matt nodded. "I see."

Laura cleared her throat. "What did she say?" She folded her trembling hands into the folds of her apron.

Clint sipped the coffee, aware that Laura wanted to get straight to the point. He wanted to hear what the sheriff said, too.

"She said she was dying and that she wanted you to raise Hope." He picked up one of the cookies and stuffed it in his mouth.

Clint released the air in his lungs, unaware he'd been holding it. He searched Laura's face for any reaction. Seeing none, he asked, "So, does that mean that Laura won't have to go before the judge to keep Hope?"

Matt looked to him and swallowed the cookie and coffee. "I believe so. He sent word that he's going to be delayed another month, so we have time to sort this all out on our own, if we can. She signed a paper saying Hope was to become your daughter, but she left a stipulation."

Laura's features turned from blank to surprise. "What kind of stipulation?"

Matt took his time and drank from his cup. His eyes searched Laura's. He lowered the cup and said, "You are not to tell anyone who Hope's mother is."

She sighed. "Not even her grandparents?"

Clint blurted, "You know who her grandparents are?"

Laura nodded. "Yes, Priscilla and I spoke earlier today." She turned her attention to the sheriff. "Did she mention that Hope's father is still alive?"

He rubbed his chin. "No."

Clint frowned. "I wonder where he is. And why hasn't he come for Hope and her mother?"

Laura sighed. "According to Priscilla, Jerry abandoned her and the baby. She said he wanted to blackmail Priscilla's parents. When she refused to help him, he up and left her."

"I wish she'd told me all that," the sheriff said, setting his cup down. He reached into his pocket and handed Laura a piece of paper.

Clint watched her expression as she unfolded and read it. Once again, she gave nothing away of how she was feeling. She refolded it.

"This is wonderful, Matt, but will it hold up in court, if Hope's father comes to claim her?" Laura unfolded then realized what she'd done and refolded the paper. She then slipped it into her apron pocket.

"I'll ask the judge when he arrives. You might have to come in and talk to him, but I don't believe he'll take

Hope from you as long as you have that." He indicated the note in her pocket.

Clint cleared his throat to remind them he was still there. Getting their attention, he asked, "Would it help if Priscilla talked to the judge?"

"I'm not sure she will. When Priscilla left my office, she was pretty shaken up, and she doesn't want anyone to know she's given up her child. Especially her parents, and since her father's the town banker, he'd know if she went to talk to the judge. Our town is small." He looked at Clint. "You knew she'd been to see me."

It was true. Not much got past folks in town. How many others knew she'd been to see the sheriff? And now that he knew that Priscilla was the banker's daughter, Clint knew the gossips would be all over this story, if they figured out she'd had a child and given it away.

The sheriff continued. "It might help if Laura was married and legally adopted Hope." He looked from Clint to Laura. "I guess that would be a question for a lawyer or the judge." When neither Clint nor Laura commented, he set his cup down. "Well, it's time for me to get back to town. Thanks for the coffee and cookies, Laura."

Clint moved aside and let Matt pass. "Thanks for coming out, Matt."

Laura looked up. "Yes, thanks." She stood to go back into the house.

"Laura, would you wait here for me? I'll see Matt off and be right back." Clint searched her face, but still couldn't read her thoughts.

She eased back on to the rocker. "All right, but hurry. I'm not sure how much longer Camelia will watch the girls."

That explained where the children were. He nodded and hurried off after Matt. Catching up with the sheriff as he unwound the reins from the hitching post, Clint asked, "Will it really help her keep Hope if she is married?"

Matt turned and looked at him. "Honestly, I'm not sure, but I do believe the judge will lean more toward letting her keep Hope if she is."

"But there is a chance?"

"Since Hope's father abandoned Hope and her mother, I'd say yes. He's more likely to let her stay with a couple who love her, than to give her to a man who doesn't." He swung into the saddle. A grin touched his lips. "And here I thought you weren't going to remarry."

Clint watched him ride away before he could respond. His gaze moved to Laura, who sat on the porch, reading the note in her hands. Would he marry her so that she could keep Hope? He cared about them both, and life on the ranch wouldn't be the same without them. He straightened his shoulders. He would, but in name only.

Chapter Thirteen

Laura studied Priscilla's signature on the paper. Would it be enough for her to hang on to Hope? She glanced up as Clint returned to the porch. His face was set as if he were going to a hanging.

She'd learned from her late husband, Charles, that when a man looked like that, it was best to wait him out and let him speak first. In her experience, whatever came out of his mouth wouldn't be pleasant. Was he going to ask her to leave, now that he was aware that Hope's father could show up?

Clint's boots sounded like thunder to her ears as he climbed the porch steps once more. He sat down in the rocker beside her and sighed. He took his hat off and crushed the brim in his hands. "Laura, I've been thinking, and if you think it will help you to keep Hope, I'll marry you."

Shocked, Laura stared at him in muted silence. He proposed even worse than Charles had. Charles had fumbled over the words like a schoolboy. Clint simply blurted out what he thought was his duty.

"Well?"

Laura opened her mouth and then shut it again. She couldn't just marry him for Hope's sake. Could she?

She shook her head in answer to her own silent question.

"Before you say no, think about it. You might be able to keep Hope. But—" He stopped.

She looked at him. What was the *but* about? Was he going to say, "But I expect you to quit your teaching job?" Laura wasn't sure she was ready to quit teaching. When he didn't finish she prompted, "But what?"

He inhaled deeply and released the air as if saying the next few words took more out of him than a mule's kick. "But it would be a marriage in name only."

Laura understood his guilt at losing his wife, but she thought, in time and when the right woman came along, he'd heal and want a real marriage. "I can't marry you, Clint. I've my own reasons for not wanting to remarry. Besides, we aren't sure the judge won't let me keep Hope." She stood. The relief on his face told Laura she'd answered correctly.

He reached out and grabbed her hand. "I'm willing to help you keep her any way I can."

She looked deeply into his eyes and saw the truth of his words. Clint Shepard was a good man, but if she were to marry him and he found out her secret, he might become bitter toward her and she couldn't live with that again. "Thank you, Clint. I appreciate your willingness to marry me, but I'm going to trust in the Lord to see this through."

Clint nodded and stood. "Then I'll get back to work." He left the porch without a backwards glance in her direction.

She silently prayed that the Lord would see fit to

work everything out for Hope and her. Laura couldn't imagine giving the little girl up now. She loved her.

Laura entered the house and walked to her temporary room. The sound of the girls playing in the kitchen hurried her steps. She tucked the note in a small box on her writing table. Maybe it was enough to hang on to Hope. Her gaze moved out the window.

Clint stood beside the barn, his gaze fixed on something in the distance. Was he thinking about his narrow escape from marriage? Laura almost wished she could marry him.

He had a nice home, land and a precious child that she already loved. In the month that she'd been here, he'd never raised his voice or his hand to anyone who lived in his home.

She studied his profile. He was a handsome man with wide shoulders, narrow hips and long legs. But it was his eyes that drew her like a kitten to yarn. The gentle way he spoke and the teasing manner he had with the girls only added to the attraction she felt toward him. Laura sighed. If only things were different. If only she weren't barren. But she was, and there was nothing anyone could do about it. Except the Lord God Himself. She'd once begged Him to let her have children, but He'd been silent and she'd remained childless. Laura fought her old enemy, bitterness, before returning to the kitchen to relieve Camelia.

Was this woman for real? It had been a week since Clint had placed his advertisement, and Mrs. Eunice Green was the result.

Laura watched as she spat tobacco juice on to the clean porch floor. Her gaze moved to Camelia, who cringed at the rudeness of the woman. If this was the type of character that Clint's advertisement brought out to the ranch, Laura thought she might offer to move Grace to town with her and Hope.

"I think I can take care of the little mite. I've been takin' care of kids for over forty years. This one can't be much worse than any of those." She spat again, barely missing Laura's skirt hem. "When will the mister be in? I'd like to talk to him. You ladies seem a mite squeamish to me."

Camelia stood. "There's no need for you to stay and wait for him. I've decided that you are not suitable to watch our Grace."

The woman pushed out of the rocker so fast it hit the wall behind them. She placed both hands on her hips and scowled down at Camelia. The fabric of her dirty trousers pulled tightly against her oversized belly. "Not suitable?"

Laura stepped up beside Camelia, silently offering her support of agreement. "Yes, ma'am. What I think Camelia is trying to say is that we don't want Grace learning that it's appropriate for a lady to dress and spit like a man." It wasn't the pants that bothered her as much as the spitting. After all, she'd worn Clint's pants when they'd gone out riding with the girls.

The woman made a huffing noise. "And I suppose you don't want me teaching her how to shoot a gun, neither." She shook her head as if the two women in front of her were daft.

Camelia made a gasping noise.

Laura decided she'd best be the one who answered again. Camelia looked as if she were ready to shove the woman off the porch. "No, if her pa wants her to learn to shoot a gun, I'm sure he'll teach her." She held her breath, waiting to see if Mrs. Green was going to leave or if they were going to have to call Richard from the barn to escort her off the ranch.

"Well, I reckon it's best her pa teach her that." Mrs. Green agreed. She walked off the porch, spat on the ground and remounted her horse like a man. "It's probably for the best. I'm getting too old to be chasing a kid around."

In a way, Laura envied Mrs. Green's spunk. But she wasn't ready to dress and act like a man every day. The other woman probably thought there were a lot of benefits to her style of life, and Laura figured there were, but again, she'd continue to be a lady. Her dresses fit her nicely, and even the thought of chewing tobacco turned her stomach.

"You ladies have a nice day." Mrs. Green turned the horse and rode from the ranch.

Laura smiled at her. "You, too, Mrs. Green. I hope you find suitable employment soon." She waved as the woman spun her horse about and galloped from the ranch.

The sound of the screen door shutting behind her drew Laura's attention. She prayed the girls weren't awakened from their nap by the sound. A few seconds later Camelia returned with a mop and bucket in hand.

"If that's the kind of women who respond to his nanny advertisement, I'm not sure if I can handle this. Did you see the way she was dressed? And that nasty habit of chewing. What woman in her right mind would take up such a habit?" She slapped the mop over the first dirty spot.

Laura sat down in one of the rockers and waited

for Camelia to settle down. She knew there was no way she'd be able to answer the other woman's questions. Using the heel of her boot, Laura set the rocker into motion.

Camelia mopped at the brown splatters on the porch. She rinsed the mop several times in the water. "Disgusting, that's what this is. I'm tempted to go find Clint Shepard and give him a piece of my mind."

It was all Laura could do not to laugh. Yes, Mrs. Green had been different, but to give Clint a piece of her mind, well, that sort of made Camelia odd, too. Why was Camelia so upset? So, Mrs. Green wasn't the nanny for Grace. Another woman might be just perfect.

"What do you think Clint is going to say when we tell him his first nanny arrived today and we sent her packing?" Laura felt a light breeze cool her brow.

Camelia picked up the bucket and started off the porch. "He said I could decide and I did." She walked to the side of the house mumbling, "I hope this 'bacca juice don't kill my wee plants."

Laura laughed. She rocked in the chair for a few moments longer and then got up. Grace's quilt still needed the binding sewn on. Binding was Laura's least favorite part of the process of quilting.

Camelia stomped back around the house. She marched up the porch steps and looked at Laura. "That woman just curdled my cabbage."

The expression struck Laura as funny, and she smiled to keep back the belly laugh she felt bubbling up. "I can see that."

"Imagine spitting like a man when seeking employment to watch a little girl." She plopped down in the other rocker. "Grace would be spitting in no time." Camelia shuddered. "So unladylike."

The countenance on the Irishwoman's face and the way she spoke with a heavy accent was simply too much. Laura couldn't control it. She howled with laughter. Bending over at the waist, she let her merriment explode.

Camelia looked at her like she'd grown two heads, causing Laura to laugh even harder. Tears of joy spilled from her eyes and down her cheeks. She could just picture little Grace spitting like a cat as she walked about the house. The image kept her laughing.

A giggle sounded beside her. "I guess I did get a little carried away."

Laura couldn't help it, she laughed more. Her cheeks were beginning to hurt from the merriment. "I can just picture our little Grace spitting and trying to keep her drawers up while Clint watched. Can you imagine his face?"

Camelia joined in her merry laughter. "He'd have a fit!"

That calmed Laura. She'd never seen Clint have a fit. Did he get angry and become violent? She shuddered.

"What's wrong, child?" Camelia had stopped laughing also.

Laura looked to her. "Has Clint ever lost his temper?"

The other woman shook her red head. "Not that I've ever seen. Why do you ask?"

"Oh, when you said he'd have a fit, I assumed you

meant he'd lose his temper and yell." Laura stood up. Embarrassment washed over her.

Camelia followed her inside the house. "Oh, no, it was just an expression. In all my years of working for him, he's never even raised his voice."

"Not even at his wife?" Laura moved to her sewing basket and pulled out her needle and thread.

"No. I'm sure he wasn't pleased with her all the time, but he never became angry enough to yell at her." Camelia walked into the kitchen.

Laura sat down and sighed. Clint seemed almost too perfect. He didn't yell, didn't get angry, and as far as she knew, he'd never raised a hand to Grace. She'd thought about marriage to him a lot over the past week but knew she couldn't marry Clint. Still, he seemed like the perfect man for the job. Would he understand if she told him she couldn't have children?

She pushed such foolish thoughts aside. Laura had turned his marriage proposal down. How foolish she would look if she went to him and said, "I've changed my mind. I will marry you, but I can never have children. Are you all right with that?"

He might say yes, but deep down she'd know it wasn't true. Clint had Grace, but what man didn't want a little boy to carry on the family name? As far as she knew, none.

It was best that she help Camelia find another nanny so that she and Hope could move back to town. Sadness enveloped her like a heavy fog. When the right nanny did arrive, she and Hope would be leaving the Shepard ranch.

Her gaze moved out past the barn and toward one of the many ranch pastures. Where was Clint now?

Was he cutting cows for branding? Or plowing a field someplace? She missed him and could only imagine what her life would be like without him and Grace in it.

Chapter Fourteen

Clint entered the kitchen door where he stopped and pulled off his muddy boots. The house was quiet. He assumed everyone was in bed.

The coffeepot and a covered plate sat on the back of the stove. He walked toward it, hoping it was still warm. His gaze took in the clean kitchen. Camelia worked hard to keep the house in tip-top shape.

His thoughts moved from there to what would have happened if Laura had agreed to marry him last week. Would Camelia have stayed as the housekeeper or moved on? Not that it mattered now. Laura had turned him down. At the time, he'd been relieved, but for some reason, he couldn't seem to get Laura off his mind.

As if she'd heard his thoughts, Laura appeared in the doorway. She wore a long housecoat. Her hair was braided and hung over one shoulder. "Oh, I'm sorry. I didn't mean to disturb you." She started to back out of the kitchen.

"Laura, you are not disturbing me." He watched her turn slowly around.

"Are you sure?" She played with the tip of her braid.

Clint tore his gaze from her and carried the covered plate to the table. "I'm sure. It will be nice to have company while I eat my supper."

She smiled. "You don't like to eat alone?"

Clint returned to the coffee pot and poured himself a cup. "Not really. Would you like a cup?"

Laura nodded. She walked to the cookie bin and pulled out two. "Yes, please." Then she returned to the table and waited for him to hand her one of the coffee mugs.

He sat down, bowed his head and said a silent prayer over the meal. When he looked up, Clint asked, "Couldn't sleep?"

"No, I kept thinking of Mrs. Green. She answered your nanny ad." A sweet smile parted her lips.

Clint uncovered the plate and discovered roast, baby potatoes and carrots. A large biscuit sat in the center. He reached into the crock that sat in the center of the table and pulled out a fork and knife. "Was she nice?"

Mischief danced in Laura's eyes. "I'm sure in her own way she was."

"How so?" He took a bite of the still-warm meat and chewed.

Laura nibbled at edge of her cookie. "Well, have you ever met her?"

He swallowed. "I'm not sure."

A giggle escaped her lips. "I think you would remember her if you had. She's about your height, wears men's clothes and spits."

He choked on his bite of potato. "What? She spits?"

Laura snickered. "Yes, she spits. Just like a man, and she did it on Camelia's clean porch."

His eyes widened. "Please tell me she didn't do this in front of Camelia."

A big grin split Laura's face as she nodded. "She did."

Clint chuckled. "How long did it take for her to tell Mrs. Green she wasn't the kind of woman we were looking for?"

"Not long, especially after she said she'd teach Grace to shoot a gun. You should have seen Camelia's face." She took a bite of her cookie and tried not to laugh around it.

"I can just imagine. She hates guns and the thought of Grace holding one…well, if she hadn't run her off, I would have." He looked up at Laura with a grin to show he wasn't angry, simply stating a fact.

"Well, that's more or less what I told her."

Curiosity filled his voice. "What exactly did you tell her?"

She grinned across at him. "I said that if you want Grace to learn how to shoot a gun, you'll be the one to teach her."

"You handled that quite nicely." Clint finished his bread and pushed the empty plate to the side.

Laura handed him her uneaten cookie. She pushed away from the table. "Thank you. Now I'm off to see if I can sleep." She yawned but covered her mouth with her hand to hide the action.

Clint took his plate to the washtub and laid it inside the shallow water. Camelia always left a little water in the tub so that in the morning whatever sauce or gravy that might still be on the plate wouldn't harden and make washing it more difficult. He looked to Laura. "Have a good night."

"You, too." Then she was gone.

He grinned as he thought of her tale of the nanny. It was obvious that Laura had enjoyed Camelia's reactions to the other woman. Laura had a sense of humor that he enjoyed. It was too bad that soon she'd be back in town and he'd miss her. Grace would miss her, too. He hoped the change in nannies wouldn't bother his daughter too much.

Laura gasped as the smallest of the three boys began falling from the top rail of the corral.

Their mother glanced their way and yelled, "Boys! Get off that fence!" Mrs. Lindy Crock turned her attention back to Laura and Camelia. "As you can see, I have experience with children."

Laura watched as two of the boys headed for the barn. The littlest one was making another attempt at staying on the top rail of the fence. She could see that Mrs. Crock was ignoring her children. Laura wasn't sure if that qualified as experience in raising them.

"Did you just move here, Mrs. Crock? I don't believe I've seen your boys in school." Laura watched the little one straddle the top rail and then his gaze moved about the yard. He was probably looking for something else to get into.

"Not recently. We've been on the Jones place for a couple of years now. The boys are taught by me at home, Mrs. Lee. I understand you are the schoolteacher." Her words dripped with sweetness, but Laura sensed there was vinegar in the mix.

"I am."

"Then I will be replacing you as the child's nanny." She tilted her head up and proceeded to look down her nose at Laura.

From this angle, Laura decided the other woman reminded her of a horse. Her face was long and her hair hung to the side like a horse's mane. Did she always wear it down? Or had the boys just been so active she hadn't had time to fix it before coming out to apply for the job of being Grace's nanny?

"Yes, I will resume teaching at the end of summer." Laura watched as the little boy began climbing back down. With his brothers not there, she assumed he no longer felt the need to prove he could get on the top rail and stay there.

"Precisely what I thought." With a nod of her head, Mrs. Crock turned her attention and focused all her energy on Camelia. "My husband and I are hoping to add a little girl to our family someday. Being a nanny for Grace will give me experience in how to raise a little girl." She smiled and took a sip from the tea that Camelia had served moments earlier.

Camelia frowned. "If you are married, how are you going to take care of Grace, your husband and teach three boys what they will need to know when they grow up?"

Mrs. Crock waved her hand as if the words Camelia had just uttered were nonsense. "Oh, I'll arrive in the morning with the boys. We will expect to eat breakfast with Grace. My husband may stop by around lunchtime, then he'll return to the farm and take care of things until supper. Of course, I'll head home and fix my family's final meal of the day."

The boys came screaming out of the barn with Richard behind them. His voice carried to the porch. "You kids stay out of this barn and away from the stallion.

You're fortunate he didn't hurt you both." He shook his pitchfork at them.

"Boys! Leave the nice man alone!" Mrs. Crock didn't even bother to turn around to see if they were obeying.

Laura shook her head. Those boys were sure to get hurt or cause someone else to be hurt, if they didn't settle down. "Mrs. Crock. Watching Grace is a full-time job. I'm afraid having other children distracting you might be a problem." The thought of those three boys coming to her school caused her to cringe. Not that she couldn't handle them, but they were going to be a handful if their mother ever decided to send them to school.

Mrs. Crock looked down her regal nose at Laura once more. "Am I mistaken, or don't you also have a child that you have here every day with you?"

Laura gave tit for tat. She raised her head, looked the other woman in the eye and replied, "I do, but Hope is a quiet little girl. Not three rowdy boys."

The chickens began to squawk and cackle as the boys explored the henhouse. They chased the hens out into the chicken pen and flapped their arms. Feathers filled the air as the chickens raced to get away from the boys. One of them grabbed a hen by the wing and proceeded to swing it around in a circle. The other two were still in hot pursuit of the other hens.

Camelia jumped to her feet. "Mrs. Crock, get control of your children!"

Mrs. Crock turned to see what they were doing. She huffed and then walked regally toward the hen-house as if nothing were out of the ordinary. When she got within hearing distance of the ruckus, the woman waved her arms and screamed, "Boys! Boys! Stop! Boys, stop!" Mrs. Crock stopped outside the fence and continued yelling at her children.

The boys ignored their mother and proceeded with their mischief. The littlest one slipped and fell. The other boy leaped over him and spotted one of the roosters. The youngest began to wail his unhappiness at being on the ground.

The rooster refused to act like a hen and run. He faced the older boy with spurs at the ready. The third continued to torment the hen he still hung on to and swung about. Mrs. Crock screamed their names over and over. "Logan! Bradley! Billy! Boys, stop that this instant!"

Laura had had enough. She walked from the porch and calmly entered the chicken yard. Grabbing the ear of the boy who still swung the hen about, she twisted it and ordered, "Let it go." She knew she wasn't hurting him, he'd just be startled.

The boy yelped and released the injured chicken.

Without freeing the boy's ear, she proceeded to the baby. Pulling him up by his belt loop, again as a schoolteacher, Laura knew she wasn't hurting the child. She ordered, "Go to your mother and stay there."

The boy she still held on to yelled. "Let go! Let go! Let go!"

Laura tugged him closer to her. "You be quiet or I might just pull this ear off." She gave it a warning tug. He hushed and the baby went running to his mother.

The other boy and the rooster were having a standoff. The rooster made deep, grumbling warning sounds as he faced the boy who by now wasn't so sure he was up to this fight. Laura used his moment of indecision to grab his ear with her free hand.

The rooster gave a crow of triumph. Laura ordered the rooster, "You behave yourself or I'll see you reach the bottom of a cooking pot tonight." The rooster unfluffed his feathers and moved to check on his flock.

Then, with both boys firmly in hand, Laura marched them back to where their mother stood. She'd had all she could take of this family. It was bad enough that her children were undisciplined, but the woman had actually forgotten about the two older boys in her rush to comfort the youngest.

Mrs. Crock had gathered the baby to her and was fawning over him. "Oh, my poor baby, did those bad ole chickens hurt you?" Using her apron, she wiped at the dirty tears on his face.

Disgusted with them all, Laura pulled the boys through the gate and ordered the one nearest to close it. He did as she said with a whimper. Still holding both boys in place, Laura turned to their mother. "Mrs. Crock, I believe this interview is over. Mrs. Murphy and Mr. Shepard will decide on the position soon. If you don't hear from them, you may assume you didn't get the job." She released the two boys, who hurried to their mother's side, rubbing their red ears.

The woman gathered her children about her and hurried them to the wagon that she'd arrived on. She climbed up on the seat and looked down at Laura. "I don't believe I want the position any longer, Mrs. Lee. This place is too dangerous for my boys."

Laura nodded. "I'll let Mrs. Murphy and Mr. Shepard know you are pulling your application."

Mrs. Crock huffed, slapped the reins over the poor

horse's back and turned the wagon toward town. She pressed the baby against her side while the older boys scuffled about in the wagon bed.

Laura walked over to the chicken pen. The little hen that the boy had swung about stood by the fence with her head down and her broken wing touching the ground. Careful not to spook the chicken, Laura entered the gate. The animal raised its head and gave out a small cry. Her heart went out to it.

Camelia walked from the porch with a grin. "You sure took that situation in hand. No wonder the school board wants you to return in the fall."

Laura gently picked the little hen up. "Have you ever set a wing before, Camelia?"

"No, and I'm not going to start now. Richard can take care of her in a few minutes, and we'll make dumplings for dinner." Camelia frowned. "But it's a shame. That's one of our best layers."

"If it's all the same to you, I'd prefer not to kill the poor little thing. It's not her fault those boys are a menace to everyone and everything around them." Laura smoothed the little hen's feathers. She was amazed that the chicken seemed to understand her actions and leaned her body more fully into Laura's.

Camelia shook her head. "I don't really want to clean a chicken anyway. But the final say will come from Clint." She turned around and walked to the house.

Laura stood there holding the chicken. She'd left the girls in their room playing when Mrs. Crook had arrived. Now she didn't know what to do. She couldn't stand out here in the hen yard all day, but she couldn't let the chicken continue to be in pain either.

Richard stepped out of the barn. He tsked and shook

his head. "What are you going to do with her? Want me to put it out of its misery?"

She couldn't do it. The hen hadn't asked to be injured. Laura looked at Richard. "Would you mind keeping her in one of the empty stalls until Clint gets back from the field?"

"Naw, don't reckon I do." He held his big hands out for the chicken.

Laura handed it over. It squawked weakly. "Be careful with her."

"I'll do my best, ma'am." Richard cradled the injured bird in the crook of his arm.

She heard him mutter as he walked away, "Women ask the strangest things. If it were up to me, we'd be having chicken soup tonight."

Walking back to the house, Laura wondered if Clint felt the same as Camelia and Richard. Would he want to kill the hen and eat her? Or would he side with her and fix the injured wing?

For reasons she couldn't explain, Laura prayed he'd side with her. If he didn't, she knew her feelings would be hurt, and she'd be skipping supper tonight.

Chapter Fifteen

Clint frowned. "You want me to set the chicken's wing?"

Laura nodded. She handed Grace a hot roll. "It's not her fault she got hurt."

"Wouldn't it just be easier to make chicken pie?" He looked to Hope, who was playing in her potatoes. His daughter sat across from him, tearing the bread into little clumps and making them into balls.

Her eyes searched his face. "Not for me. Look, I know this is a ranch and you raise animals for food, but that little hen isn't going to die. She just needs her wing set." As if grasping for straws, she continued. "Camelia says she's our best laying hen."

Camelia buttered a roll and nodded. "She is at that."

Clint heard her but could only focus on the word *our*. Laura had used the word *our* as if she were a part of the family. He looked deeply into her eyes. Something told him this wasn't just about the hen. It was as if she were waiting for something. Something from him. But what?

Her cheeks turned pink under his watchful eyes. "I

know I'm being silly, but I feel bad for the hen." She turned her back on him and began gathering up the little balls of bread from around Grace's plate. "Sweetie, we don't play with our food, we eat it." She patted the top of Grace's head.

Clint sighed and looked down at his supper plate. "After the girls are in bed, we'll go to the barn and see what we can do for your chicken," Clint said. He didn't know why he'd given in, but there was something in Laura's manner that told him it was the right thing to do.

Her soft reply sent his heart to pumping. "Thank you."

He looked from Camelia to Laura. "How did the hen get a broken wing?"

Camelia told the tale. She chuckled when she told about Laura grabbing those boys by their ears and forcing them to walk to their mother. Pride shone in her face when she looked at Laura.

"So that's two nannies who didn't work out," he said. He'd known the moment that Camelia had mentioned that the woman was Lindy Crock that she wouldn't work as a nanny for Grace.

Everyone in town knew the woman and her raucous boys. Lindy Crock liked for everyone to think she knew what she was doing. Unfortunately, even if she was good at some things, raising a houseful of boys wasn't one of them. They were wild and disrespectful. It amazed him that she was unaware of how her youngest acted. Of the three boys, he seemed to be the worst of the lot.

Clint sighed. Thankfully, he hadn't had to deal with the woman or her children. It probably wasn't fair that he'd turned the hiring of a nanny over to Camelia. So far, she'd had to deal with one rude woman and another with a pack of wild boys. Neither were good candidates for a nanny.

"Come along, girls." Laura helped both Grace and Hope from their chairs.

He pushed back from the table. Clint noticed that Camelia had already started clearing it and was stacking the dishes in the washtub. His gaze followed Laura and the girls as they left the room.

"She did good today," Camelia said as she picked up his plate.

Clint felt guilty that Laura and Camelia had had to deal with the strange events of the day. "Maybe I should start interviewing the women myself."

She shook her head. "No, I'm the one that is going to be stuck with her all day while you are out working. I should get to choose the best fit for Grace and myself." Camelia put his plate in the tub and began washing the dishes.

He had to admit that she was right. Clint walked over and stood beside Camelia. "What do you think about setting a hen's wing?"

Camelia grinned at him. "I think it's fine. If it were her leg the boy had broken, we'd have no choice. I'm not sure why, but for some reason Laura has become attached to the little chicken. It would break her heart if you killed it."

He nodded. "Thanks." Clint went into the sitting room where Laura and the girls had retired.

Laura sat with her sewing box by her side while the girls played with their rag dolls and blocks. It was a nice scene and one that he'd grown to love.

Clint went to his chair that sat beside the fireplace and picked up the big family Bible. He searched the chapters for something fun to read to the little girls. The book of Daniel opened before him, and he began to read about Daniel in the lion's den.

Camelia entered a few minutes later and went to her favorite rocking chair. She picked up her mending and was soon rocking and working the needle back and forth through the cloth of one of his shirts.

His gaze moved to Laura, who had her head bent close to a square of blue fabric. He recognized the pattern on the blue square and grinned. It was from one of his papa's old shirts. Laura hadn't asked if she could use the other clothes in the chest, but he didn't mind that she had.

Grace dropped her doll and went to sit at his feet. Hope followed but hung on to her baby doll. She tucked her finger in her mouth and looked up at him expectantly.

Laura smiled at the girls. Love shone in her eyes. She cared for the children, and from the look on her face, Laura loved them like a mother.

Did she realize how hard it was going to be for her when she left the ranch and Grace? And how was Grace going to react at the loss of her nanny? He'd thought at first it would be easy to replace Laura; now he wasn't so sure. Would they ever find a nanny like Laura? Clint snuck a quick look at her. She was more than a nanny to him and Grace. And he knew there'd never be anyone like Laura Lee.

Laura held the little hen while Clint tucked her wing into a natural position. He stood close enough that she could smell the peppermint candy he'd shared with the girls earlier on his breath.

"Now you'll need to hold her still so that I can wrap the cloth around her body to hold the wing in place." Clint placed her hand on the wing and then reached for the strips of cloth that Camelia had supplied.

His hands brushed hers as he wrapped the chicken's wing tightly. The little hen squirmed and made sounds in the back of her throat. She didn't like them handling her and began to voice her discomfort more loudly.

"How long will we need to leave the cloth on?" Laura asked, trying to ignore the fact that her pulse was racing at his nearness.

Clint tied the fabric and sighed. "I have no idea. I guess until she can hold her wing up herself." He moved back. "Go ahead and set her down. I want to see if she can get the wing out of the sling we've made for it."

Laura did as he asked. The little bird flopped about unhappily. She tried to pull her wing from her body and couldn't. The bandage was on nice and tight. Laura looked up at Clint and found him watching her. "Um, thank you."

He grinned. "You're welcome."

"You must think I'm crazy, wanting to bandage a chicken up like that." She rubbed her arms.

Clint reached out and brushed her hair from her eyes. "No, I think you are sweet."

Breathlessly, she asked, "You do?"

He stepped closer. "I do." His hand stayed in her hair.

Laura stepped back. What was she doing? She'd thought he was going to kiss her, and for a moment she'd welcomed the idea. But that was ridiculous. "I really should get back inside and make sure the girls are sleeping."

His hand dropped to his side. "Yes, I suppose you should. I'll make sure the chicken gets into the coop."

She wanted to say something that would make them both feel less awkward. "I think I'll call her Miss Priss."

"Miss Priss?" He looked at her as if she'd lost her mind.

Laura nodded. "Yep, Miss Priss. She's the only girl in the coop with a special bandage. I'm sure the other hens are going to be jealous, and then she'll just sort of strut around and be, well, and act like a Miss Priss."

Clint leaned his head back and laughed. True laughter that brought a smile to her face.

Laura left on the happy note, aware that she'd almost reacted to his nearness tonight. She vowed before going to bed that she'd put some space between herself and Clint. Even though, deep down, she wished it didn't have to be that way.

Chapter Sixteen

L aura and the girls studied the hook and can of worms that Richard had dug up for her that morning. He'd also found her a cane fishing pole and plenty of strings and hooks.

She'd wanted to get away from the house and spend some time out in the sunshine. This fishing adventure had been her idea of how to do just that. Plus, thanks to the picnic she'd packed, she was assured to miss Clint at lunch.

"Ick." Grace wrinkled her nose at the wiggling worms.

Hope mimicked her. "Ick." She smiled broadly at a surprised Laura.

Laura grabbed them both and hugged them tight. When she released them, they both were smiling broadly. Her gaze moved back to the can of worms. "Ick or no ick, the only way we are going to catch fish for dinner is if we put one of these worms on our hook."

Grace nodded. Hope nodded. Laura took a deep breath and picked up the biggest worm she could find. She'd gone fishing lots of times with her father, but now that the time had come to bait the hook, Laura remembered that he had done that part for her.

She quickly threaded the worm on the hook, walked to the water's edge and cast it out into the water. Laura looked to the girls. "That wasn't so bad."

Hope curled her lip and wrinkled her nose. "Ick."

Grace laughed and shoved Hope. The two girls giggled and rolled about on the grassy ground.

Laura squatted down, laid her pole on the grass and rinsed her fingers off in the cool water. She motioned for the girls to come join her.

They toddled to Laura, giggling and shoving each other.

"You two better settle down or you are going to fall into the water with the fish." She grabbed Grace around her little waist and plopped her on to the right side of her, then helped Hope sit down on the left hand side of her.

They looked up at her as if to say, what now?

Laura laughed. She picked up the pole and then lay down on her back. She looked up into the sky. "Lie down here by me and let's see if we can find any clouds shaped like animals."

The little girls lay back, wiggled about and then looked up. Laura's gaze followed theirs. The sky was a brilliant blue with big, fluffy white clouds floating about.

For several long moments, Laura simply enjoyed the quietness of the bank. She'd loved doing this as a child but knew at the ages of one and two, the girls would get bored with it fast.

Grace pointed up at the sky and said, "Bird."

Laura's gaze followed the little girl's finger and saw

that there was a bird flying above them. "Oh, how pretty! You found a bird, Grace." She turned her head and looked to Hope. "See the pretty bird?"

"Hey!"

Laura sat up at the sound of Clint's shout. He was sitting on his horse a few feet away and was pointing toward the bank. She looked and saw that her fishing pole was quickly traveling down toward the water's edge.

Grace squealed at the sight of her papa.

She ignored the child and scrambled to get the fishing pole before it hit the water and sank with the fish on the other end. Just before it went under, she grabbed the pole and began running back up the little embankment.

Clint's rich laughter sounded behind her.

Laura looked behind her and saw Hope sitting where she'd left her. Clint held Grace in his arms and his horse stood behind them. A tug on the line reminded her she had caught a fish.

She jerked the pole, and the line, with a fish dangling on the end of it, shot out of the water. "I got one!"

Hope stood up and clapped her hands.

Grace pushed against her papa's chest until he released her, then she joined Laura on the bank. "Ish!" She pointed at the squirming fish on the end of the hook.

"Yes, fish." Laura couldn't seem to stop smiling. It had been a long time since she'd gone fishing, let alone caught anything.

Clint scooped up Hope and walked to where they stood. He looked about. "Did you bring a bucket to put your catch in?"

Laura's smile slipped from her face. "No, I forgot." She'd have to release the fish back into the stream.

"Not to worry. I may have a small piece of rope we can use for a stringer. "You might want to hold him over the grass and not the water. If he jumps off that hook he'll swim away." He flashed a white grin in her direction before turning to his horse's saddlebags.

Grace jumped up and down. She wanted to touch the fish. Laura bent over and held it in front of her.

"Don't touch its mouth. There is a sharp hook in there."

The little girl bobbed up and down on her feet. She reached a single finger out and touched the scales on the fish's back. A squeal issued from her when the fish flipped around. She jerked her hand back and laughed.

Clint returned with a nice size piece of rope. He laughed at his daughter. "We'll make a tomboy out of you yet." His large hand ruffled her brown hair.

Laura stood, giving him better access to the fish. Within minutes, he had it off the hook and on to the thin rope.

"This one's a pretty good size." He looped one end of the rope around a nice size rock and then slipped the fish into the water. Secured to the rope, it wasn't swimming away.

"I was hoping we'd catch enough to have a fish fry tonight," Laura confessed with a grin.

He wiped his hands on his pants. "Then it's a good thing I came along when I did, isn't it?"

For the first time, Laura noticed a cane pole across the back of his horse. She nodded. Inwardly, she groaned. So much for keeping more distance between them.

* * *

Clint enjoyed the rest of the morning and part of the afternoon with Laura and the girls. She was easy to be around and not the least bit skittish about touching the worms or fish.

Grace yawned and stretched. Hope had already curled up on the blanket.

Laura took Hope by the hand and pulled her up from her resting place. "Come on, little one. Let's go to the house where you can rest better." She gently pulled the sleepy child off the blanket they had all sat on while they'd had lunch.

Clint picked her up. "If you don't mind, she and Grace can ride on the horse on the way back."

Grace jumped around and giggled. She ran to the side of the horse. "Up."

Laura laughed. "I don't mind as long as they stay awake and don't fall off."

Clint carried Hope to the horse and set her in the front of the saddle. Then he reached down and plopped Grace behind Hope. "Grace, Hope is younger than you, so you need to hold on to her tight. Can you do that?"

The little girl bobbed her head and babbled. Her little arms slid around Hope's waist. Then she looked at him with a big smile, seemingly looking for approval.

"That's good." He patted her leg. "Hope, you have to hold on to the saddle horn so that you and Grace don't fall off. Can you do that?"

This time Hope nodded shyly and babbled like Grace. He smiled. Something had changed in Hope. She now seemed more confident and ready to start talking. The little girl grabbed the saddle horn and hung on tight.

Clint patted her leg and said the same thing to her. "That's good."

His gaze moved to Grace, who released Hope and stuck her little hand into the pocket of her dress. What did she have? Trying not to be too obvious, he snuck a peek. Several wiggly worms could be seen hanging from the little girl's hand. He looked away as Grace tucked them back inside her pocket.

He couldn't wait for Laura to find Grace's little surprise. It was all Clint could do not to give the little girl's secret away with a knowing grin. Clint turned to see Laura picking up her newly refilled picnic basket. "All we have left to get is our fish." He looked to where they flopped about in the water.

"I'll get them." Laura walked over and pulled them from the water. She carried the basket in one hand and the fish in the other back to where he stood beside the horse and the girls.

They began walking back to the house. "Today was fun," Laura said.

Clint nodded. "Yes, I should have helped Richard and a couple of the men clear brush from around the water hole."

"The water hole?"

He grinned. "That's what we call the main pond in the west pasture."

"I see. What made you come find us?" Laura looked up at him as they walked.

Clint steadied the little girls by resting a hand on Hope's leg. "Richard came out and told me you were fishing today. I haven't been fishing in a long time and thought it would be fun." He didn't tell her that he was concerned about her and the girls being away from the house alone.

When he'd returned to the house, Camelia had already packed him a lunch and had the cane pole sitting on the front porch. The little Irishwoman had admitted to sending Richard out to get him. She hadn't voiced her concerns to Laura and had asked him not to tell the nanny it had been her idea for him to go fishing.

"It has been a long time for me, too." She handed him the fish.

Clint took the fish with a frown. "Why are you giving them to me? You caught the majority of them."

"Yes, well, they stink." She looked to the little girls.

Hope yawned and mumbled, "Ick."

He chuckled, then sobered. "Oh, I see what you are up to. If you give them to me, you think I'll clean them."

Laura turned large, innocent eyes on him. "That's a great idea. Thank you."

Confusion filled Clint's mind. "What?"

She smiled mischievously. "Didn't you just volunteer to clean the fish?"

He laughed. "No, but since you are so sweet, I'll do it for you." Immediately Clint wished he hadn't called her sweet.

Her cheeks reddened and Laura ducked her head. She remained quiet the rest of the way back to the house. The little girls chattered to one another unaware that the adults were feeling uncomfortable with each other.

Why did he feel the need to tease her? And say what

he was thinking? Last night, he'd come close to kissing her. Why? He knew it would lead to nowhere, and still, he simply couldn't stop himself around her.

Chapter Seventeen

Laura looked to the house and sighed. "Looks like we have company." Did the wagon in front of the house belong to another woman wanting her job?

Clint led the horse to the barn after handing Laura the fish. As he tied the horse to the hitching post, his gaze moved to the front porch where Camelia sat with another woman. He pulled the girls off the horse's back and set them on the ground.

Grace started walking to the house. Laura returned the fish and picked up a tired Hope. Together they walked to the house.

Camelia stood to welcome them. "I see you were able to catch a few fish." She waited for them to get on the porch. "Clint, Laura, this is Millicent English. She likes to be called Missy."

Clint reached across and shook the young woman's hand.

Laura smiled her greeting, aware that the other woman never took her eyes off Clint Shepard. Her light brown hair was swept up in the latest style. The dress she wore was pressed and starched to perfection.

Little button-up shoes covered her tiny feet. Her skin was clear as a newborn baby's, and green eyes as big as a dessert plate stared up at Clint.

"It's nice to meet you, Mr. Shepard."

Even her voice dripped with sweetness. Laura decided to leave this interview to Camelia and Clint. She took Grace's little hand and started toward the door.

"Oh, you must be Gracie," Missy exclaimed as if she'd just noticed the child. "You are so cute. You look just like your daddy." Missy held out her hand for Grace to shake.

Grace smiled at her and put small muddy fingers into the other woman's clean hand. She babbled happy to talk to a new adult.

Missy flinched away from the child when she realized how dirty her hands were. Her face took on a look of disgust. Gone was the sweet voice, and in its place was a sharpness that grated. "What is all over you?"

Too young to notice the change in the woman's attitude, Grace reached into her pocket and tried to hand Missy her newest treasure. What was Grace trying to give Missy? It looked like mud, but Laura couldn't remember any mud at the riverbank. The area where they'd fished and had lunch had been grassy and there were rocks along the shoreline. She'd thought the girls had stayed relatively clean.

The young woman moved back in her seat. Her big eyes took on a look of horror. She jerked away from Grace. "Get those away from me!" she shrieked.

Laura caught Grace's arm and turned her around to see what she had in her hand. Big, red worms wriggled in the little girl's dirty hand. She smiled. "Grace, what have you got there?"

"Whumms." Grace smiled.

"Worms?" Laura looked to Clint, who smiled broadly at his daughter. Had he known she had worms in her dress pocket?

Disgust sounded in Missy's voice. "Well, young lady, we do not play with worms. If you were my child, I'd spank your bottom for bringing those to the house."

Clint's head swung in the direction of the young woman. "Thank you, Miss English, for coming out, but I don't think you would be a good fit for our Grace."

She looked at him in shock. "I—" Her gaze met his. "I see." Missy stood up and smoothed imaginary wrinkles from her skirt. She walked past him and out into the yard. Missy got into her wagon and rode away.

Laura was glad to see her go. She'd been more of a dewy-eyed schoolgirl than a proper nanny.

Camelia tsked. "I thought she was the one."

Grace yawned and held out her worms to Laura, who took them and asked, "Are there any more worms in your pocket?"

The little girl put her hand into the pocket once more, then pulled it out empty. She tried to look inside the pocket but didn't see anything. "Aw gone."

"Come along, Gracie. Let's wash your hands. Laura will take care of your worms." Camelia opened the door and let Grace go in first.

Hope laid her head on Laura's shoulder and sucked on her finger.

Laura stood and rested her chin on Hope's head. The soft baby blond hair tickled her. She walked out to the chicken coop and tossed the worms inside. Miss Priss hurried forward with her friends, and they clucked and scratched at the ground.

Clint followed her. "I don't know if we'll ever find anyone to replace you." He sighed, then continued on toward the hitching post where his horse waited.

Laura tilted her head. Was he talking about as a nanny? Or in their lives? She had no reason to think he meant their lives. He'd given her no indication that she was that big a part of the family. Yet the question continued to nag at her as she made her way back to the house.

Clint had learned to listen to his gut years ago. Right now he sensed real danger. Seeing the rustlers below only added conviction to his gut reaction. He squinted harder and focused on the cow thieves below. All ten or twelve had covered their faces with bandanas, leaving only their eyes showing.

Every crisp sound from below swept up the steep incline where he crouched in a stand of cedar to the right of an old, gnarled oak. He'd hidden his horse a short distance away and prayed the animal stayed put.

"Hurry up with those cows! We've gotta get out of here. Shepard and his men are close enough I can smell 'em!" the ringleader yelled.

Where were his men? Richard had reported that a head of cattle had gone missing this morning, and they'd pulled together all the ranch hands they had to go in search of them. Seven men including him worked on the Shepard ranch. He'd sent them two by two to all four corners of the property except the east side, and he'd decided to come check out the gullies here himself.

Letting the outlaws escape took everything Clint Shepard had. But to his way of thinking, there were too many of them for one man to try to stop alone. Surely his men had realized by now that he hadn't returned to the barn and would be coming out to find him.

He peered closer as the rustlers tried to drive the bawling cattle up the draw. But the ornery cows seemed to be smarter than the outlaws. The rustlers yelled obscenities at the animals and each other as they tried to drive them out of the canyon. The cows broke away from the group, scattering this way and that. Clint allowed a grin. These rustlers were definitely not cattlemen.

Clint adjusted quickly to the situation. His mind whirled as he searched for some kind of a plan. One shot in the air would alert the other men to his position, if they were near. But would they arrive before the outlaws got to him?

The hot sun bore down. Sweat trickled into his eyes, making them sting. He wiped it away with an impatient hand.

From his hiding place, Clint watched the rustlers. He couldn't afford to lose those cows to outlaws. His livelihood and Grace's depended on him hanging on to the herd. Slowly, he drew his gun and prepared for the fight.

He hated shooting at men and prayed his bullets wouldn't kill anyone, simply injure them enough to keep them from rustling his cattle. Clint knew he had only one chance to scare off the outlaws. But if they decided to fight back, it was all or nothing.

His first shot ripped into a man's shoulder. As the outlaw screamed, Clint quickly swung to the next target and caught the rider's thigh. A third shot grazed another's gun hand. The next man leaned from the saddle just as Clint pulled the trigger.

Before he could fire again, cold steel jabbed into Clint's back. A hand reached for his gun. "Let's have a look at ya. Don't turn around. Just show me your face."

The order grated along Clint's nerve endings and settled in his clenched gut. He listened for any sounds to indicate his men were nearby. If they weren't, he was as good as dead. He heard nothing except the bawling of cows and rustlers yelling to each other over the chaos that he'd caused with his bullets. He silently prayed the noise below was the reason he couldn't hear his own men.

Clint turned his head slowly. Cold, dark eyes glared over the top of the rustler's bandana.

He narrowed those eyes at Clint. "Well, whadda ya know? I got myself the owner of the Shepard Ranch."

Though Clint couldn't see the outlaw's mouth, the tone of his words told him he wore a sneer. Clint straightened his spine. "I'm not here alone. My men are here, as well. I suggest you tell your partners that they'd best clear on out."

"That right? Well, from what I can see, no one is firing at us but you." The gun barrel poked harder into Clint's back. "Get on down there."

Clint could have managed without the rough shove. The soles of his boots provided little traction in the gravel. Slipping and sliding down the steep embankment, he glanced for any sign that would suggest help had arrived, but saw nothing.

At the bottom, riders on horseback immediately surrounded him.

"Good job, Spence." The outlaw pushing to the front was the ringleader. He was dressed all in black, from his hat to his boots. "Let's teach this cattleman not to mess with us. I've a special party in mind for him. One of you, find his horse and get a rope. Spence, march him back up the hill. The rest of you drive those cattle to the makeshift corral."

Clint's mouth grew dry as the man named Spence bound his hands in front of him, then pushed him up the steep incline.

Any minute, Clint knew his men would arrive. Just a matter of time, he told himself, praying he was right. His horse and a rope could only mean that the leader planned a hanging party. He'd just as soon not be the guest of honor. Somehow, he had to stall until help arrived.

"Spence, do you know the punishment for hanging a man?" he asked.

"Shut up, and get movin'."

Clint tried again. "Are you willing to throw your life away for a man who doesn't give two cents about you? The sheriff is a friend of mine, and he will hunt each and every one of you down if you do this."

Spence gave him a rough shove forward toward the oak tree. "You don't know nothin' about nothin', so keep your trap shut. One more word out of ya and I'll shoot you in the leg and drag you the rest of the way up this here hill."

Clint lapsed into silence. He could see Spence had closed his mind against anything he said. If he ran, he'd be lucky to make it a few feet before hot lead slammed into his leg. Clint was sure that the men in this group would rather see him hang than to die of a fatal gunshot wound. Even if he made it to the cover of the trees, what then? He had no gun and no horse. Maybe he could spin around and get Spence's gun.

But just as he prepared to twist around and take the weapon, the ringleader rode up beside them and shouted, "Hurry up, you two! We don't have all day." His evil laugh sent a chill down Clint's sweating back.

As they made their way up the steep incline, Clint watched an outlaw appear with his horse. The steed bobbed his head in greeting. Once they were at the top, the horse nuzzled Clint as though offering sympathy or maybe a last goodbye.

Stalling, Clint stoked the face of his faithful friend, murmuring a few quiet words of comfort, to both himself and the animal. He sent more silent prayers heavenward, asking the Lord to send his men quickly.

"Enough of this nonsense," rasped the leader with an impatient motion of his gun. "Put him on the horse."

Clint scanned the landscape anxiously, hoping to glimpse his men, but saw only the branches of cedar, oak and cottonwood trees swaying gently in the breeze. He strained against the ropes binding him but they wouldn't budge.

His heart pounded against his ribs. Panic so thick he could taste it lodged in his throat as they jerked him into the saddle. Clint refused to cower in front of them. He sat straight and tall in the saddle, not allowing them to see the fear and regret that gathered in his heart.

He regretted not allowing himself to have feelings for another woman since Martha's death. Clint knew he had cared for Laura. Not the love of a man for a woman, but it could have grown into that had he allowed it to happen.

Sitting tall in the saddle, Clint silently vowed to the Lord that if he lived through the day, he'd stop feeling guilty for Martha's death and find a true mother for little Grace. He knew Martha wouldn't be happy with him, if she knew he was raising her daughter without a mother's influence.

The leader laughed as he threw the rope up and over one of the gnarled oak branches. "Better pray hard, Shepard. You are about to meet your maker."

Shots rang out close by. The sound of horses crashing through the trees filled Clint's ears. He could hear the men yelling below and the sound of gunfire. Had his men split up, and were they attacking both the ridge and the gully below?

Growling a foul word, the leader looked up at Clint. "It's your lucky day, Shepard." Then he jumped on to his horse. He raised his gun. Clint felt sure he was about to die, and then Richard burst through the tree line.

The leader of the rustlers spun his horse and ran. Richard waved as he passed, in heavy pursuit down the steep incline.

Clint's horse snorted as Clint struggled with the bonds that held his hands in place. "Steady, boy." From the hilltop vantage point, he watched as Richard and his men chased after the outlaws. He prayed for their safety as he continued to work at the rope around his hands.

He still couldn't believe all that had transpired since breakfast. Richard had reported a large field of cattle missing. They'd all gone in different directions with Clint going off alone to the east. He'd no idea that the band of rustlers had been so large. In his mind, he'd thought there would only be about three men to deal with, not the twelve he'd encountered. Now his men were fighting for their lives.

Finally, his hands were free. Clint tore off after his

men and the rustlers. He could no longer hear gunfire and prayed that his men were all safe.

Clint arrived just as the last outlaw was being shoved up on to his horse. He rode up beside Richard. "Is everyone all right?" His eyes scanned the condition of his men.

"Luke took a bullet to the arm, but it went straight through so I'm sure he'll be fine." Richard hooked his thumb over his shoulder. "Looks like we got them all."

Clint's heart sank. "No, the leader isn't here. You didn't get them all." He spun his horse around. "Richard, get them into town to the sheriff. I'm going to the house to check on the ladies."

He didn't give Richard time to answer but sped back toward the house. If the leader came across the house, what would he do to Laura, Camelia and the girls? With his heart pounding in time with his horse's running feet, Clint prayed over the women and children in his care.

Chapter Eighteen

Laura hung the last of the wash on the line. She yawned, wishing she could take a nap like the little girls. Wash day wasn't her favorite, but it had to be done. Camelia walked up beside her with another basket of wet clothes.

"Is that the last of it?" She reached in and pulled out one of Grace's little dresses.

"Yep. I could have done this by myself." She set the basket down and walked to the other clothesline.

Laura hid her grin. "I know, but you wouldn't have had much time left for all your other chores. Besides, when Clint hired me, he didn't say I couldn't do my and Hope's laundry."

Camelia chuckled. "You are one stubborn woman."

She revealed her grin around the little dress hanging on the line. "Maybe I'm part Irish."

At that Camelia did laugh. "You know, you just might be at that."

The sound of horses coming into the front yard at a fast clip had Laura and Camelia exchanging worried looks. "What do you think is wrong now?" Laura asked, turning to walk to the front of the house.

"With our men, there is no telling. How do you lose a whole herd of cattle?"

Laura shook her head. "Cattle don't get lost, they get rustled."

Camelia frowned. "Rustlers?"

They hadn't talked about Richard's earlier visit, but now that new trouble seemed to be brewing, the ladies frowned and continued.

"Only way to really lose cows, at least as far as I know." Laura stepped around the front of the house just as Clint's horse slid to a stop.

His voice sounded urgent. "Where are the girls?"

Camelia walked up beside Laura. "Napping inside."

"Good. That's where I want you ladies, too." He walked to Laura and Camelia and took each of them by the arm.

Laura pulled away from him. "Hold on one minute, Clint. What is this all about?"

"Rustlers." He grabbed her arm again.

Richard tore into the yard. His gaze took in the scene of Clint trying to get the women into the house.

Clint barked at him. "I told you to stay with the other men."

"And let you run off on your own again? Sorry, boss, couldn't do it. I sent Luke with them into town. He's angry at being shot and has put fear into those rustlers. They'll get to town, all right."

Camelia covered her mouth with her free hand.

"Someone shot Luke?"

As if he remembered the ladies, Clint proceeded to

pull them toward the house. "Yes, and I want you inside so you don't get shot, too."

Camelia needed no more urging. She practically ran inside.

Laura, on the other hand, wanted answers. She dug her heels in and jerked away from Clint once more. Her gaze moved to Richard, waiting for him to answer her question.

He swung from his saddle. "Yes, he got himself shot. He's fine, just angry." Richard faced Clint. "The women are probably fine. I don't think the rustlers came anywhere near the house."

So that was the problem. Clint was worried the outlaws had come to his home to cause more trouble. She picked up her skirts and calmly walked up the front porch steps. "We haven't seen or heard anyone, and we've been outside most of the morning." Laura turned to face Clint.

He stood in the yard, looking up at her. Worry lined his face. Did he really think they were in harm's way? "The leader got away. Please, keep the girls inside until the sheriff captures him."

She shook her head. "No. If I made that promise, I'd have to break it. What if he heads for another territory and never comes back? Do you want us to be cooped up in the house forever like chickens afraid there might be a wolf at the door?"

Richard laughed. "She's right, boss."

Clint shot a mind-your-own-business look at Richard. He sighed and turned to Laura once more. "All right, will you at least stay in the house for the rest of the afternoon?"

She nodded. "But only if someone will help us get the wash in before sundown."

Richard's lips twitched. "I'll help you."

"No, you won't. We have to feed the rest of those cows and someone will have to stand guard. I'm thinking we should move the remaining herds up to the house."

Richard smiled at Laura. "Sorry, Miss Laura. The boss has spoken."

Laura turned on her heel and entered the house. She wasn't going to cower in the house. When the clothes were dry, she'd go get them. Decision made, Laura continued on into the kitchen.

Camelia sat at the table nursing a cup of coffee. Worry etched her face. "What do you think we should do?"

"About what?"

Green eyes searched hers. "About the rustler."

Laura laughed. "Nothing. I doubt he's anywhere near the house. He's after cows, not women and children." She filled a mug full of coffee and took a sip.

She understood Clint's desire to see them safe, but she really felt he was overreacting. Was it because of his feelings over his wife? When would he learn he couldn't control everything and everyone around him?

Clint felt bad. The sun had descended, and he'd not made it home in time for Laura to take the clothes off the line. He walked around the house to take them down for her. Only they weren't there.

He stomped to the kitchen door and entered the quiet house. Didn't she realize the danger she'd put herself in? What if the leader of the rustlers had been out there waiting for her?

A plate sat on the back of the stove just like before. Only this time there was no Laura up and waiting for him to come home. Did she think he'd be angry with her and yell? Is that why she'd already gone to bed?

Camelia came into the kitchen. "Good evening, Clint. Did the sheriff catch the cow thief?" She poured him a cup of coffee and placed it in front of him.

"Thanks." He took a sip and sighed. Weariness weighed on his shoulders. "No, I have men guarding the cattle in shifts tonight."

She grinned. "You took the first shift?"

He nodded. "Me and Parker." Clint picked up a chicken leg and tore the meat from the bone.

"Should I fix a plate for Parker?"

He swallowed. "No, he's having ham and beans. I made sure he ate before I left the bunkhouse."

"Good."

They sat in comfortable silence for several long minutes. He finished his supper and pushed the plate back. "Thank you for holding supper for me. Sometimes I forget how blessed I am to have you in my life."

Camelia reached over and patted his hand. "You are like a son to me, Clint."

He placed his hand over hers. "Thanks." Clint smiled at her, then released her hand. "How was your day?"

"Well, up until we found out there were rustlers on the place, it was pretty good." She smiled. "Laura refused to stay in the house, though. She said we aren't cows and that cattle rustlers weren't interested in stealing women and children."

"So she did take the wash in?"

Camelia chuckled. "She sure did. Although, I noticed she didn't take any longer than was necessary and made the girls stay inside."

Clint sighed. "Maybe I should have told her to stay outside, and then I would have gotten the results I wanted from her."

"Possibly." Camelia stood and yawned. She took the plate and silverware to the washtub that Clint had been using. It didn't take but a couple of minutes for her to wash and dry them. She returned to the table. "Clint, I need a few supplies from town. Do you think it would be all right if Laura and I took the girls and went to town?"

He studied the bottom of his cup. If Laura was in town, she wouldn't be running around outside here at the house. Was that what Camelia thought, too? Clint nodded. "Yeah, but you'd better ask her to go with you. If I tell her to go, she will dig her heels in here for sure."

"Good, and can you send one of the men with us? I don't feel comfortable on the road alone."

He stood and yawned. "Yep. I think I'll ask Parker. He's been hinting he'd like to go to the general store for another charcoal pencil and pad of paper."

"Good. I like that young man." She pulled her housecoat tighter about her waist. "Good night, Clint."

"Good night, Camelia." He sipped on his coffee. Maybe it would do both him and Laura good if they spent a whole day apart. She was too familiar with him, so much so that she'd disobeyed his order to stay in the house.

The next morning, Clint walked to the bunkhouse to find Parker and to tell him he'd be going to town with the women. He'd wrestled all night with letting them go. Worry ate at him like a rat ate away at a piece of cloth.

What if they ran into the rustler? Would Parker know what to do? He was young but seemed to be able to take on anything Clint and Richard threw at him. Yesterday he'd managed to help capture the rest of the rustlers, without getting shot. Luke was a good ten years older than the younger man and he'd not been so blessed.

Parker was just leaving the bunkhouse when Clint arrived. "Just the man I wanted to see," he said as a means of greeting.

"Morning," Parker replied.

Clint grinned. "Morning. I have a special job for you today."

The young man straightened his shoulders and stood a little taller.

"The women have decided they want to go into town today. I need you to escort them." He watched to see Parker's reaction.

The boy gave nothing away.

"When do they want to leave?" he asked.

"Within the hour." Clint wasn't sure if he should impress upon the boy the importance of keeping the women safe on this trip or not.

Parker looked him square in the eye. "Your family will be safe with me, sir. I'll keep a close lookout for that rustler."

That's what Clint wanted to hear, but he didn't think it would keep him from worrying. He nodded. "I appreciate that."

He returned to the barn where Clint decided he'd muck out stalls until the women left.

As he worked, Clint silently prayed. *Lord, please keep them safe.*

Chapter Nineteen

Laura sighed with relief as they entered town. Leroy Parker, or Parker as everyone referred to him, had her nerves wound so tight she could almost scream with the tension. His body language said he was as nervous as a cat in a room full of rocking chairs. Maybe now that they were in town, the young man would lighten up.

She prayed the sheriff would catch the leader of the rustlers because the men on the ranch were behaving irrationally.

"Thanks for seeing us into town, Parker. Feel free to go relax while we shop. I'm sure there's something you'd rather do than wait around while we shop." Laura smiled what she hoped was her most encouraging smile.

"Oh, no, ma'am. My orders were to stay with you and Mrs. Murphy until I got you home safe and sound." He shifted in the saddle and looked about as if expecting someone to jump out at them from between the buildings.

Laura sighed. She set the brake on the wagon and looked at Camelia.

The Irishwoman was almost as bad as Parker. She'd jumped at every snap of a twig or rock under the wheels of the wagon. Her face looked pinched and unsure. She held Hope in her arms as if afraid to let the child go.

Grace sat between them. She leaned against Laura's side.

Laura gazed about the small town. She'd hoped to find Priscilla and see how the young woman was doing. She couldn't believe a whole month had passed, and she hadn't heard from Hope's mother or her grandparents, or that she'd spent so many hours worrying that one of them or both would come and take Hope away.

Parker got off his horse and tied it to the hitching post in front of the general store. He then hurried to Camelia's side of the wagon. "Here, let me help you down."

"Thank you, Parker. Take Hope and I'll follow."

Laura didn't wait for the young man to finish with Camelia and Hope. She eased down from the wagon and then turned to help Grace. Grace's eyes looked tired as she reached for Laura.

Once the little girl was in her arms, she tugged at her ear.

"Ear huts." She laid her head on Laura's shoulder as Hope had done many times in the past.

Heat radiated from her little body. Laura felt her forehead and found it hot to the touch. She turned to Camelia, who had joined her on the sidewalk. "Grace is sick," she said. "She's burning up with a fever."

"We should take her to the doctor." Camelia looked at Hope. "Are you sick, too?"

Hope shook her head and frowned. She tucked her fingers into her mouth.

Laura sighed. "Camelia, would you mind taking Hope with you? You can get the supplies you need, and I'll take Grace to the doctor. I have a feeling if we are in town too long, Clint will become worried and come looking for us. This way, we can get both our shopping done and Grace can see the doctor in the same amount of time."

"Yes, that's a good idea." Camelia turned in the direction of the general store. "Come along, Hope."

Laura grinned. Hope really had no choice as Camelia was carrying her.

Parker stepped up beside her. "I'll go with you. Mrs. Murphy will be safe enough in the store."

Laura tried not to be irritated. "Thank you, but didn't you have some shopping you wanted to do, as well?"

He ignored her protest and began walking beside her. "Yes, and I'll get what I need when we come back for Mrs. Murphy." Parker smiled a rare smile.

As they walked, Laura asked, "If you don't think I'm being too nosy, what is it that you are shopping for today?" She thought engaging him in conversation might take his mind off of guarding her and Grace.

"I'll be buying charcoal and paper." He continued to keep an eye open for danger.

Laura grinned. "You are an artist?"

"I wouldn't say that." He shrugged. "I just enjoy drawing."

They arrived at the doctor's office. Parker opened the door for her. A little bell above the door jingled, announcing their arrival. The doctor came out with a frown. He took one look at Parker and said, "Tell me you didn't bring another man to patch up."

"No, sir, I brought Mrs. Lee and Grace Shepard this time."

The old man looked at Laura and Grace. His gray eyes swiftly assessed them. "She's sick?" He indicated Grace.

Laura answered, "She has a fever."

"Then bring her on back." He looked to Parker. "Have a seat, young man."

Parker did as he was told.

Laura followed the doctor into his examination room. She looked about at the many bottles and things there. It was clean but cluttered.

"Just set her on the table over there." He poured water into a washbasin and began scrubbing his hands. "When did the fever start?"

Laura knew Grace hadn't been sick when they left the house. "About an hour ago, I'd say."

He nodded. His gray eyes softened when he looked down at Grace. "Hi, Gracie. Are you sick?"

"Uh-huh."

He touched her forehead.

"Ear huts." She tugged at her right ear.

The doctor moved to a candle and lit it. "Well, that's not good." He returned with the lit candle. "Be real still so I can have a look see."

"Otay." Grace tilted her head so that he could use the candle for light and look inside her ear.

He tsked. "No wonder you have a fever. That ear is mighty red inside." The doctor patted her on the head. "Good thing for you, I know how to make the fever and the hurt go away."

Big brown eyes looked at him. "Ear huts." She pulled at it again.

"I know." He moved to a cabinet and pulled out a little brown bottle. "Mrs. Lee, would you be so kind as to get this child a cup of water?"

Laura looked to where he pointed at a pail of water. She saw the ladle and two coffee cups sitting beside it. "Yes."

The doctor continued talking. "I'm going to give her some powders and oil for her ear. She'll need to take both for about a week. Then I want to see her again. Understood?"

Laura nodded as she handed him the cup of water. He turned to Grace. "Gracie, you need to take this and let me put warm oil in your ear and after a little while it won't hurt anymore. All right?"

"Aw white." She took the powder he had on a small spoon, made a face and then grabbed the cup. The little girl gulped at the water.

He laughed, then returned to his cabinet where he pulled out a small peppermint stick. "This will help with that yucky taste." He handed Grace the candy.

Laura watched, fascinated, as he filled the same spoon with a little oil and held it over the candle's flame to warm.

The doctor grinned at her. "This doesn't take long to warm up so don't overheat it." He touched the oil and then motioned for her to do the same.

It felt almost hot but not hot enough to burn her finger. She looked up at him for further instructions.

"That's how warm it needs to be when you put it in her ear." He pulled a couple of cotton balls out of a glass jar and returned to Grace. "Tilt your head sideways, child, so I can pour this in."

Grace did as she was told, all the while sucking on

the candy stick. Her eyes widened as he poured the oil into her ear, but she didn't cry or fuss.

He poked cotton into her little ear and hummed.

Laura waited until he was done and then asked, "Will the fever go away soon?"

"She'll need to take the medicine to keep it down, but yes, as the infection leaves her body, the fever will, too." He put the bottle of powders in a paper bag, a small bottle of oil and a handful of cotton balls. "Just give her the powder with meals and fill her ear with oil in the morning after she wakes and before bedtime." He grinned over his shoulder at the child sucking away at her treat. "You might get some more peppermint sticks if you go to the drugstore. It will help the other medicine go down."

Laura laughed. "Thank you, doctor. I'll make sure to get plenty." She opened her small purse. "What do I owe you?"

He shook his head. "Nothing. I'll put it on Clint's bill. He can pay me next week."

Laura shut her purse and walked over to get Grace. She looked to the doctor. "Sir, I was wondering how Priscilla Maxwell is doing. Last time I talked to her, she seemed very sick."

Sadness entered the doctor's eyes. "I'm sorry to be the one to tell you that she passed away a few days ago. We buried her in the town cemetery yesterday."

A few minutes later, Laura, Grace and Parker left the doctor's office. Her heart was heavy at the loss of Hope's mother. She was so young. Her parents were probably beside themselves. Had Priscilla told them about Hope? If so, would they want their granddaughter now that their only child was gone?

Laura felt torn. What would she do if they came to take Hope away from her? Fresh heartache filled her.

When they got back to the store, Laura went inside. She sighed as a sense of heaviness filled her. This was the last place she'd seen Priscilla alive. She spotted Camelia and Hope standing in front of the toy section.

Camelia had turned when she heard the bell over the door ring. Once Laura was close enough, she asked, "How is our wee one?"

"She has an ear infection." Laura watched as Parker walked to the shelf holding books and paper.

"Oh, our poor, wee baby." Camelia stroked Grace's cheek.

She squeezed Grace's hand. "The doctor prescribed peppermint sticks twice a day." Laura grinned at Camelia's shocked look. "He said they help the medicine go down."

Camelia knelt in front of Grace. "Well, if the doctor ordered it, it must be important."

Hope reached for Laura, who took her with ease. Camelia looked relieved not to have to stand still holding the child.

"I'll get the candy when I go to the counter. I've only a few more items on my list and then we can head back," Camelia said.

In a very soft voice, that Laura hoped Parker wouldn't hear, Laura said, "I'd like to take the girls to the wagon to wait for you. I've just learned that Priscilla, Hope's mother, has passed."

Camelia nodded. "You go on, honey." She patted Laura's shoulder. "I'll keep an eye on Parker."

Laura took Grace's hand. She slipped out onto the

boardwalk, thankful that Parker hadn't seemed to notice her departure.

She put the girls in the bed of the wagon and then climbed up on the seat. Laura watched both the girls. Grace lay down on the blanket and closed her eyes. Hope looked at her friend and then to Laura.

Hope stood and toddled over to the seat. She held her arms up for Laura to lift her onto the seat with her.

Laura picked her up and held her close. This little girl would never know her real mother. The sadness of the thought caused her eyes to burn with unshed tears.

"Excuse me."

Laura looked to the sidewalk where Elizabeth Maxwell, Priscilla's mother, stood.

"Hello, Mrs. Maxwell. How are you today?" Laura wasn't sure how she got the words past her tight throat.

"I'm well, Mrs. Lee. I couldn't help but notice how cute the girls look today." Her eyes shone up at Hope. She hugged her handbag closer to her side.

She said the only thing she knew to say in this situation. "Thank you." Would Mrs. Maxwell take Hope from her?

Tears filled the other woman's eyes. "She looks so much like Prissy did at that age." She reached up and touched Hope's small hand.

Hope pulled it away and clung to Laura.

"I'm sorry for your loss." Laura prayed that neither of them cried. She looked about the busy town. What would the gossips in town say?

Mrs. Maxwell swallowed hard. "It is for the best. Priscilla is in a better place."

Laura prayed that Priscilla's mother was correct and

that Priscilla had gone to be with the Lord. She looked at Hope. The little girl smiled shyly at her grandmother.

"I'm glad I ran into you today. I've been hoping you'd come into town so that I could see little Hope." She smiled up at Laura. "Dear, I know Priscilla wants you to raise her. My husband and I have a little house here in town that we'd planned to give to Priscilla but…" Mrs. Maxwell paused and swallowed. "Well, we'd like to give it to you and Hope when you move back to town."

She offered a smile. "Thank you, Mrs. Maxwell." What more could she say? It sounded as if the Maxwells weren't going to try to take Hope from her, but they were going to give her a new house. Laura wasn't sure she should accept it. What if they changed their minds and decided they wanted Hope to live with them?

Chapter Twenty

The moon drooped low in the sky. Clint stomped up the steps of the house. Laura sat in one of the two rockers. She'd been quiet over the last two days and he was starting to worry about her. He slid into the rocker beside her and yawned. "I'm sorry I didn't get back in time to put Grace to bed. Was she upset?"

"No, she was pretty tired. I think the powder that the doctor gave her makes her sleepy. Thankfully it also keeps her fever down." Laura looked up at the full moon. She wore a light sweater and had tugged it tightly about her waist.

"What's troubling you, Laura?"

She glanced over at him. "Am I that obvious?" Laura pushed the hair that had fallen out of her bun behind a shell-shaped ear.

"Probably not to anyone but me. I've noticed you've been pretty quiet since you went to town. Are you concerned that the leader of the rustlers might still be out there?" His gaze moved to the shadows.

She shook her head. "No, I've about forgotten him."

Clint nodded. "Well, that's good, because we don't have to worry about him any longer."

Her eyes searched his.

"Part of the reason I had to leave after supper was because one of the bulls had gotten out of his pasture. On our way back from fixing the fence and getting him back inside, the sheriff rode out and said they'd captured the last of the rustler gang. They are all behind bars tonight." He pushed his hat back and leaned farther down into the rocker.

Laura smiled. "That's wonderful news. Now maybe you'll stop shadowing the house."

He peeked up at her from under his hat. "I haven't been shadowing you."

"Yes, you have. Every time I looked up, there you or one of your men were." She smiled. "Thank you for caring about us."

Clint wondered if he cared too much. What she said was true. He'd made sure that he or one of his men could see the house at all times. "You're welcome."

He watched as Laura tilted her head back and stared at the moon again. The air outside was cool but not cold. He sat watching her for a moment and then remembered he'd been trying to find out what was bothering her. Clint cleared his throat and asked, "If it's not the outlaws, then what is it?" He was persistent. Whatever was bothering her, he wanted her to talk to him about it.

She sighed. "The other day, when we went to town, I found out that Priscilla had passed away."

"I'm sorry to hear that." Clint sat up a little taller in his chair, praying he'd be able to find words to comfort her, if that was what she needed. Maybe she just needed him to listen. He knew he could do that.

"Her mother saw me and the girls and stopped by to say hello." She turned fear-filled eyes to him. "Clint, she recognized Hope and offered us a house in town to live in."

Clint was at a loss. To him, that sounded like a good thing. But obviously, Laura wasn't happy. "That was generous of her."

"It was, but I'm afraid that she might change her mind when I go back to town." Tears began streaming down her face.

He was out of the chair and had pulled her into his arms before Clint realized he'd even moved. She sobbed against his shirt. Her tears seeped in and touched his chest.

"I don't want to lose her," she cried. "I know I'm being selfish, but I love her."

He hugged her tight. "You aren't being selfish. I can't imagine that the Maxwells would want to take her from you, knowing how much you love her."

She hiccupped. "But they might."

Clint let her cry until she was all cried out. Laura stepped out of his arms. He continued to hold her around the waist.

"I'm sorry." She buried her face in her hands.

He gently removed them. "Laura, I will do all I can to make sure that you keep Hope." Clint grinned at her. "You could marry me and we could legally adopt her." This was the second time he'd proposed to her. Clint knew he meant it. He'd protect her and Hope forever, if she'd let him.

Laura shook her head. "No, I can't marry you because I want to keep Hope. You deserve a wife who loves you and wants to create a family with you."

Her words cut deeply. He knew she didn't love him, but her words reminded him that he'd started to fall in love with her. Clint released her and offered what he hoped looked like a friendly smile and not a pain-filled sneer. "Well, I had to offer. I'll do all I can to help you keep Hope, even if you won't marry me." He watched as she hugged the sweater close to her body and nodded.

Clint couldn't stand the thought of being on the porch with her any longer. "Good night, Laura." He turned and walked into the house. He stood just inside the door and took a deep breath.

Now that the danger of the rustlers had passed, Clint decided it was time to look more seriously at finding a new nanny. If Laura stayed on the ranch any longer, he was sure she'd take his and Grace's hearts with her.

The sound of a wagon coming up the driveway brought Laura's head up from the beans she'd been sorting. She knew dark circles rested under her eyes from her sleepless night. Camelia had even gone so far as to suggest she take a nap with the girls.

Laura had refused. Her mind wouldn't stop its fearful racing that the Maxwells were going to take Hope away. It was just silly of her to think such a thing, but she couldn't still the thoughts that pushed at the edges of her mind. Even now she wondered if the approaching wagon contained the Maxwells. Were they coming to get Hope?

As the wagon came closer, Laura could see that a young woman with raven black hair was guiding the mare into the yard. She didn't look very old. The woman set the brake on the wagon and then climbed down.

Laura stood up and walked to the top of the steps on the porch. "Hello."

A soft smile touched the other woman's lips. "Hello, I'm Selina Morgan. I've come in response to Mr. Shepard's advertisement for a nanny. I hope the position hasn't been filled yet."

Laura motioned for Selina to come up on the porch. "It hasn't. I'll get Mrs. Murphy and Mr. Shepard. Please have a seat." Laura indicated the rocker she'd just vacated.

Selina did as asked. "Thank you."

Laura hurried into the house in search of Camelia. She found her in Clint's room, dusting. "Camelia, there is a Selina Morgan here to interview for the nanny position."

"Well, that's just great. Why do they always choose to come during the girls' nap times?" She frowned and laid down the dust rag. "That baby hasn't been feeling well, and I'm not about to get her up to meet this newest woman."

"I'll go send one of the men to go get Clint. He can decide about this one." Laura smiled. She didn't want to wake Grace either.

Laura and Camelia walked back to the front of the house together.

In a low voice, Camelia asked, "What do you think of this one?"

"Well, so far I've only said hello, but she seems awfully young." Laura shrugged. "But that doesn't mean she wouldn't be good with Grace."

Camelia nodded and headed out the front door. Laura went through the kitchen and out the back door. She walked to the barn, where she found Richard mending a halter.

He looked up from his work at her and smiled. "What brings you out here, Laura?"

"Camelia would like for you to go get Clint. It seems we have another young woman who'd like to be Grace's nanny." She smiled back at him.

Richard laid the halter to the side. He stood and stretched out his back. "I don't see why you don't just stay on."

"Because I'm a schoolteacher, and I have a town full of children to teach." Laura grinned. Even though she wished she could stay on here at the ranch, it wasn't possible.

He nodded. "Clint isn't that far away. I'll be back in a little while."

Laura turned and left the barn. Sunshine beat down on her as she walked along the well-worn path. In no hurry to get back to the house, she turned toward the chicken coop. Miss Priss stood off to the side. Her wing had healed, but not as straight as Laura had hoped.

Her thoughts were on the night before and Clint's proposal. If she had said yes, there would be no need for the new nanny. But she couldn't marry Clint. She cared about him and might even love him a little, but the truth of the matter was she was barren and he'd want a son.

She sighed and headed back to the house. Entering the kitchen door, Laura gathered up a tray; she placed a dessert plate on it and added small slices of pound cake. As soon as she'd finished adding the cake, Laura made a fresh pot of coffee. She placed three cups on the tray with the coffeepot and then headed back to the front porch.

Clint stood on the top porch step. His hat was in his hand and his fingers were working the brim. He looked to her and smiled as she pushed through the door and handed Camelia the tray. "I thought you might like refreshments."

"Thank you, Laura." Camelia set the tray on table.

Laura turned to go back inside.

Clint's voice stopped her. "Laura, Miss Morgan tells us she's from Denver."

She looked from him to Selina. "That's nice. What brings you here?"

"I got tired of the big city life and wanted a change." She smiled at Clint and batted her long eyelashes. "I was a nanny in Denver so when I saw your advertisement I thought it a blessing."

Laura couldn't help but wonder if Selina had known Priscilla while in Denver. She started to ask but then stopped herself. Denver was a big city, and the chances of the two girls knowing each other were slim to none. "Did you attend college in Denver?" she asked instead.

Selina took the cup that Camelia was offering her. "No, I didn't have the money for school. I worked for the Blanchards. They have two rowdy young boys."

Camelia shot the next question at her. "Why did you leave? Didn't they pay enough?"

"Mr. Blanchard got a job in New York, and the family was moving there. They offered to take me with them, but I just couldn't stand the idea of moving to another big city." She took a sip of the coffee and grimaced.

Laura tried not to smile. Everyone on the ranch

drank their coffee black. It hadn't occurred to her to bring out cream and sugar for Selina.

Clint took the cup Camelia offered him and stared into it. "When would you be able to start?"

Camelia looked at him, startled. "What I believe Mr. Shepard is trying to say is, if we hire you, when would you be able to move out here?"

Selina smiled. "I can move in now. Everything I own is in the buggy."

Laura felt as if she were in shock. Was Clint going to hire her on the spot? From the straight line of Camelia's mouth, she wasn't happy with this turn of events any more than Laura. If he hired Selina, did Clint expect her and Hope to be moved out by this evening? Her hands began to tremble as well as her lower lip. Laura fought the urge to cry. How had things progressed so swiftly?

Chapter Twenty-One

Clint could tell that two of the three women on the porch were not happy. Anger radiated from Camelia like steam off a hot teakettle, and Laura looked as if she would burst into tears at any moment. This wasn't at all what he'd had in mind. He walked toward Selina. "Thank you for coming out. I will talk to the ladies and let you know first thing in the morning what our decision is." He held out his hand for her to shake.

Selina frowned but stood to leave. "Thank you." She shook his hand and offered a sweet smile. "I understand."

He wondered if she truly did. Clint walked her to her wagon and helped her back on.

She smiled and waved as she left the yard. Selina was a pretty girl, but he couldn't help but compare her sweetness to the beauty that was Laura. The women were as different as night and day in appearance, but he thought she might have the same sweet disposition that Laura had and that Grace loved.

Clint walked back to the porch. He waited to see if either of the ladies were going to speak first. When it became evident that neither had anything to say, he said, "I think I'll hire her."

It was Camelia who responded. "Why?"

"Well, she's smart, she has been a nanny before, and she's not..." He searched for the right words. "Um, unlikable."

The Irishwoman shook her head. "Clint Shepard, Selina's smart. She knew exactly what you wanted to hear and so that's what she told you. As for her being a nanny before, we only have her word for that." Camelia took a deep breath. "But you are right in the fact that all the ladies who have arrived for the job, she is the most likable."

Laura stood quietly beside the door. She had a look of relief on her face that hadn't been there before.

"Laura, what did you think of her?"

She gazed at him. "It's not my place to decide what is best for Grace. It's yours." She turned to walk into the house. Sadness shrouded her like a storm cloud on the horizon.

His voice stopped her. "It is your place." Clint waited for her to turn back around. "You are her nanny now. Would you hire Selina for Hope?"

Laura blinked several times as if she'd been hit in the face with a cold bucket of water. "I'm not sure. We don't know anything about her."

Camelia nodded. "My point exactly."

He grinned at his housekeeper. "All right. I can see your point of view. How about this? How about we hire her for a week? If she works out, she stays, and Laura will be free to move back to town."

"Where will she sleep? We don't have a lot of rooms in this house," Camelia was quick to remind him.

Laura sighed. "She can have my place in the nursery."

Camelia's eyes narrowed. "And then where will you sleep?"

Clint grinned as he watched the women face off.

Laura's shoulders came back, and her eyes narrowed. "There is a small closet right off the kitchen. We can toss a straw mattress in the floor. I'll sleep in there."

Camelia opened her mouth to speak, but Clint beat her to it. "How about I pull one of the bunks from the bunkhouse and you sleep on that? If you are sure that's what you want to do."

She nodded. "I'm sure and..." Laura looked at Camelia. "There really is no other place in the house, and I want to make sure that Grace is happy before I leave."

The older woman sighed and picked up the coffee tray. "Well, if you both are set on giving this gal a chance, who am I to stand in the way?"

Clint stopped her from walking away by stepping up in front of her. "Camelia, you are a part of my family. If you don't want me to hire her, I won't. But if the only reason you aren't happy about this is because Laura will be leaving..." He paused and looked to Laura. "Laura and I agreed on this from day one."

Camelia made a sniffing sound. "We'll give her a week. She might not be too bad." Then she walked around both Clint and Laura and went into the house.

As soon as she was out of earshot, Laura said, "Camelia will be all right. She doesn't like change."

Clint nodded. "What about you? Will you be all right?"

"Like you said, this is what we agreed on from the beginning." Laura turned and followed Camelia.

He stood on the porch and sighed heavily. What was it about women and change? Martha had hated change, as well. His thoughts traveled to what the women didn't like changing. They ran straight into Laura. Neither woman looked forward to her leaving. Come to think of it, he didn't care much for the change either. Had Laura become such a part of their lives that she now felt like family? How was Grace going to take the changes that were coming?

After the girls were in bed and sleeping, Laura began to pack up her things. There was no reason to wait until morning to do it. Maybe if she did it now, Grace wouldn't get to upset when Selina arrived and began to unpack.

She carried her clothes to the closet off the kitchen and looked about for a place to put them. The pantry was being used for canned goods and dishes that weren't everyday items. Laura laid the clothes on a stool and began to move things about.

"You can stay in my room, if you don't mind snoring."

Laura smiled at Camelia over her shoulder. "Thank you, but I think we'll both feel better if I stay here."

Camelia gave an unladylike snort. "I don't know why you don't just give up that teaching job and stay out here with us."

"You know I can't do that. In a few years, Grace will be going off to school, and then what need will Clint have of a nanny? I'd be without a job and no prospects of finding another one." Laura placed her clothes on the newly cleaned off shelf. "I think I'll leave everything else in the bedroom with the girls."

"I would. It's going to be crowded in here when the cot gets added." Camelia stepped out of the doorway.

Laura followed. She watched her friend go to the sink and start washing the last of the pots from supper. They'd gotten into a routine of having dessert after the dishes were done and the kids put to bed. She moved to the table and sat down.

"You know what I think?" Camelia looked over her shoulder at Laura.

She gave her friend a cheeky grin. "Never."

"I think that gal won't last the week." She turned back to the dishes.

Laura laughed. "That's probably what you thought of me, too."

"No, I knew you were made of strong fibers. But that girl, I don't think she will be able to handle our Gracie." She set the pan on the counter to dry.

Laura gave the Irishwoman one of her firmest looks. "Camelia, promise me you won't make this job hard on that girl."

The older woman cut them each a slice of cake and turned to face her. "I won't make it any harder on her than I did on you." She set the cake in front of Laura.

"That's what I mean. You were mean to me when I first came here. Don't be that way with Selina. She's coming into a house with two women and two little girls. She'll be nervous and maybe even a little scared. I don't think that she's even twenty years old." Laura reached for a fork from the crock in the center of the table.

Camelia returned to the counter and poured two cups of coffee. "I believe you are right about her age. She seemed awfully young to me." She sat down with the cups and searched Laura's face. "What do you think her story really is?"

Laura shook her head. "I don't know. She may be running from her family, a new husband or—" she grinned "—she told the truth and just got tired of city living and wants a simpler life."

Camelia handed her one of the cups. "Maybe. Something just didn't set as true to me."

Laura shrugged. "I wasn't with her long enough to make that decision."

They ate their treat in silence. Laura couldn't help but think how young Selina looked. Once more she thought of Priscilla and the fact that they both were young, they both came from Denver, and they both seemed to have something to hide.

Banging on the back door had Camelia jumping out of her seat. She stared at the door as if she thought a cattle rustler was going to break in.

Clint's voice called to them. "Camelia! Laura! Open the door. This cot is heavy."

Laura shook her head at Camelia and hurried to the door. She pulled it open with a grin. She moved back to let Clint and Parker enter. "Here I thought I'd have at least one more night sleeping on a soft mattress."

Clint walked backwards into the pantry. Parker followed, carrying in the other end of the cot.

Laura returned to the table and sat back down, aware Clint hadn't answered her. She picked up her fork and shoved a huge piece of cake in her mouth.

Parker walked toward the back door. "Good night, ladies." He closed it behind him.

Clint walked to the table and sat down. "You do have another night in the girls' room. I just thought it might be best if we moved the cot in tonight so as not to upset the girls in the morning."

Camelia nodded toward the cake pan. "Help yourself to cake and coffee."

He didn't have to be told twice. Laura watched as he crossed the room and helped himself to a generous piece of the cake. It amazed her that like her, he'd thought not to upset the girls with the changes that were taking place.

"Would either of you like to ride into town with me in the morning?" He returned to the table and snatched a fork from the crock before sitting down.

Laura wanted to say no and could have used the girls as an excuse not to go. But she also thought it might be good for Selina and Grace to meet. They could get to know one another on the way back to the ranch. And she needed to visit Mrs. Maxwell and see if she were still willing to let her stay in the house meant for Priscilla.

Camelia shook her head. "No, thanks, I've had enough of town to last me another month."

Clint looked to Laura.

"It might be good for Grace to meet Selina in town."

He chewed and swallowed. "Is that a yes?"

She nodded with a sigh. "I suppose."

"Good. I'm sure the girls will enjoy the trip." Clint ate his cake happily as if he'd been dreading making the outing alone.

A few minutes later, Laura stood up. "If you will excuse me, I'm going to go check on the girls and call it a night."

Clint nodded. "We'll leave for town right after breakfast."

"Um, are you in a hurry to get back here?" She hadn't thought to ask him if he minded waiting for her while she spoke to Hope's grandparents.

Confusion laced his features. "Why?"

"I have some business I need to take care of. I'm not sure how long I'll need." She twisted her hands in the blue floral apron around her waist.

"Oh, of course, you can have as long as you need." He picked up his plate and carried it to the washbasin.

"Thank you. Good night." Laura hurried to her room. Her nerves felt as if a hundred ants were parading up and down them. Fear and uncertainty troubled her as she dressed for bed.

Tomorrow, would she find out that the Maxwells had decided to take Hope from her after all? Or would they show her the house that Mrs. Maxwell had said she and Hope could use? Would Grace like Selina? Laura wasn't sure she was ready to take the steps that would lead her farther and farther away from Grace and Clint.

Chapter Twenty-Two

Laura took a deep breath and stepped into the bank. She looked about the rich interior. Every piece of wood shone, every worker was dressed to perfection. She felt out of place in such a place. A classroom was where she felt at home, and knowing that Mr. Maxwell not only worked here but owned the place sent rocks into her stomach.

Maybe this was a mistake. She turned to leave.

"Mrs. Lee?"

At the sound of her name, Laura turned with a smile. She didn't feel like smiling. She felt like the rocks had just grown and she was going to be sick. "Yes?"

An older gentleman with silver hair and beautiful blue eyes smiled at her. He held out his hand as he approached. Laura didn't have to be told that Hope's grandfather was about to shake her hand. "I'm so glad you stopped in today. I was about to go to the house for lunch. The Missus would love it if you joined me." He shook her hand as if they were old friends.

Laura took a deep breath, aware that he only had

eyes for Hope. She offered her best smile and nodded. "Thank you."

He looked to his left. "Mr. Jones, I'm going to lunch. If you need me, I'll be at the house."

"Yes, Mr. Maxwell."

His gaze turned back on her. "Shall we?" He indicated the door.

Laura turned with a nod. She'd only taken two steps when she felt his hand in the small of her back. Unaccustomed to having men escort her from a building, Laura wasn't sure how to react to his touch. She straightened her shoulders and walked faster.

He held the door open for her. Once on the boardwalk, Mr. Maxwell pointed to the right. "Elizabeth has been talking nonstop about you and the baby. I hope you don't mind that I thought she would like to see you both."

Hope studied her grandfather with big eyes. She sucked her finger and patted Laura's shoulder with her free hand as if offering her comfort. Did the child realize Mr. Maxwell was her grandfather? Probably not.

Laura nodded. "No, that's why I came to the bank today, to see you both." She knew the Maxwells were the wealthiest family in town. She knew that he was one of the school board members and that they were a large part of the community church, but for the first time she realized she didn't know where they lived. Laura allowed him to gently guide her to his house.

"I'm glad." He hurried her up the street and then down two others. They stopped in front of a tall two-story brick house with blue shutters. Mr. Maxwell used his hand in the small of her back to propel her up the walkway and to the front door.

It opened as soon as they stepped onto the porch. A heavyset woman wearing a stark white apron over a black dress held the door open for them. She addressed the banker, "Mrs. Maxwell is waiting for you in the dining room, sir."

"Thank you, Harriet." He handed her his hat, then turned to Laura. "The dining room is right down this hall and then to your left."

Laura swallowed. She'd never been in a house this big and never one with servants. Her feet felt as if they were caked in mud as she walked to the dining room.

Mrs. Maxwell stood beside a side bar. She turned at the sound of footsteps and then gasped when she saw Laura and Hope. "Oh my gracious, please come on in, Mrs. Lee."

Mr. Maxwell's warm chuckle had Laura looking to him once more. "I knew you'd be pleased, dear." He walked over and kissed his wife lightly on the cheek.

Laura followed him. She looked about the dining room with interest. It wasn't that different from other homes, only everything was bigger. Paintings covered the walls and a large table sat in the center of the room.

Hope popped her fingers out of her mouth and smiled sweetly at her grandmother. She babbled something and pointed to Mrs. Maxwell.

"She remembers me." Mrs. Maxwell said, coming to stand in front of Laura and Hope.

Laura nodded. "I believe you are right."

Mr. Maxwell walked to the table and held out a chair for her. "Please, sit."

Laura did as she was asked. She placed Hope on her lap, facing her grandparents. It was time she stop acting like a frightened little girl and find out what the

Maxwells' intentions were toward their granddaughter. She took a deep breath and said, "Thank you both for seeing us."

Mrs. Maxwell turned to another woman who'd entered the room. "Mrs. Jefferies, please set two more places at the table. We have lunch guests."

"Yes, ma'am." The servant quickly left the room.

Priscilla's mother turned back to face her. "Nonsense, you're family."

"No, ma'am, I'm not. Hope is." She looked them both in the eyes. "I'd like to know what your intentions are toward your grandchild." There, she'd said it. Now they knew why she was here.

Mr. Maxwell's eyes hardened. "Are you asking us for money?"

"No. I'm asking what role you want to play in your granddaughter's life. I'm not sure where I stand here and want to find out. I do not want your money." Laura meant it. She didn't come for their money, hadn't even thought about asking them for money.

Mrs. Maxwell sighed. She pulled a chair from the table and placed it in front of Laura. "We simply want to be grandparents to her."

Mr. Maxwell moved to stand behind his wife. He placed a hand on her shoulder which she quickly reached up and took.

Laura's voice shook as she asked. "How?"

Hope looked over her shoulder at Laura. Her big blue eyes filled with tears as she sensed Laura's distress. She looked back to her grandparents and puckered her lips.

Laura hugged Hope close. "It's all right, Hope. We're just talking."

"Maybe we should go to the sitting room for our talk. Hope can get down and move about in there," Mr. Maxwell suggested.

The kitchen servant chose that moment to reenter the room with two more place settings. Mrs. Maxwell stood. "Mrs. Jefferies, would you be a dear and tell cook not to serve lunch for another thirty minutes?"

She answered, "Yes, ma'am," and left the room.

The older woman stood. "I agree. We need a more comfortable room for our talk." She walked out the door with her head held high.

Feeling as if she had no real choice in the matter, Laura followed. This was taking forever. All she wanted to know was if they intended to take Hope from her.

The windows in the sitting room windows were open, allowing a cool breeze to blow through the large area. A couch and two chairs made for a nice sitting area. Mrs. Maxwell took one of the chairs and indicated that Laura sit down on the couch.

Laura sat down and then set Hope down. The little girl smiled up at her. Gone was the stress from the child's face. She walked around the table that sat in front of the couch and smiled at her grandparents.

"To answer your earlier question," Mr. Maxwell began, "we want to be grandparents to Hope. Priscilla chose her deathbed to tell us of the child's existence and that she felt you were the perfect replacement for her."

Mrs. Maxwell picked up where her husband left off. "I know we don't really know each other, but we do know that you are a good woman with a good reputation. Our Priscilla said you would be the perfect person to raise Hope, that you were kind, fair and still strict enough not to let Hope hurt herself or to let any-one hurt her."

Laura didn't know what to say. She held her tongue and waited for them to continue.

Mr. Maxwell shook his head. "Of course, Priscilla didn't always make good choices, so I hope you can understand that we took it upon ourselves to make sure you are the woman she thought you were."

"And, how did you go about doing that?" Laura knew they'd snooped into her past, without them say-ing so.

"We hired a man to research your past." Mr. Max-well answered matter-of-factly.

Since she didn't have anything to hide, Laura simply nodded. Would she have gone to such lengths to guar-antee that her child was safe? Or in their case, grand-child was safe? If she were honest with herself, Laura would have had to answer, yes.

"And, are you satisfied with what you learned?" she asked.

"Yes. From every person he interviewed, all he got were good reports. I'm sorry if it upsets you that we went to such lengths, but I hope you understand," Mrs. Maxwell said as she watched Hope play with the doily on the table.

Laura smiled. "I believe I would have done the same, if I were in your shoes." She watched them vis-ibly relax. "Look, I'm not trying to take your money or even keep Hope from you."

Mr. Maxwell eased into the chair beside his wife. His gaze followed Hope as she walked around and around the table. "Why do you think she chose you?"

Laura shook her head. "I don't know. All I know is

that Priscilla put her baby on my doorstep. She asked me to take care of her. I told her to talk to you, to be honest about what happened in Denver. I pray she did." Laura pressed on before she lost her nerve. "But I also promised to take care of Hope and tell her someday about her mother and that she loved her enough to give her to me to care for."

"We hope you will allow us to be a part of her life," Mrs. Maxwell said with tears in her eyes.

Laura looked from one of them to the other. "So, you aren't going to take her away from me?" She searched their faces, looking for the truth.

"No, dear. Our daughter wanted you to raise Hope. All we are asking is that you let us be a part of her life." Mrs. Maxwell reached out and touched Hope's soft curls. Tears filled her eyes.

Mr. Maxwell nodded. "We'll give you however much money you think you will need to raise our grandchild."

Laura shook her head. "Mr. Maxwell, I said it before. I don't want your money."

He opened his mouth to say something, but Laura butted in, "All I want is for you to love Hope. She is your grandchild. I have no intention of keeping her from you."

His eyes misted over. "We already love her."

Hope turned around and looked at him. As if her soft heart couldn't take the thought of him being upset, she toddled over to him and rested her little hand on his arm.

He looked to Laura.

"She's your grandchild. If you want to pick her up,

hug her or simply touch her, do so." Laura watched as he nodded and pulled Hope up into his lap.

Mrs. Maxwell leaned toward them and touched the child's head, shoulders and back. It was as if she couldn't believe that Hope was real.

Priscilla would have been happy to see her daughter and parents coming together as a family. Laura had to trust that they'd let her raise the child. But if they did choose to take her, she knew she wouldn't stop them, not that she could. With their wealth, Laura felt sure she'd not be able to fight them for the baby she loved.

He passed Hope over to his wife and then Mr. Maxwell looked at her. "Thank you. We were so worried you'd hold Hope away from us or demand payment to be in her life."

She shook her head. "I will never do that. Hope needs her family, Mr. Maxwell."

"Please, call us John and Elizabeth." He smiled. "We're practically family now."

Elizabeth looked up at her. "We've been talking and are hoping that you will take Priscilla's house."

Uncertainty hit Laura. They'd been so concerned she was after their money but once more were offering her a home for herself and Hope.

"Please, we want our grandchild to grow up close to us, and we're hoping you'll allow us to keep her from time to time."

Laura knew it wasn't easy for Mr. Maxwell to use the word please twice in less than two minutes. She nodded. "Only if you understand that I am not after Hope's inheritance."

"We understand, dear." Elizabeth Maxwell kissed

the top of Hope's head. She put Hope back down on the floor.

Hope toddled over to Laura and lifted her arms. She giggled as Laura picked her up and hugged her close. "Thank you. I really should be getting back to the bank. Mr. Shepard is going to pick me up there." Laura stood to leave.

"Are you sure you can't stay for lunch?" Elizabeth asked hopefully.

Laura shook her head. "No, I'm afraid not. But I will be returning to town next week. Mr. Shepard is in the process of hiring my replacement. I'll come by then, so that you can show Hope and me our new home."

Elizabeth smiled. "We'll have the house ready for you to move into."

"Thank you." Laura walked to the hallway.

The Maxwells followed closely behind. "Thank you for coming to see us."

Laura stepped out on the front porch. She turned and allowed them to say goodbye to Hope. The little girl shyly waved and laid her head on Laura's shoulder.

Things had gone much better than Laura had hoped. She now had a home, Hope's grandparents weren't going to try to steal her away, and life would be returning to normal soon. Laura knew she should be happy, but for some reason she wasn't.

Chapter Twenty-Three

Clint had never been so glad to be home in all his born days. In her excitement, Selina had talked all the way back to the ranch. She'd thanked him for the job and played with the little girls in the bed of the wagon. Laura had suggested she sit up front with him and her, but Selina had insisted this would give her a chance to get to know Grace better.

He'd tried to figure out what Laura was thinking all the way back to the ranch. She'd been quiet and seemed at times to be in deep thought. How she could ignore the incessant chatter from the back of the wagon, he had no idea.

Laura climbed down from the wagon and turned to Hope. "Come along, sweetie," she said. She gathered Hope from the wagon and walked away.

Clint stared after her. Why had she not taken Grace? Or at least helped him get Selina into the house and settled?

Camelia met them at the door. She smiled at Laura, who asked, "Is there any lunch left? Hope and I are starved."

Why hadn't he realized she hadn't eaten? He'd taken Grace and gone for a quick bite to eat before gathering the chatty Selina from the boardinghouse.

"There are fried potatoes and biscuits on the back of the stove. You're welcome to them," Camelia answered.

"I have so much to tell you. As soon as Selina and Grace are settled, maybe you could join Hope and me in the kitchen?" Laura asked.

So much to tell her? Laura had said less than ten words to him all the way home. Why hadn't she talked to him? Was she angry that he'd hired Selina? He pulled Selina's bags from the wagon bed and tried to listen to Camelia and Laura's conversation over Selina and Grace's chatter.

"I will be there as quickly as possible." Camelia grinned as Laura dashed into the house.

"Come on inside, Selina, and I'll show you to yours and Grace's room." Camelia held the door open for Selina to pass with Grace on her hip.

Clint put all the bags and things on the porch, then began setting them inside the door. Selina had brought more things than Laura had. He could hear her talking to Camelia in the bedroom. Exclaiming over every piece of furniture and toy that Grace showed her.

Camelia came down the hall with a shocked look on her face. She looked at him and sighed. "I don't remember her talking like that when she was here before."

He picked up an armload of bags and shook his head. "Me either. I don't think she's stopped talking since town."

"Well, at least Grace seems to like her." Camelia walked to the kitchen.

Clint would have loved to join them, but he had luggage to deliver. His mind worked as he made trip after trip to Laura's—no, Selina's—room. He set the bags down, all the while wondering what Laura was telling Camelia in the kitchen.

"Thank you, Mr. Shepard." Selina took the last bag and laid it on the bed.

He smiled. "You're welcome. I hope you will be comfortable here." His gaze moved to Grace, who was playing with a pile of wooden blocks.

Selina smiled sweetly at him. "I'm sure I will."

Clint glanced once more at Grace and then walked away. He liked Selina all right, and Grace seemed to be comfortable with her. This might just work out. If the rest of the week continued to go as it was now, Laura would be free to return to town.

He'd miss her. Maybe since she'd be leaving soon, he'd spend more time with her. With that thought in mind, Clint walked to the kitchen.

Laura handed Hope a biscuit with jelly in it. "They offered me a house and seem to want to be with their granddaughter, but they didn't act as if they were going to take her away from me."

Camelia set a cup of milk a little in front of Hope. "That's wonderful. It sounds like you will go back to a good life."

Laura nodded. "I'll be able to teach, and I'll have Hope."

She didn't voice her concerns about Hope's father showing up. After all, if he had followed Priscilla here, wouldn't they have seen him by now?

"Are you taking her to school with you? Or leaving her with Elizabeth Maxwell?" Camelia pulled out a chair and sat down.

Laura swallowed the potatoes in her mouth. "I was thinking I'd take her with me, but if Elizabeth asks to take care of her while I'm at school, I see no reason why she can't."

"That would probably be easier for you." Camelia reached over and touched Hope's chubby little cheek. "I believe she's gained a little weight since you came out here."

Laura stood and carried her plate to the washtub. "So have I. I'm going to miss your cooking, Camelia."

Camelia smiled. "Thank you. It won't be the same without you here." Her green eyes sparkled.

Afraid the older woman might cry, and cause her to cry, Laura changed the subject. "With Selina taking over the care of Grace. I think I'll have a little more time on my hands. Is there anything I can do to help you?" She went to get a small rag to wash Hope's face.

"No, if you start helping out now, I'll get used to it and then won't want to do my own work once you're gone." Camelia stood. "You've worked hard the last few weeks. Why not take off some time for yourself this week?"

Clint came through the kitchen door. "I think Selina and Grace are getting along just fine." He stopped and looked at the two women.

"I'm sure they are," Laura said, she finished washing Hope's face and then picked her up. Laura smiled at the little girl who yawned. "Come along, Hope. I think it's time for your nap." She turned and walked toward her room in the pantry.

"Shouldn't she sleep in her own room?" Clint asked.

Laura shook her head. "No, I'm not sure what Selina's schedule will be like with Grace. Hope can nap in my room but will need to sleep at night with Grace, if that's all right."

Her voice came out a little crisper than she'd intended.

Laura still smarted from the lack of attention that Clint had given her on the way home. It seemed to her that all he could do was pay attention to the new nanny. He'd been silent, simply listening to the young woman go on and on all the way to the house.

"That is fine with me." His brow furrowed as if confused.

She nodded, then walked to the closet. It didn't take long to get Hope asleep on the little cot. Laura pressed her pillow against the child to keep her from rolling to the edge and falling off. She wished it were bigger so that Hope could sleep with her in the evenings, but the cot was only built to sleep one.

Laura stayed in the room for half an hour to insure that Hope was sound asleep. Laura peeked out the door of her new room. Not seeing Clint or Camelia, she walked out the kitchen door. What was she going to do with so much free time?

She walked to the henhouse and watched as the chickens scratched about in the dirt looking for worms or seeds. There was so much on her mind. Soon she'd have a new house but very little to put inside it. Laura grinned. Maybe she and Hope wouldn't need a lot to start.

Her gaze moved about the ranch yard. Everything they needed was right here. Grace, Camelia, even Clint. Miss Priss walked up to the fence and looked up at

Laura. As crazy as it sounded, she would miss the little hen, Miss Priss.

Tears filled her eyes; change was hard. Laura dashed the moisture from her face. She told herself that it was the changes in her life that made her sad. But deep down, Laura knew the sadness came from leaving Clint.

Chapter Twenty-Four

"So this is where you got off to." Clint walked across the yard and joined her beside the fence. Had she been crying? He studied her profile.

"I just thought I'd check on Miss Priss." She continued to stare down at the little hen.

He grinned. Laura had come to the henhouse every day since the Crock boys had terrorized the ranch. Usually with the pretense of gathering eggs. "You know, if you'd like, I'll build you a small chicken coop at your house in town, and you can take Miss Priss and a couple of the other hens."

A grin tilted her lips. "Thank you, that's very nice, but I'm not even sure what the house in town looks like or if there is room for chickens."

He turned around and rested his elbows on the fence as he surveyed the main entrance to the ranch. "When we were in town, I ran into Mr. Smith. He and a group of men are going out to the Mason farm and rebuilding his barn." Clint glanced toward her. "I asked Camelia if she would like to go, but she doesn't think it's wise to leave Selina alone with Grace just yet but suggested you might like to go."

Laura tilted her head sideways and smiled. "Are you asking me to come?"

He shoved his hat back and grinned. "Why not? You could visit with the other ladies and eat good food all day." Clint realized he'd just tried to bribe her to come with him with food.

She laughed. "You didn't mention that I'll have to cook a lot of that food." Her eyes challenged him to deny that she'd be working at the barn raising, too.

"Well, if you can't cook." Clint shrugged. This was new territory for them, and he wondered how Laura would take to his teasing.

Laura turned and faced the main entrance also. "Oh, I can cook." She gave him a sideways glance. "I just haven't because you would want me to stay forever, and that just wouldn't do."

He watched her sashay back to the house. She did have a teasing nature. Unfortunately, it just made him love her all the more, and he knew he'd miss her when she returned to town.

"She really is something, isn't she?"

Clint turned to look at Richard. "That she is." He pushed away from the fence. "We'd best get on with our day, what's left of it."

Richard laughed. "I suppose."

Keeping his mind on running the ranch was harder than usual. Clint did his chores and made sure everyone else was doing theirs, too, but his mind wouldn't stray far from Laura Lee.

He was pretty sure she'd been crying when he'd approached her earlier. Her eyelashes were moist. Was she sad about leaving the ranch? Was it possible that Laura had begun to care about him and Grace?

The next morning, Laura sat on the wagon bench with Clint. They were headed to the Smith farm with lots of food and little Hope. She'd spent the afternoon the day before baking and cooking dishes for the noon-day meal. Barn raising was hard work, and the men always had large appetites.

Hope sat between her feet. She played with her rag doll and a little blanket Laura had made that matched the doll. Laura and Camelia had made several little dresses to go with each of the girl's dolls. The baby seemed to be Hope's favorite toy.

Clint glanced over his shoulder at the boxes of food, Laura had set in the bed of the wagon. "Looks like you made enough for a small army."

"Everyone will be hungry come lunchtime. I hope it's enough." She had fussed as to what all to bring. In one box there were fresh breads and cakes. In another she'd put canned jars of pickles, green beans and various fruits. Laura had also made a meat loaf, a pot of chili and a platter of fried chicken.

"You do realize there are other women coming who will be bring food, too." He chuckled and set the wagon into motion.

"I know. Maybe I overdid it." She worried her bottom lip. She knew that Mrs. Smith would be there, but besides her Laura hadn't given any thought to how many other ladies might attend. Had she done too much? Camelia hadn't commented that she thought so.

Clint bumped her with his shoulder. "I was teasing. You did good."

"Thanks." Laura wasn't as confident as she'd like to be. The Smith family were kind and had several children that went to her school. She knew they'd welcome her, but in the past, she'd stayed away from events like this because she didn't feel comfortable in crowds. Now Laura felt trapped and unsure how to act.

He draped an arm around her shoulder. "You'll do fine."

How did he know how she was feeling? Had it shown on her face? Laura nodded. "I know. I'm just a little nervous."

Clint squeezed her shoulder. "I don't know why. You deal with parents all the time. Don't the Smiths have a couple of boys in your class?"

"They do. I'm just being silly." How could she explain that being the teacher was different than just showing up to help with the food at a barn raising party. That even at church she'd kept to herself, arriving a little before service started and leaving as quickly as possible.

Hope pulled on her skirt. She held up her baby with its dress half on and half off.

Laura grinned. "Little one, do you want the dress on or off?" She took the baby and pulled the dress the rest of the way on.

The little girl frowned and pushed it back to Laura when she tried to give the toy back. Her pretty blue eyes searched Laura's.

"Oh, you want it off." Laura pulled the dress the rest of the way off and handed them back to Hope.

Clint chuckled again. "Still don't see why you are concerned. You can communicate with kids just fine. Adults really aren't that different."

Laura smiled. "You're right. I normally don't have any trouble. I'll be fine." Inwardly she sighed and thought, I'll do what I always do and put on a good front.

They continued on. Clint pulled his arm from around her shoulder and concentrated on his driving. Laura assumed he didn't want to jar the boxes in the back too badly.

Thankfully the Smith's ranch bordered Clint's, and they were there in a matter of minutes. Other wagons were parked around the front yard under shade trees. The horses had all been unhitched and were milling about in the corral a few yards away.

Laura allowed Clint to help her down and then pulled Hope and her baby from the wagon. She set Hope on her hip and looked about. The women were working on the side of the house, setting up make-shift tables.

Several men hurried out to help Clint carry her boxes to the ladies who waited. Laura followed them to the side of the house. She swallowed the lump of uneasiness.

"Mrs. Lee!"

At the sound of her name, Laura turned to find a large group of children running to her. The older ones stopped and talked all at once. The little children grabbed her about the legs and hugged tightly.

She patted each child and answered their many questions. Some wanted to know when school would be starting back. The girls looked disappointed that it would still be a few weeks, while the older boys looked relieved. Laura laughed and walked toward the group of women who were watching their children greet the schoolteacher.

"Kids, go play while you can," Mrs. Smith instructed once they were close enough that she didn't have to yell.

The children took off running as fast as they had arrived.

Mrs. Smith came around the table and smiled. "Mrs. Lee, we are so glad you could come today."

She returned the older woman's smile. Mrs. Smith was in her early forties, and her youngest child was ten. "Thank you. But I'm not the schoolteacher today. Please, call me Laura."

All the ladies seemed to visibly relax. Laura smiled. Maybe she didn't always have to be the schoolteacher. Maybe, just maybe she could be herself.

Chapter Twenty-Five

Clint tried to keep an eye on Laura. He could tell she felt a little overwhelmed when they'd first arrived. It amazed him that such a confident woman could be so skittish around a group of other women.

He hammered several nails into the board that would soon be a part of the doorframe. His gaze moved about the group of men while he worked. Mr. Smith, Mr. Carson and Mr. Daniels all worked on one wall. They'd put up several barns in the last few years. It seemed as the community grew, the barns wore out.

Other men were working on other frames for walls. Each man had a job, some were crew chiefs. They'd been around long enough to have learned some things, make good decisions and guide the younger men. Some were what he referred to as "go-getters" because they were young, had strong muscles and were the ones who were told to "go get this or lift that." Normally a barn took a full day to get up, and even then, sometimes, depending on the weather and the man power, they'd have to return the next day to finish it up.

His gaze moved to Laura. He knew the women had

a similar way of doing things. The barn hostess gave everyone jobs. Clint half expected to see Laura with the young children, since she was the schoolteacher, but instead saw her organizing the dessert table.

She looked to him and grinned. Gone was the nervousness in her eyes. The stress lines in her face had disappeared, as well. Laura Lee's inner beauty had worked its way out and painted a picture of her in his mind. A picture he'd probably never forget.

Pain exploded into his thumb. Clint yelped and stuck the throbbing member into his mouth. His gaze shot to Laura, who looked away.

Male laugher filled the morning air. "Keep your mind on the job, Shepard," his crew chief, Mr. Lawrence, yelled from his supervision spot under a big oak tree.

Mr. Lawrence knew how to put up a barn. As one of the old-timers, who played a lot of checkers at the general store, this position was one of great respect.

"Yes, sir," Clint called back. He bent his head to look at the damage to his thumb. He'd probably lose the nail in a few weeks or at least have a purple thumb for a few days.

But it had been worth it to see Laura look away with a faint blush on her cheeks. The women had all stopped what they were doing and glanced from her to him. He could see the speculations growing and prayed they'd not hound her about them.

"Now you've gone and done it," Eli Porter said as he came to help Clint line up another board.

Clint looked to the young man. He was probably in his early twenties. His baby face still hadn't seen the edge of a good razor. "Done what?"

"Opened the door for a whole mess of worms." He grinned at Clint. "I might be young, but everyone here now knows you are sweet on Mrs. Lee."

"As far as I can tell, that's not so bad. It will keep the other bachelors away." He winked at the younger man.

"Yes, sir. And, it will get the women into a match-making mood. Mark my word, before the day is up there'll be a barn dance in this here barn in a couple of days, and it's all your fault."

"Eli, quit your jawin' and go help Mr. Carson with that wall!"

The young boy yelled back, "Yes, sir." Then he lowered his voice for only Clint to hear. "Mr. Lawrence is having fun. Isn't he?"

Clint laughed. "He sure is." His thoughts returned to Eli's speculations on a barn dance. Would the women really start planning all that, simply because he hit his thumb and Laura blushed?

A few hours later, Clint's stomach growled. Thankfully his wasn't the only one, and the crew chief called for the lunch break. He got in line with the other men, aware that Laura stood at her place at the dessert table.

Mr. Smith blessed the food and announced they could all dig in. Clint looked for the meat loaf he knew that Laura had made. In the weeks she'd been on the ranch, Camelia had done all the cooking. He was looking forward to seeing for himself that Laura could make a good meat loaf.

When his plate was full, he went to join Eli's table. The young man had piled his plate to overflowing. His brown eyes met Clint's when he sat down. He held a drumstick in one hand and a biscuit in another. "This chicken is so good. You should have got a piece." He waved the leg around as if it were a grand prize.

"I went for the meat loaf."

Eli looked at Clint's plate. "No dessert?" he asked, frowning.

Clint laughed. "Not yet. I like to eat the good foods first, and if there is room, go back for dessert."

"That's too bad. Mrs. Lee said her peach pie was all taken."

He hadn't known she'd baked a peach pie, too. No wonder she'd been working in the kitchen half the night as well as all afternoon. "That's too bad. I would have liked to try it."

"She doesn't make peach pie at your place?" Eli snickered with a couple of the other boys who also sat at the table.

Clint chose to ignore their childish ways. "Afraid not." He dipped his fork into the meat loaf. Flavors danced over his tongue like rain on a still pond. He smiled. Laura could cook, and she did a far better job on meat loaf than either Camelia or Martha ever had.

He turned around and looked to the dessert table. Laura was no longer there. He sighed and returned to his meal.

Eli leaned over and whispered, "She went to get a little girl." He nodded to a group of children standing not far off. "See?"

"Thanks." He felt his neck grow red. Clint picked up his plate and drink and walked to where Laura was gathering Hope.

Clint smiled when Laura looked up at him. "Where are you going to eat?"

She smiled and pointed to an unoccupied space

under one of the many trees. "That's our blanket over there."

If people were going to gossip about them, they might as well have material to use in their conversations. "I'll take Hope while you go fix your plates." He moved his drink to the crook of his arm and reached down to take Hope's little hand in his and walked to the tree.

Hope's steps were slow, but they finally made it to their spot for lunch. He sat down and sighed. His thumb throbbed and so did his heart. What was it about Laura that made him wish for a wife and more children? Was it her sweet nature? Or the fact that he'd been alone for two years?

Laura filled her plate. She was one of the last ladies in line, and the pickings were slim. Choosing to share a plate with Hope, Laura noticed that her meat loaf was gone but that there was a pan of sliced beef with brown gravy. Laura forked out a little of that for herself, and for Hope she got a chicken wing with mashed potatoes, gravy and a spoon full of green beans. Two small biscuits completed her plate. Then she walked to the dessert table where she spooned out a small helping of vanilla pudding for Hope.

As she walked back to where Clint and Hope now sat, she wondered what had changed his mind about sitting at the table with the men. He'd caught and held her gaze several times during the morning hours. She'd secretly watched his muscles work as he hammered and lifted wood in the process of completing the door to the barn.

The women had teased her mercilessly when he'd

hit his thumb with the hammer because his focus had been on her instead of the job. She'd taken their teasing in stride and assured them that there was no love interest between the two of them. It wasn't exactly a lie. Yes, she loved Clint but told herself that it was like the love between friends. No more.

She handed him the plate and smiled. "Thanks for watching Hope for me."

"She is no trouble to watch."

As soon as Laura was seated with her legs tucked under her, Hope began reaching for the food. "Hold on, you little one." She put the plate a little out of Hope's reach and then tore the wing apart. Laura handed Hope the little drumstick part of the wing.

"Tan to."

Laura smiled. "She's picking up more and more words."

Clint nodded. "I think we can thank Gracie for that." He finished off the meat loaf and then moved on to his vegetables.

"Yes, I believe you are right. Soon we are going to have two talkative children." She looked to the barn.

"How much longer do you think it will take to finish?"

Laura saw that he was watching Hope as she tried to reach for the mashed potatoes on the plate. "I'd say about another four hours."

"That's really fast." Laura scooped up a spoonful of potatoes and offered them to Hope. The little girl opened her mouth like a bird and smacked her lips around the vegetable.

Clint reclined back on his elbows. "Haven't you ever been to a barn raising?"

She nodded. "Once, but I was a kid and don't remember much about it." Laura added green beans to the next spoonful that she offered to Hope.

Hope wasn't as happy about that bit as she had been the first. She curled her little nose at Laura.

"Sorry, little one, but you have to eat the green stuff, too." She tickled Hope's belly. Laura had given up on eating herself. With Clint present, her stomach seemed to be all knotted up in a tangle of nervousness.

He reclined the rest of the way and put his arms behind his head.

Hope mimicked his actions and yawned.

Laura enjoyed the soft chattering of the families near them. Everyone had either branched off as family units or as friends. She heard the soft snores of Clint as he fell asleep.

Her gaze moved to Hope, who had snuggled up against his side and gone to sleep also.

Her gaze moved to the tables that needed to be cleared and cleaned. Since none of the other ladies were rushing to clean up, Laura decided to enjoy this time. She scooted until her back was against the tree trunk, leaned against it and closed her eyes.

Children laughed and played as a cool breeze drifted about the tired adults. What would it be like to be a wife and mother who stayed at home and kept house in the cold winter months?

She remembered the first year of her marriage to Charles, it had been full of laughter and fun. Giving up teaching had been easy, but then things changed as they always do. Laura breathed in deeply through her nose. It was best not to dream of not working as a teacher, since she could never go back to the life of just being a wife. No matter how badly her heart longed for those days.

Chapter Twenty-Six

Laura tried to enjoy the rest of the afternoon. Her own thoughts and desires had put a damper on her happiness at being a part of the small farmland community. She cleaned the tables and packed away the extra food. Not that there had been a lot of extras. The men and children had eaten as if they were at a feast. She smiled, happy that her dishes had just about been licked clean.

"Laura?"

She turned to see Mrs. Smith standing behind her. "Yes?"

"The other ladies and I were wondering if you would like to help us plan the barn dance?" She waved her hand to indicate that the other ladies had left one table standing and were all sitting around it.

"Um, sure. I've never been to a barn dance before, so I'm not sure how much help I will be in the planning of one." She followed Mrs. Smith back to the other women.

"Oh, don't worry about that. We've all had our first barn dances and many more since. We'll be happy to help you understand what we're going to do." She motioned for Laura to sit down.

Laura did as she was bid. Her gaze searched out the children and saw that Hope was playing happily with one of the older girls. She turned her attention back to the planning committee.

Mrs. Smith stood at the front of the table. "Who would like to bring three dozen cookies?"

Several hands shot into the air. She raised hers slowly. How was Camelia going to react to this? Laura thought if she had to, perhaps she could go to the bakery in town and buy them. But would she have time?

"Mrs. Smith? When is the barn dance taking place?" Laura asked before the older woman could press on with her plans.

"Day after tomorrow, dear. And please, we are all friends here, I'm Doris." She smiled at Laura and then continued going down her list of things that needed to be done.

Laura listened as each lady volunteered to bring various things. So far all she was responsible for were three dozen cookies. Others were bringing drinks, cakes, tablecloths and whatever else Doris Smith thought she'd need.

"Now for the decorating committee. Laura, Shelly, Esther and Beulah, I would like you ladies to arrive around noon and help me set up. I'll supply a luncheon with all the trimmings in appreciation of your help."

The other three ladies nodded happily. Laura simply didn't know what to say. She wanted to help, but she was also concerned about what to do with Hope. "Um, can we bring our children?"

"Of course, dear."

Laura smiled what she hoped was a confident smile. "Then I'll be happy to be a part of the decorating committee."

The men gave a triumph hoop. Laura and the ladies all turned to see that the barn was complete. They clapped their hands, and the children cheered.

Doris turned back to the table. "We better get everything loaded up. Those men will be ready to go home now."

Laura was amazed at how the ladies all jumped up to do Doris's bidding. She followed the others and gathered her boxes up and carried some of them to the wagon. On her return trip, she noticed that Hope had wandered off by herself and was standing with a big stick in her hand.

Clint seemed to notice the little girl at the same time because he took off running toward her. Laura frowned. Why run? She had a stick; it wasn't like she had a snake by the tail.

She followed and saw him jerk Hope up and carry her toward the rest of the children. He took the stick and scolded. "Hope, we do not poke sticks in big holes in the ground."

The little girl's bottom lip pooched out and she began to cry. Laura hurried to them. "What's wrong?" She went to cradle Hope close, but Clint stopped her.

Laura turned angry eyes on him. What did he think he was doing? He'd made Hope cry, and now he didn't want her to comfort the child? Before she could say anything, Clint spun on his heels.

"Eli! Get Mr. Smith and a hoe!" he barked, returning to the place where Hope had been playing. Laura didn't understand. It wasn't that big of a hole, and what in the world did he need a hoe for? Was he planning to dig and make it bigger?

Laura wanted to comfort Hope but didn't. She wouldn't embarrass Clint by disobeying him, but she had a few choice words for him when they were alone.

The other kids crowded around them. They too watched the men scramble about the hole. Soon the other mothers had joined them.

"What's going on?" Shelly asked, hugging her son close to her skirt.

"I don't know. Clint just pulled Hope away from that hole, and now the men are digging in it as if searching for gold." She looked at Shelly with a frown. "Do the men out here do that often?"

Shelly shook her head.

One of the older girls gasped.

Laura turned to see what she was looking at and gasped also.

Clint had a rattlesnake on the stick he'd taken from Hope earlier and was pulling it from the hole. He tossed the snake on the ground and jumped back. Mr. Smith moved in with the hoe and chopped at the slithering reptile.

Her gaze clashed with Clint's, and Laura now understood he hadn't been angry with Hope, but scared of what could have happened to her.

He turned his attention back to the hole. His face paled as several baby snakes came out of the ground. Men jumped back and children screamed. The women gasped, and Mr. Smith went to work with his hoe.

When everyone had calmed down, ten snakes were lying on the ground, dead.

Clint walked back to them and picked up Hope. He

took Laura by the hand and walked back to the snakes and the hole. "Hope, never play in a hole. Snakes live in holes, and they are dangerous."

Laura thought she was going to be sick. Mr. Smith had taken out his knife and cut the rattlers from the snake. He held it up for everyone to see. She would guess that it was over five feet long and had been the mother to all the babies lying around.

She looked to Clint. "I'm ready to go home now." Laura swallowed hard. Hope could have been killed. One strike from those sharp fangs. She shuddered.

He nodded. "Let's get the rest of your boxes." Clint kept Hope with him.

Laura assumed it was because he didn't want her to be afraid of him but to understand that he'd raised his voice in fear, not anger. She watched as he patted her back and kissed her wet cheek. The action thawed out another piece of her heart.

Clint thanked the Lord that he'd been right in jerking the child away when he had. For a split moment he'd seen the rattler's head rise, just as he'd grabbed Hope out of harm's way. It wasn't in his nature to go after a snake, but this one's den was too close to the house and barn.

From the look of the ground, the Smith boys had been digging at that hole earlier. Clint didn't know if it were today or days before, but he did know that it was a deadly spot for children to be playing.

He'd given Hope to Laura and nodded his consent for her to comfort the baby. Then he'd finished loading their wagon and saying his goodbyes. Paul Smith had offered him the rattlers; he'd declined taking them.

What must Laura think of the way he'd scolded Hope? She still cradled the child close but hadn't said a word since they'd left the ranch. He reached over and touched Hope's soft baby curls. His heart still skipped a beat at how close she'd come to getting snake bitten.

"Thank you, Clint." Her words were so soft, he'd almost missed them.

He smiled with relief that she wasn't angry at him for the way he'd handled the snake situation. "You're welcome. I'm glad she wasn't hurt."

Laura grew silent as Hope drifted off to sleep in her arms. He inched a little closer to her on the bench in pretense of shifting his weight. The sun was setting on what had turned out to be a very long, tiring day.

Her voice drifted to him on the evening breeze. "Did you know that there is going to be a barn dance in two days?"

So Eli had been right. Clint almost laughed but decided it would just confuse Laura and possibly wake the baby. "No, but I'm not surprised."

"No?"

"No, Mrs. Smith likes to be the center of attention." He slowed the horse down wanting to spend more time with Laura.

Laura giggled. "I got that impression today. She asked me to bring three dozen cookies."

"Did she say what kind?" Clint asked. He was partial to oatmeal raisin.

"No, but I was thinking I might do a sugar cookie or maybe an oatmeal one."

Clint hid his grin. "Since you have to make three dozen, why not make both?"

She yawned. "I suppose I could." Laura eased Hope

around into a more comfortable position in her arms. "I also have to go over there at noon the day of the dance and help decorate."

"Mrs. Smith is taking advantage of your good nature." He frowned into the darkness.

Drowsiness filled her voice. "No, she asked everyone to pitch in. I think she took it easy on me, since this is my first barn dance." Laura's head bobbed.

Clint scooted a little closer. Soon they'd be touching, he was so close. He worried she and the baby might fall off the wagon, if she fell asleep. "This is your first barn dance?"

"Yes." She slid on the bench.

He scooted closer and put his arm around her shoulder. Clint relaxed when she didn't pull away. The gentle rocking of the wagon and Hope's steady breathing soon had Laura leaning into his shoulder.

Clint enjoyed the sweet scent of her hair. Laura smelled of vanilla and cinnamon, probably from the baking she'd done the day before. Her slow, even breathing told him, she'd fallen asleep.

Only an exhausted person could sleep on a moving wagon. It seemed no matter how careful he tried to be, Clint hit a chug hole of some kind. He marveled that she and little Hope slept on.

Just before they pulled into the yard, Clint woke Laura by removing his arm from around her and baby Hope. He stopped the wagon and turned on the seat. "Laura, we're almost home. Wake up, honey." Immediately, he realized he'd given her an endearment.

She blinked her eyes and looked about. "I'm sorry. Are we home?"

Did she think of the ranch as her home now? Clint

leaned in and kissed her lightly on the lips. Whatever possessed him to do so, he didn't know. She just looked so sweet and innocent half asleep. He leaned back and looked into her wide eyes. "Almost."

Clint turned around in the seat and gently urged the horse to continue home. He didn't regret kissing her. She seemed a little baffled but not unhappy with him. He had lost his heart to Laura weeks ago. But his head still told him it wasn't right. What was he going to do with a warring heart and mind?

Chapter Twenty-Seven

Laura spent the next two days in a daze. Clint Shepard had kissed her, that was her foremost thought. He didn't act any different at breakfast, lunch or dinner the next day. But she felt different. Not a bad different, just different, as if she were special.

She shook her head and pulled the last batch of oatmeal cookies out of the oven. Camelia hadn't been too pleased when she'd ask to take possession of the kitchen again. But she'd grudgingly allowed it, and now the house smelled of sweetness. So much so that Laura had decided to make an extra dozen for home.

Grace came into the kitchen with Selina right behind her. "Cookie!" Grace begged with an impish grin.

A weary-looking Selina shook her head. "I'm sorry. I tried to keep her out of here. I promise."

Camelia looked up with a frown. "You have to be in charge of the child, not the child of you." She shook her head and went back to polishing the silverware.

Hope squealed and pushed herself up from the floor. She toddled over to Grace and fell into her, giggling and hugging her. The two little girls babbled. Every so often, Laura made out the word, "cookie," and little fingers pointed up to where Laura had been setting them on racks to cool.

Laura knew the little girls missed each other. She smiled at Selina. "It's all right. We'll give both the girls cookies and milk for a morning snack today."

Camelia huffed. "Yep, and they'll both skip their nap today, too." She gathered up her silver and took it back to the silverware drawer.

"Cookie!" both girls pointed in unison up at the fresh cookies.

"Did I hear someone say cookie?" Clint asked coming through the door behind Selina.

"Well, goodness. It's a regular family reunion in here," Camelia grumbled.

But no one heard her over Grace's squeal of "Papa!"

He hugged both little girls and kissed their little cheeks. Clint looked up at Laura from his kneeling position and winked.

She felt heat enter her face and neck and looked away. "Clint, if you will go and get the milk out of the well, I'll dish up these cookies." Laura looked to Selina. "You get the girls up to the table."

Camelia turned. "I'll come back when it's a little more quiet in here." And with that statement, Camelia left the room.

Laura and Selina shared knowing grins, then went to work preparing snack time for their charges. Selina got them in their chairs while Laura put several cookies on a plate and sat it in the center of the table.

"Is Camelia always that mean?" Selina asked, once both the girls were in place with their cookies in hand.

"Have you heard the saying, 'her bark is worse than

her bite'?" Laura asked, pulling down cups to pour the milk into. She looked to the door. Clint should have been back already.

"Yes." Selina's gaze followed Laura's.

Laura turned back around. "Well, that's our Camelia. It takes her a while to warm up to you. Just remember to treat her like you want to be treated, and you'll be fine."

Selina finger-combed her hair, pinched her cheeks, and then poured two cups of coffee. She carried them back to the table all the while staring at the back door. Distracted she said, "Thanks, I'll keep that in mind."

Clint hurried back inside. He stomped his boots on the rug just inside the door to remove dirt. Camelia would be beside herself, if he tracked dirt inside. "I'm sorry. One of the men had a question for me that couldn't wait." He walked the rest of the way into the kitchen and handed the milk to Laura.

With a wicked grin, he reached around her and snatched one of the hot cookies from its cooling rack. Taking a big bite, he sighed. "These are so good. You'll have to make them again, soon."

Not to be outdone, Selina purred, "I've set you a place at the table, Mr. Shepard." She smiled and indicated one of the cups of coffee she'd just poured.

Laura turned away. She'd thought the girl had poured it for her. Did the young girl think Clint was interested in her romantically? Was she hoping to rope herself a rich rancher?

"Thanks." Clint pulled the chair back, making a scraping sound across the floor. When Laura turned around he grinned.

Laura poured each of the girls a cup of milk and

then poured a glass for herself. She walked to the table and set the cups just out of reach of the girls. Hope still needed a lot of help, and Grace needed a little.

"What time do you want to leave, Laura?" Clint asked, around a mouth full of cookie.

She hadn't expected him to ride over with them. "Um, probably as soon as Hope is done with her snack and I get these cookies boxed up."

He nodded. "I'll get the buggy ready."

Selina looked from one to the other. "Are you going, too?"

Her eyes were fixated on Clint. She batted her eyelashes and smiled boldly.

Laura waited for his answer, trying not to let him see how much Selina's flirtations bothered her. "No, I'll ride over later this evening to pick her up. I'm sending one of the men to make sure she gets there safe." He looked to Laura.

Could he read the disappointment on her face? She tried to conceal it by telling Hope. "You are doing better at holding your cup, good girl."

Selina purred again, "So I guess that means you'll be having dinner with us tonight."

"If I'm not too busy." He looked to Laura. "You know, it might be better if you left Hope with Selina and Grace while you go to the dance. I'm sure the girls would love to play together, and you'd have a little time to yourself with the other women."

Selina looked as if she wanted to object but instead smiled sweetly. "I'd love to watch her for you, Mr. Shepard."

Laura sighed. Why had she thought he'd attend the dance? The thought of dancing with him had filled her mind all day. Disappointment hit her hard and fast. She took a deep breath and told herself that the week couldn't be over soon enough, and then Selina and Clint could play house all they wanted to. Bitter jealousy ate at her; Laura tried to push it away. She had no claim on Clint Shepard.

Clint sat on the front porch nursing a cup of hot coffee. Two days had passed since the barn dance. He'd arrived early, hoping to secure a dance with Laura before the night ended. Only, when he'd arrived, so many young farmers had claimed her that he'd not had a chance to dance with her. Not that he'd tried too hard. He'd stood in the shadows and watched her laugh and smile with the other men. Her beauty outshone all the other women there. Laura hadn't seemed to notice him until the dance was over.

She'd helped clean up and then spent the whole ride home talking about how wonderful barn dances were and how much fun she'd had. Laura had thanked him for letting her leave Hope with Selina and Grace. The little girl had been so happy to spend the afternoon with them that she'd almost forgotten to give Laura a hug goodbye.

Clint knew the coffee would keep him awake all night, but since he figured he'd be up anyway, it didn't matter. A cool evening breeze couldn't soothe the ache in his heart.

He loved Laura but still fought the feeling that he should tell her. No matter how hard he tried, fear that she'd die before him kept him from confessing his love. He'd asked her twice to marry him, and each time she'd refused. Now he wished she hadn't. If she had said yes then, before he'd fallen in love with her, well then, he wouldn't be hurting now. But as his mama used to say to him, "Son, if wishes were kisses, you'd always be kissed."

The door made a soft screeching sound. He looked up to see Camelia come out on the porch. She too held a cup of coffee and was dressed in her night robe.

"Oh, I'm sorry, Clint. I didn't mean to disturb you." She turned to go back inside.

"Please, stay." He pointed to the other chair on the porch.

Camelia took the chair and sent it into a gentle rock. "Normally, I would be in the kitchen but I didn't want to wake up Laura."

Clint grinned. "Same here."

A twinkle came into her eyes. "Remember when it was just you, baby Grace and me? Life seemed simpler then," she teased.

He looked out across the moonlit yard. "Yes." Clint heard the sorrow in his voice and feared Camelia would detect it, too.

"What's eating at you, Clint?" Her voice held that comforting tone that she'd used after Martha's death.

Her use of it now told him that she'd heard it. "Laura will be leaving in a couple of days, and I really don't want to let her go." There, he'd said it, confessed he'd miss Laura.

"Then why don't you tell her?" Camelia didn't look at him. She sipped her coffee with her head bent down.

As much as he wanted to tell Laura how he felt, Clint confessed. "I can't."

"Why not? She's a bright, beautiful woman with lots of love to give. I've seen her with you and the girls."

Clint sighed. "You know I can't."

"Do you love her?" Camelia's rich Irish accent drifted to him in a soothing manner.

He nodded. "But even so, I can't tell her."

Again she asked, "Why not?"

Clint looked across at her. He looked into the depth of his cup and confessed. "I'm not sure I could handle it if Laura died before me. When Martha died, a part of me went with her."

Sadness filled her accent. "I know that feeling." Camelia gazed out into the darkness.

He realized that with all the time that Camelia had been here, he really didn't know much about her. She'd come out to the ranch looking for a housekeeping job right after he and Martha had married. Martha had hired her on the spot, and Clint had never been happier.

Martha was a good wife in the sense that she was kind, loving and tried to do everything a wife was supposed to do. But, he'd soon learned, she couldn't cook, wasn't the best house cleaner and hated getting dirty. Camelia had been a blessing.

He studied her profile. "You do?"

Her emotions caught in her throat. "Yes, I've loved and lost three husbands to death." She sipped from her cup, avoiding eye contact with him.

Three? Why would anyone marry three times? She'd said loved and lost. Clint couldn't imagine loving three women who died. Could his heart take that much abuse?

Camelia put her cup down and turned to face him. "Clint Shepard, if you love that woman—" she paused and held his gaze "—you need to tell her. If you don't, you will spend your whole life wishing you had."

"But it hurts so badly when the one you love dies."
He swallowed. Was he a coward?

Camelia sighed. "Yes, it does. But think of all the
time you spent with Martha and how wonderful those
times had been."

Clint leaned his head back and closed his eyes. He
remembered Martha and wouldn't take away one moment of being with her, loving her. But she was gone.
Had been for two years. Martha's image seemed to
dissolve, and Laura's face filled his mind. Her smile
and the way she talked filled his emotions. She loved
Hope deeply. How much more would she love a child
of her own?

His thoughts turned to Grace. Together he and Laura
could give the little girl sisters and brothers, friends to
grow up with. But, more important, he'd have a com-
panion again. Someone he could share his dreams and
plans with. A friend that wouldn't betray him.

Camelia's soft voice broke through his thoughts.
"See? You need to tell her how you feel. I wouldn't be
surprised if she said she loves you, as well."

He had seen a look of love in Laura's eyes. Maybe
like him, she was afraid to express those feelings. And
when he'd stolen a kiss from her, Laura hadn't shoved
him away or acted as if she never wanted to see him
again.

Perhaps, Laura had gone to love him, as well.
With that thought in mind, Clint opened his eyes and
grinned. "Thank you. I'll talk to her first thing tomorrow."

She stood and yawned. "In that case, I'm going to
turn in now."

"Camelia?"

She turned to face him.

"Thank you. And whether she says yes she'll stay or not, you will always have a home with us."

Tears moistened her lashes. Camelia seemed to be at a loss for words; she simply nodded, then closed the door softly behind her.

Clint sat on the porch and listened to the locusts in the trees. How was he going to tell Laura that he loved her and wanted her to stay on the ranch? Would she turn him down again if he proposed? He frowned. Well, so much for being content with his decision to confess his love. Now he had a whole slew of new questions barging in and making him feel wide awake.

Chapter Twenty-Eight

Laura felt as if she'd worked three days without sleep. As soon as they'd gotten home from the barn dance two days ago, she'd checked on Hope and then hurried off to her room where she'd let her real feelings flow. Her heart still ached, but she had no more tears to shed.

Clint hadn't come to the dance until the last minute. She'd tried to put on a good front by dancing with everyone who asked her. Laura wasn't very good at dancing, but her partners didn't seem to mind. She'd shared laughter with her dance partners and had stepped on every farmer in the county's toes in the process of learning to dance.

Even as she'd danced, Laura had watched for Clint's arrival. How many times had she searched the barn doors waiting for him to enter? What had she expected? Him to swoop in and take her in his arms, swing her about the dance floor and tell her how beautiful she looked? That was silliness, and she knew it. But Laura also knew she loved Clint.

Looking for something to occupy her sleepless night, Laura slipped from her bedroom, crossed the dark kitchen and quietly eased down the hall to Selina and the girls' room. She'd heard Camelia close her door earlier, and then shortly after that, Clint had retired to his room. She felt pretty sure they were both in their rooms and wouldn't catch her up checking on Hope once more.

The door to Selina's room was open. Laura tiptoed inside. She didn't want to wake the young woman, but when she glanced toward her bed, Selina wasn't there. Laura assumed she'd gone outside for a breath of fresh air or to the outhouse.

Either way, she was glad to find her gone. She walked to the bed where Grace and Hope slept. Expecting the little girls to be curled together like kittens, Laura stood staring down at Grace, only Grace.

Where was Hope? Had Selina taken her to the outhouse or perhaps the kitchen for a last drink of water before going to sleep? Laura hurried to the kitchen, knowing they weren't there since she'd just passed through on the way to their room. As she expected, the kitchen was dark and empty.

She ran to the outhouse, only to find it empty, as well. Fear crept up her spine and into her heart. Where were they? "Don't panic. Camelia may have taken Hope to her room," she whispered as she hurried back to the house and down the hall to Camelia's room.

At the sound of her knock, a sleepy Camelia opened her door. She blinked sleep-filled eyes at her. "What's wrong, Laura?"

"Is Hope with you?" Laura blurted, trying to see around the Irishwoman. *Please, Lord, let her be safe with Camelia.*

Camelia's eyes opened wide. "No, why would she

be in my room?" She pulled her housecoat on over her gown.

Renewed panic caused Laura to squeak. "Because she's not in her bed and I can't find Selina."

"What? How long have they been gone?"

Laura forced herself to calm down and answered, "I don't know. I went to check on Hope just now. Grace is the only one there. Selina and Hope are not in the room. I looked in the kitchen and the outhouse. They are gone."

Camelia's eyes narrowed. "Do you think Selina took her away?"

"I don't know what to think." Laura shook her head. "Why would she take Hope and leave Grace?"

Camila pushed past Laura. She hurried to Clint's room and pounded on the door. Laura followed.

He answered it with his shirt half on. "What's wrong?" he asked, looking at the women's frightened faces.

"Hope and Selina are gone," Laura said, wringing her hands.

Clint ran his hands through his hair. "Maybe they are outside."

Laura shook her head. "No, I checked."

He walked back into his room, sat down on the side of the bed and began pulling on his boots. "How long have they been gone, and where is Grace?"

"We don't know how long, and Grace is asleep in her bed," Camelia answered.

"I'm sure they are around here somewhere." He stood and began buttoning up his shirt. "We'll find them. Maybe Hope was fussy, and Selina thought she needed fresh air to calm her down."

"If Hope was fussy, why didn't Selina just bring her

to me?" Laura answered. Her cheeks heated up as she realized that she'd been crying in her room. Had Selina heard her and thought it would be better to take Hope somewhere else?

"I think she took that baby and left," Camelia stated. "You need to get on your horse and get to town. Maybe the sheriff can get a group of men together and go find her."

Clint patted the frustrated woman's shoulder. "Don't go getting yourself all riled up, Camelia. I can't believe that Selina would steal Hope."

Laura was sick of hearing how wonderful Selina was from Clint. This was important. Her baby was missing, and she expected him to help find her, not say how Selina wasn't capable of taking the child.

"I don't care if you believe it or not, Clint Shepard. My child is missing, and I want her back." Laura knew she was being unreasonable. Maybe she was wrong.

Clint walked up to her and pulled her close. "I'll find her, Laura." He released her and started walking down the hall. "Stay here and take care of Grace. I'll be back as soon as I can."

Laura watched him leave. She didn't have any intentions of sitting back and waiting for him to find her baby. "Will you watch Grace, Camelia?"

Camelia reached out and touched her arm. "Of course, I will. You go on."

"Thank you." Laura hurried to her room and pulled on the trousers that she'd worn once before. Then she hurried to the barn.

Clint had just finished saddling his horse. His eyes narrowed when he saw her. "Did you find them?" he asked.

"No. I wish I had."

"Then why are you out here?" Clint looked as if he were going to ride out, instead of waiting for her answer. He pulled the horse out of the barn and swung into the saddle.

Frantic to find Hope, Laura shouted, "I'm going with you!" She placed both hands on her hips and continued. "Hope is my baby, Clint. I have the right to go looking for her with you. Camelia is going to stay here and watch after Grace."

Clint nodded. "You'll have to ride double with me." He kicked his foot out of the stirrup.

She nodded and put her foot into the stirrup he'd just taken his boot out of. He reached down and pulled her up.

Once she was in the saddle, Clint set the horse to trotting out of the yard. "One of the horses is missing from the barn. I'm afraid you were right."

"I don't understand. Why would she take Hope? Other than at night, she hardly saw Hope." Laura laid her cheek on Clint's strong back.

His voice sounded as stressed as she felt when he said, "I don't know, but I'm going to find out." Clint sent the horse into a gallop.

She tightened her arms around his waist. Tears pricked her eyes but she refused to let them fall. Laura knew that she had to be strong. She closed her burning eyes and silently prayed, asking God to watch after her baby and to keep her safe from all harm.

They rode in silence. Getting to town was faster by horse than by wagon. The horse's hooves ate up the ground. Laura realized they were getting close to town when Clint pulled the horse to a walk.

He shrugged his shoulder to get Laura's attention. "Look." Clint pointed to something beside the road.

Laura squinted in the semidarkness. From where she sat, it looked like someone had lost a pile of old clothes on the road. She swallowed, when she realized it wasn't just clothes but a person. She couldn't tell in the darkness if it were a man or a woman, but Laura could tell that it wasn't Hope.

Clint pulled her arms from around his waist and slid off the horse. He handed Laura the reins and proceeded to walk toward the slumped figure. Laura and the horse followed. As they drew closer, Laura realized it was a woman.

Clint knelt down and brushed her hair from her face. "It's Selina. She's bleeding and unconscious." He picked her up.

Laura urged the horse to walk faster. Where was Hope? What had Selina done with her? She looked down on the woman who had stolen her baby.

"We've got to get her to the doctor," he said, pushing Selina up on to the horse in front of Laura.

Laura held Selina's limp body on the horse, wishing she would wake up and tell them where Hope was. Blood dripped from the wound on Selina's head. "We'd better hurry. The sooner she's awake, the sooner she can tell me where Hope is."

Clint grabbed the horse's bridle. "I know you want to hurry, but we can't jar her too much. She might have broken bones."

Even though Laura wanted to race into town, she knew Clint was right. If she did have broken bones, such as a rib, it could be fatal to the other woman.

Clint walked beside the horse, helping Laura hold

Selina upright in the saddle. The young woman practically laid across the horse's neck, but there was no helping that.

Laura chewed on the inside of her lip as they slowly advanced into town. With each clop of the horse's hooves, Laura asked herself, where was Hope? Had someone stolen the baby from Selina? Had Selina hid the little girl somewhere? It was obvious that Selina had run into someone who had beaten her up. But who? Who would do such a thing to a woman with a child? There were so many questions racing through her tired mind.

Tears slipped from Laura's eyes as she realized Hope could be lost to her forever. What would she do if the baby was hurt somewhere? Or worse, dead?

Clint patted her leg. "Don't cry, Laura. We'll find her."

He prayed he was telling her the truth. His own heart ached at the fact that baby Hope was missing.

Thankfully, they arrived at the doctor's office and Selina was still breathing. They needed her to give them some answers. "Stay with Selina while I get the doctor." At her nod, Clint hurried to the front door and knocked loudly.

A sleepy doctor answered the summons. "What's going on out here?" he asked, looking past Clint to Laura and Selina on the horse. A tired sigh escaped him.

"I've brought you a patient. We found her on the road to town," Clint said. He stepped to one side so that the doctor could get a better look at the women.

Now fully awake, the doctor pushed past Clint.

"Well, don't just stand there. Let's get her inside where I can look at her."

Clint followed him to the gelding. Together the doctor and Clint moved to take Selina from Laura. The horse took a step sideways, throwing the two men off. Clint patted the mount's neck. "Hold him steady, Laura, while we get her down."

Laura nodded. Her jaw was set, and tears no longer flowed down her cheeks.

The doctor stood back as the young woman slid into Clint's arms. "Bring her inside," he ordered, leading the way.

Clint was aware of Laura climbing off the horse and tying the reins to the hitching post in front of the doctor's house.

The doctor followed him inside and walked past him. "Bring her into the examination room. Who is she?"

"Selina Morgan."

Laura entered and shut the front door. Clint looked over his shoulder and saw her slump into a chair beside the door.

"What happened to her?" The doctor was examining the cut on Selina's forehead.

Clint turned his full attention back to the doctor. "We don't know. She kidnapped Hope, and we were following her to town. We found her lying in the road like this."

The doctor took a cloth and washed the cut above Selina's eye. Satisfied it was clean, he tossed the cloth into a nearby basin. "Where's Hope?" he asked, running his hands up and down Selina's arm.

"That's what we'd like to ask her. Can you get her

to wake up?" Clint watched as the doctor ran his hands down Selina's sides.

"I can, but I'm not sure it's a good idea. She has a head injury and a couple of broken bones." His gaze met Clint's.

Laura rose and came into the room. "Doctor, I realize you don't want to cause her pain, but I need to know what she did with my daughter. Hope is out there somewhere, alone."

He nodded. "I'll wake her up."

Clint looked to Laura. His brown eyes begged her to believe and trust him. "We'll find her. I promise."

Laura tried to smile. "You will try, but until she can tell us where Hope is, I'm afraid we won't be able to find her."

Selina gasped as she came to. The doctor stood beside her holding a cloth close to her nose. Whatever was on the rag the doctor held was enough to wake Selina. Her gaze jerked frantically around at the people in the room.

From the look on Laura's face, Selina was in for a tongue lashing of the worst kind. Clint said a silent prayer that the woman would tell them where to find baby Hope.

Chapter Twenty-Nine

"Where is Hope?" Laura demanded.

Selina looked at her. Tears streamed from her eyes and into her hair. "I don't know."

Panic dripped from Laura's lips. "How can you not know?"

Selina wept harder and curled onto her side. "I gave her to my husband. I'm so sorry, but he made me."

Clint stepped up beside Laura. He placed an arm around her shoulder. "Who is your husband?" His arm offered comfort.

Selina kept her eyes locked with Laura's. "Jerry Roberts, Hope's pa."

Laura sagged against Clint. Jerry had come to get Hope, but as her pa, why hadn't he just come and claimed her? Why send Selina to kidnap her?

The only person who had answers to those questions looked as if she might be drifting back to sleep. Selina closed her eyes.

Straightening her spine, Laura used her best school-teacher tone and demanded, "If that's true, why didn't he come get her himself?"

Selina jerked at the sharpness in Laura's voice. "He is going to demand that the banker pay to get her back."

So that was the reason he'd had Selina kidnap Hope—money. As her father, didn't he realize Hope's grandparents would have given him help in raising their granddaughter? She didn't have time to question Jerry Roberts's reasoning. Instead she snapped at Selina to get her full attention, once more, "Where did he take Hope, Selina?"

She shook her head. "I don't know." Fresh tears flowed from her eyes. "He never told me that part of the plan." Selina reached up and touched the side of her head. "All I know is he wants the money. I told him I didn't want to do this anymore, but he wouldn't listen." Fresh tears of pain and regret poured down Selina's pretty face.

Clint asked. "How did you end up hurt?"

Selina cried bitterly. "I met him as planned but told him I didn't want to take Hope from Laura. I told him we could give her back and go back to Denver. He wasn't as loving as I remembered and said that if I didn't want to continue with the plan I didn't have to. Then he hit me."

The doctor spoke up. "I'd say he hit you several times."

Laura swallowed. Jerry Roberts had beat his wife so that he could take Hope and then demand a ransom from his child's grandparents. What kind of parent did such a thing?

Selina sank back into the blessed darkness where she no longer felt pain. Laura wanted to wake her up again but knew that would be unkind and that the young woman had probably told her all she knew about

Hope's whereabouts. Which, from what they'd gathered, was nothing.

The doctor looked to Clint. "I won't wake her again. She's been through a lot tonight. You need to get over to the sheriff's office and let him know what's happened. Tell him I'll hold Mrs. Roberts until he tells me to let her go."

Clint nodded. "I will tell him." He looked at Selina. "Take care of her, Doc. She might be able to help us yet." Clint pulled Laura from the room.

"How can he do that to his wife and child?" she asked, looking up at him. Confusion filled her mind; even when Charles had been the most angry over his loss of an heir, he'd never hit her.

Clint shook his head. "I don't know, but the doctor's right. We need to get to the sheriff's office and let him know what is going on."

Laura felt as if she were in a daze. So much had happened in just the last day. What were Hope's grandparents going to say when they found out she'd allowed Hope to be kidnapped? And, if they did get her back, would they give her back to Laura after what had happened? But, right now, Laura decided that wasn't important. What was important was finding Jerry and freeing Hope from him. It didn't matter that the Maxwells might take their granddaughter from her; what mattered was that Hope be returned and in good health.

Laura was surprised when they got to the sheriff's office. She hadn't even realized they'd walked the short distance. Mentally she told herself to wake up. Hope needed her to have a clear mind. She preceded Clint into the sheriff's office.

Matt looked up from a stack of papers on his desk.

One glance at their faces and he was standing. "What's happened?"

Clint pulled out a chair for Laura to sit down in. His warm brown eyes looked at her with worry. Was she scaring him by her distractedness?

"Thank you." She tried to gather her wits about her but couldn't seem to get past the screaming thought, Hope is gone. Laura swallowed hard, forced herself to focus and said, "Jerry Roberts had his wife kidnap Hope. He's planning to ask a ransom for her from her grandparents."

"Well, I'll be dogged." The sheriff sat back down. "When did this happen?" He began digging through the papers on his desk.

Clint answered, "This evening."

"Was he working alone?" A frown marred his handsome features.

Laura shook her head. "No, his new wife was helping him."

"How do you know this?"

Clint sighed. "We found her on our way into town to see you. He beat her up and took the baby from her. She claims she was going to bring Hope back, but he stopped her."

Matt unearthed a piece of paper. He studied it for several long moments. "Where is she now?"

"The doctor's office," Laura answered.

The sheriff looked up. "Jerry Roberts is wanted in Denver for bank robbery." He held the wanted poster for them to see.

Laura started to cry. She looked to Clint for support. He gathered her into his strong arms and rubbed her back. "We'll find them."

Laura prayed he was right. She couldn't stand the idea of her baby alone with a wanted criminal. Was she safe? Had he harmed her?

The door to the sheriff's office opened once more. Laura sniffled and wiped at her eyes as she stepped out of Clint's embrace. She would have stayed there forever, if it wasn't improper to do so.

She turned to see Elizabeth and John Maxwell enter. Elizabeth's face was splotchy as if she'd been crying. Her gaze moved to Laura, and she burst out crying. "It's true," she wailed.

John Maxwell walked to the desk and thrust a piece of paper at the sheriff. "This arrived on our doorstep about thirty minutes ago. Someone is demanding money for the safe return of our granddaughter." He looked at Laura. "Please tell me this is a mistake."

"I wish I could." She held her arms out to Hope's grandmother.

The older woman hurried to her.

Matt stood and held the wanted poster out to John. "His name is Jerry Roberts, and he's Hope's pa."

"How did he know she was here? Priscilla said he didn't know where she'd grown up," Elizabeth said, searching everyone's faces, looking for answers.

John sighed. "Prissy probably mentioned it sometime during their time together and simply forgot. You know how she was." He walked over and pulled Elizabeth close to his side.

She nodded. "Yes. That is possible."

"Selina Morgan, his new wife, might have the answer to that question. Of course, she might be Selina Roberts," Laura said aloud.

The sheriff added, "Well, how he found Hope isn't the main question here. Where are they now is."

Clint and the banker moved closer to the sheriff's desk, and then the men began to discuss the possibilities in quiet tones. Laura suspected it was to keep her and Elizabeth calm as they worked to decide the best course of action.

She felt as if it were all a bad dream and she'd wake up to find Hope sleeping soundly in her little bed with Grace. Elizabeth's soft sobs didn't quite seem real either. Oh, she knew they were, and Laura knew that Hope was out there somewhere with an outlaw.

Clint looked to where Laura sat hugging her arms and rocking from side to side in the wooden chair. Her face had grown even paler over the last few minutes.

Mr. Maxwell's voice drew his attention back to the men's discussion. "There are two places he might be holed up. The Joneses moved away a couple of months ago. Their place is vacant. Or, he could be out on the Timberlake's place up in the hills. They have a shack there that the men use when out hunting. Mr. Timberlake came in and said he wanted to sell it. Asked if the bank would handle the sale."

"But would he know of either place?" Clint asked, looking down on the map that Matt had spread out over the desk.

"Selina Morgan, I mean Roberts, came to see me when she first arrived in town. Said she was looking for a place to settle. I told her about both places." He ran his hand through his silver hair. "If I'd have known then…"

The sheriff cut him off. "Did she seem more interested in one place over the other?"

His troubled gaze met theirs. "Yep, said she liked the idea of living in a cabin. I told her it really wasn't any place for a lady. Then she nodded and said she'd think on it. That was the last time I saw her in the bank."

Clint shoved his hat back on his head. "How long would it take the three of us to ride out there?"

"About two hours," the sheriff answered. He walked to a cabinet that set against the wall and pulled his gun belt off the top. As he strapped it on, Matt said, "Ladies, you are welcome to stay here until we get back, or go on home."

Laura stood. "I'm going."

Clint shook his head. "No, not this time."

"But she's my baby."

Elizabeth stood up, as well. "And my grandbaby. We have the right to go help find her."

John's voice came out strong. "No, you both are staying here. If you tag along, you'll only slow us up, and we'll be worried sick about something happening to you."

Matt handed John one of the rifles that had been hanging on the wall moments earlier. He turned to give the other one to Clint.

"No, thanks. I'll use my own pistol. I'm a better shot with it." He looked deeply into Laura's eyes. "Please stay put. I'll bring her back to you. I promise." Clint just wished he could promise he'd bring her back alive. The truth of the matter was, he didn't know how they would find the little girl.

He leaned forward and kissed her on her forehead before whispering in her ear, "Take care of Elizabeth.

She needs you right now." Clint prayed Laura would do as he asked.

She surprised him by whispering back, "Be safe." Laura looked up at him with worry and love in her eyes.

"I will." He hugged her briefly and then turned to leave with the other two men.

Mr. Maxwell hugged his wife, as well. "Don't worry, Beth. We'll find her and bring her home."

Clint saw Laura's face pale even further. He wanted to assure her that the banker had only meant they'd bring Hope back, not that he planned on he and his wife keeping the little girl.

Matt opened the door. "We need to get going." He walked out onto the porch. "Mr. Maxwell, do you have a mount?"

The older gentleman nodded. "Yes, I told Levi to have it ready at the house when I got back."

Laura followed them to the door and now stood in the frame looking small and helpless.

John reached out and patted her shoulder. "I'll bring her home to you, Laura. We'll get through this." His gaze moved over her shoulder where Elizabeth sat silently sobbing. "Please take care of her until I get back. She's lost so much already."

Clint was proud of Laura as she raised her head, put her teacher's poise on and said, "I will."

John nodded to her. "Thank you."

Clint hated leaving her but knew if they were going to save Hope, they had to leave the women behind. As they rode into the night, Clint thought about Jerry Roberts. Could he hurt his own child? The note had said he wanted a thousand dollars or he'd send Hope home in a wooden box. Surely the man wasn't so ruthless that he'd take his own child's life.

Thoughts of Hope filled his mind. She was sweet and shy. He felt the same sense of protectiveness for her that he felt for Grace. Hope was as much a part of his heart as Grace and Laura. What would he do if they found Hope dead? Rage and fear rolled up in his belly, making him a very dangerous man.

An hour and a half later, Clint knelt down behind a clump of trees. It hadn't been that long ago that he'd done the same thing. Only this time, instead of looking for cattle rustlers, he was looking for a bank robber turned child abductor. He looked across the way at Matt.

The sheriff pointed toward the other side of the house and motioned for Clint to move over there. Clint nodded his understanding and crept through the trees. They could see a light in the back of the cabin but couldn't see inside.

The banker peeked out from behind a tree. His face looked pale in the moonlight. Morning would come soon, but right now they were all in the dark. They weren't even sure Jerry was anywhere about.

But the hair on the back of Clint's neck was standing straight up. His gut was talking, and Clint was trying to listen.

He moved from the tree line and ran for the side of the house.

A shot rang out.

Clint dropped and rolled until his back hit the wood of the cabin. His eyes frantically searched for the shooter. Was it Matt or John? Or had Jerry seen them and was firing from the woods?

Matt ran for the house. His breath came hard as he asked, "Where did that shot come from?"

"No idea." Clint frowned. "Where's John?"

Matt looked about. "John!"

John stepped out from behind the tree. "I think I hit him." He pointed a shaking finger toward the tree line.

Matt and Clint inched toward the trees that John continued pointing at. Clint frowned at the banker. "John, get down."

The banker knelt but continued looking into the woods. Matt led the way and soon shouted to Clint. "He's down."

Clint hurried to stand beside the sheriff.

Jerry lay on the ground gasping for breath. He held his hand to his stomach, his eyes large. He grabbed at Matt's arm. "Hope is in the house." His hand slid to his side as Jerry's eyes closed for the last time.

John groaned. "I didn't mean to kill him. He was going to shoot Clint in the back. I just acted." His hands shook as he ran them through his silver hair.

Clint didn't take time to figure out what had happened. He ran for the house. His only thought was to find Hope and make sure she was safe.

He pushed through the door and hurried from room to room. Jerry had said that she was in the house, but where? Clint tried to remain calm and called out for her. He kept his voice low and steady. "Hope, honey, where are you?"

The toddler came out of the back room. She smiled at him and hurried to him. Hope raised her arms and said, "Papa!"

At hearing her call him "Papa," like Grace did, Clint's heart filled at her acceptance of him and his place in her life. He scooped her up into his arms and hugged her tight. "Oh, baby girl, I was so worried about you." Tears spilled down his face as he held her close. Clint hadn't realized just how scared he'd been, but now that he had Hope in his arms, he didn't ever want to let her go.

Matt entered the house. "Clint? Did you find her?"

He wiped his eyes and called back, "She's in here, and she's fine."

Matt and John entered the room. Matt stopped in the doorway, but John came to stand in front of them. He reached out and touched Hope's soft curls. "I'm so glad you are all right."

Hope smiled at the men. She looked about as if looking for Jerry. When she didn't see him, Hope captured Clint's face between her palms. Her eyes searched his.

"I'm sorry, sweetie. Your daddy had to leave."

Her wise eyes searched his. Then Hope laid her head on his shoulder. "Papa?"

Protective fatherly love filled him once more. "Yes, baby?"

"Warwa?" She stuck her finger into her mouth.

Clint smiled. "Laura is waiting for you."

Matt shook his head. "We'd better get back to town." He turned and led them all back outside into the night air.

Clint blew out the kerosene lantern and then followed the other two men out of the now-dark house. John and Matt stood beside their horses. What had they done with Jerry's body?

Matt answered his unspoken question. "We put him in the house. I'll come back later with a couple of men to help me take care of him."

He sat Hope up on the saddle and told her to hold on,

then Clint swung up behind the little girl. She leaned against his stomach once he was in the saddle with her. Clint wrapped his arm around her little waist. It was time to go home.

Home. Would he be able to talk Laura into marrying him? Clint didn't know what the outcome would be, but he planned to ask her to marry him for the third time. He wasn't sure what he would do if she rejected him again. This time he truly loved her and wanted to spend the rest of his life with her. He, Grace, Laura and Hope would be a family. The thought made his heart swell with love. He urged his horse to go faster toward home and the woman he loved.

Chapter Thirty

Laura paced. She couldn't help it. Sitting and waiting were not strong points for her. They never had been.

Elizabeth had stopped crying and now sat with her hands in her lap, watching Laura. "If you would like, we could go to the house," she suggested.

"No, thank you. They will come here first, since this is where they left us." She paused. Maybe Elizabeth would rather wait in the comfort of her home, instead of at the sheriff's office with nothing to do. "But I'll walk you home, if you want to go. Then I can come back here and wait." Laura studied Elizabeth's face. She was a pretty woman, and Laura could see Priscilla in her.

Elizabeth's smile wobbled as she said, "I didn't really want to go. I was just trying to find something to occupy our time while we're waiting."

Laura understood how Elizabeth felt. Waiting and not knowing what was going on was wearing thin. She sat back down and sighed.

"How about we talk, dear?"

It was time for lots of questions. Laura smiled to

cover her weariness. "What would you like to talk about?"

"Well, if it's not too personal, I was wondering if Mr. Shepard has asked you to marry him. It is as clear as water that the man is smitten with you." The older woman folded her handkerchief and placed it into her lap.

Laura almost laughed at the ease with which the older woman had jumped right into her personal life. "Yes, he has asked me. Twice."

"Oh, that is wonderful! When is the big day?" She sat forward in her chair. Laura was sure the other woman was ready to talk wedding plans for the rest of the evening.

"Um, I said no." She looked to the door, praying the men would return and the awkwardness of the moment would pass.

Elizabeth sat back. "You said no? Why?"

Instead of answering, Laura asked a question instead. "Why should I have said yes?"

"Well, he's handsome, rich and would make a great husband for you and father figure for our Hope." She smiled as if pleased with her quick answer.

Laura laughed. "You look like one of my students who think they have the right answer but instead are off just a little."

"Are you saying he's not handsome?" Elizabeth countered.

She couldn't deny that Clint was a good-looking man. "No, he's certainly handsome. That's the part you got right."

Elizabeth studied her for a moment. "Well, are you saying he's not rich?"

Laura shrugged. "I'm not sure if he's rich or not.

Just because a man owns a big ranch does not mean he's rich. As far as I know, he could owe your husband's bank a lot of money." She watched Elizabeth's nod and understanding cross her face. She continued. "Besides, I'm not interested in a man's wealth to consider him for a husband."

"Then your argument is that he wouldn't make a good husband for you or be a good father figure for Hope." She sat back and studied Laura. "I've known Clint Shepard for a long time. My husband tells me he's a good and fair businessman. His attendance at church isn't consistent, but that's because he works on a ranch. He is a man who lives his life according to God's principles. So, I really can't see where he would be a bad husband or father."

Laura shook her head. "I know he is a great father and was probably a wonderful husband. But I'm not the woman for him." Sadness filled her voice. Laura knew without a shadow of a doubt that she loved Clint Shepard and would marry him in an instant, if she weren't barren.

Elizabeth leaned over and placed her hands over Laura's. "Then what is the problem?"

Should she tell Hope's grandmother? What did she have to lose? It might be good to talk to another woman about her doubts and fears.

Laura lifted her head and pretended the words she was about to speak hadn't torn her heart out more than once when spoken aloud. "I can't have children."

Elizabeth studied her face. "And you believe that you should remain a widow because of that?"

In for a penny, in for a pound, Laura thought. "Yes. Not a lot of people know this, but before Charles died we were a very sad couple. I had discovered a year earlier that I couldn't have children. He said it was all right, but Charles became bitter over the following months because he realized he'd not have a son to carry on the Lee name. The man I loved died, not loving me." Tears filled her eyes, but Laura refused to let them fall. "I never want to see a man look at me that way again, ever."

Elizabeth squeezed her hands. "Oh, honey, I'm sorry." She pulled another handkerchief from her other sleeve and handed it to Laura.

A tear slipped unbidden from her lashes. "Especially a man I love."

They sat in silence while Laura tried to keep the tears at bay. She wiped them away with a heavy heart. No longer did she cry because of the hurt Charles's words had inflicted, but now she cried because she'd never be able to tell Clint that she loved him.

Elizabeth cleared her throat. "Thank you for sharing that with me. Now, would it be all right if I shared something personal with you also?"

Laura nodded and wiped the last of the tears away.

"After John and I married, we discovered we couldn't have children. I wept for the loss of something I never had. I became bitter and hurt deeply because I felt I had disappointed my husband. We almost went our separate ways, only John wouldn't give up on me. He continued to tell me he loved me and that having a son didn't matter to him." She stopped and looked out the dark window.

Laura was confused. If Elizabeth couldn't have children, then how did they get Priscilla? She wanted to ask but knew that Elizabeth would tell her if she simply waited.

Elizabeth turned a sad smile on her. "You aren't going to ask?"

"No. If you want me to know, you'll tell me." Laura missed the feeling of Elizabeth's warm hands over hers as she pulled away.

"I do want you to know. I think it will help you knowing." Elizabeth picked up her handkerchief from her lap and sighed. "I might need this in the telling," she explained.

Laura understood. What Elizabeth was about to tell her was still painful, so she nodded.

"One day, John had to go to Austin on business. He came home happy and smiling for the first time in a long time. Then a few days later, he said he needed to make another trip to Austin. Before, he'd ask me to go with him, but not this time or the many times after that. I began to think that he was seeing another woman on these business trips and became even more bitter." She stopped and looked at Laura with a grin. "But I was wrong."

Laura frowned, unsure where this story was going. "Please, continue." She hated asking but really wanted to know the rest.

"Well, one morning he got up and said we needed to go to Austin. I thought he was taking me there to see a lawyer so that he could set me aside. So, I dressed in my best, put on a big smile and pretended I was happy to go." She laughed. "Only instead of a lawyer, he took me to a hospital. We went inside and went to the maternity ward and met with Dr. Michael Burns. Dr. Burns began explaining that a young woman had had twins and that since John had started the process of adopting a child first that he could choose which baby he wanted, then the other couple could choose theirs. You can imagine my surprise. I was so stunned I simply stared at him and the doctor."

Laura mumbled, "I can imagine."

"The doctor then took us to a private room where two babies were resting in a cradle. One had a pink blanket and the other blue." Tears filled her eyes. "I knew John would scoop up that boy baby and shout for joy, but he didn't. Carefully, he picked up the girl, set her in my arms and said, 'We'd like a daughter.'" She wiped away the tears that now flowed freely from her eyes.

The story was both happy and sad. Laura felt tears prick her eyes again.

"We brought Priscilla Hope Maxwell home that day. On the ride back, I asked John why he didn't take the little boy. Do you know what he said?"

Laura shook her head.

"He said, 'Not all men need a son, but we all need a happy wife.'" She watched as Laura picked up her borrowed handkerchief.

Laura used the cloth to wipe the tears from her eyes. "That is a beautiful story, Elizabeth."

"Yes, it is. You know, dear, I think you should tell Clint Shepard that you love him and that you cannot give him a son. If he says he doesn't need a son but does need a loving wife, believe him. And, if he says he wants children and thanks you for your honesty but that he can't marry you, then come see me and we'll share my handkerchief again."

Laura didn't have time to answer. They heard horses

arriving at the hitching post outside. Both women jumped up to see if it was the men returning with Hope.

Clint smiled as Laura and Elizabeth spilled from the door of the sheriff's office. He held a sleeping Hope in his left arm, her small body cradled against him in peace.

Both women looked as if they'd been crying the whole time they'd been gone. The sheriff and John dismounted and tied their horses to the railing. Matt stepped around the women and headed to his desk.

John walked to his wife and hugged her close. "She's fine, Elizabeth."

Laura looked up at Clint. She laid her hand on his thigh. "Is she really all right?"

Clint laid his hand on top of hers. "She doesn't have a scratch on her. Her pa didn't hurt her. He only wanted the money."

"Good. Where is her pa?"

He shook his head and looked to where John held his wife as if he never intended to let her go. The older man had taken a life tonight. His first, from what Clint could see in his face.

Clint passed the sleeping Hope down to Laura.

When he was sure she had the baby secure, Clint climbed down from his horse. He walked to the Maxwells and laid a hand on John's shoulder. "I never did thank you for saving my life. You did what you had to do, and for that I am eternally grateful."

John released Elizabeth, who walked over to Laura. In a low voice he said, "Thank you, but I don't know if I will ever get that poor man out of my mind. He was so young."

"You can't blame yourself for the path he took. If you ever need to talk, I'm here for you." He clasped the man's shoulder and gave it a squeeze.

Hope woke up and cuddled closer to Laura. She smiled at Elizabeth. Her little eyes searched the area until they landed on Clint. She smiled. "Papa!"

Elizabeth and John smiled. John said, "Well, she knows you." He slapped Clint on the shoulder and walked to where his granddaughter reached out for Clint.

He took the little girl in his arms and hugged her close. Everyone was smiling but Laura. She looked confused and worried.

Clint hugged Hope once more and then said, "Here, go to Mama." He passed a smiling Hope back to Laura. Then Clint walked into the sheriff's office.

"Matt? What are you doing hiding out in here?" Clint sat down in front of his friend's desk.

Matt looked up at him. "Trying to decide who gets the reward money for Jerry Roberts." He passed the wanted poster across the desk to Clint.

When he saw the reward was a hundred dollars, Clint whistled low. "That's easy. John Maxwell."

Matt sighed. "That's what I thought, too, but he won't take the reward money. Said it felt like blood money to him. He doesn't want payment for killing a man."

Clint thought about it for a few moments. "Since Jerry has no relatives around here, besides his daughter, maybe the money should be given to her."

A smile spread across Matt's face. "Sounds fair." He stood and shook Clint's hand. "That's just what I'll do."

Clint stood also, "We'd best be getting back to the ranch. I'm sure Mrs. Murphy will be worried sick by now."

Matt followed him out the door.

The sun rose in the east, casting a fiery glow over the waking town. Clint yawned. What he wouldn't give for his nice warm bed and to see Grace's smiling face.

Hope grinned at him. John held her for a moment before passing her off to Elizabeth. Did the child feel as if she were a favorite toy being passed around? Probably. He smiled back at her.

"Papa!"

Now that she'd said it three times, Clint had to admit he enjoyed hearing it from her almost as much as he enjoyed hearing it from Grace. "Hey, baby girl, are you ready to go home?"

Hope reached out for him again. He took her from Elizabeth and smiled. "I can sure get used to this special attention." He looked to Laura.

She offered him a soft, sweet smile. "We need to get going. Camelia is probably beside herself with worry." Laura climbed onto Clint's horse.

Once Laura was in the saddle, Clint handed Hope up to her. The little girl wiggled until she was comfortable, then leaned her head on Laura.

Laura looked to John and Elizabeth. "We'll be back in a few days."

"Make sure and come by and see us," Elizabeth said. "There is always room at our house, if you should decide to spend some time in town." She smiled up at Laura. "And remember what I told you."

"How can I forget?" Laura smiled back at her. "Keep that handkerchief handy."

Elizabeth waved the handkerchief at her. "I will. I'll even launder it for future use."

Chapter Thirty-One

It bothered Laura that Hope continued to call Clint "Papa." How was the child going to cope when they left the ranch and she wouldn't be seeing him every day? Would she adapt like she had to having her mother missing from her life? It still baffled Laura that Hope had never cried for her mother. But who knew? Maybe the child was just too young to really be aware of the adults in her life. No, Priscilla had been her mother, but Hope hadn't acted as if she'd ever known her. Something wasn't right.

"Laura, you've been awfully quiet since we left." He leaned across the saddle horn and searched her face.

She felt the horse's muscles tighten under her. Thankfully the livery had offered them the extra mount so that they wouldn't all three have to ride the same mount home. "I was just thinking about Hope." She hugged the child closer. "She's going to miss you, Grace and Camelia when we leave."

He frowned. "Who says you have to leave?"

Laura chuckled. "The school board, for one body of people."

Clint reached across and pulled her borrowed horse to a stop. "I'm serious." His eyes searched hers.

She wanted to tell him she'd stay, but knew she couldn't. At least not until he heard the whole story of her past. And Laura had no intention of sharing that with him just because he'd invited her to stay on the ranch. Being Grace's nanny had been all right at first, but now Laura couldn't imagine living there and loving Clint but not able to express that love.

"Marry me. I love you and I want you to stay. I'll be a good husband, and we can raise our children together." Clint moved his mount so that his leg touched hers. He reached across and tucked a wayward strand of hair behind her ear. "Laura, I'll make you happy, or do my best trying." He smiled a nervous-looking grin.

Laura shook her head. "I can't marry you, Clint." She looked down at Hope, thankful the child was asleep once more.

Sadness filled his voice. "Is it because you don't love me? You might grow to love me."

"It's because I do love you that I can't marry you." She turned her head, not wanting to see the sorrow and disappointment in his face.

Clint moved his horse away from hers. She felt the loss of his warmth immediately, and her heart broke. Laura couldn't seem to stop herself. She turned to look at him.

He had moved away several feet and gotten down from his horse. Clint walked over to her and lifted his arms to take Hope. "We need to talk before we get back to the ranch."

She handed the baby over and then slid from the back of her horse. Laura followed him to a nearby tree with a large log leaning against it as if the tree had fallen but landed on its neighbor. When he indicated she sit down on it, she did.

He paced in front of her. "Let me get this straight. I love you and you love me, but you can't marry me?" Clint stroked Hope's back as he waited for her answer.

"Right." Laura felt heat enter her face. It was hard enough to tell another woman you couldn't have children, but to tell the man you love one of your deepest secrets was, well, embarrassing. And made it hard to get the words out.

"Why? Was it something I've done? Is it because you'd have to live out of town? Or that you can't teach?" He looked desperate.

"No, it's me." She sighed. "I can't marry anyone."

Clint sat down beside her on the log. "Can you explain to me why? You aren't dying, are you?"

Laura grinned. "No, I'm not dying." How could she explain it to him? She looked away, not wanting to face him or for him to see her face. "I can't marry you because it wouldn't be fair to you."

"Honey, you are circling the wagons again. Why don't you just tell me why not? I'm sure it's not as bad as you think." He wrapped his free arm around her waist and pulled her closer to him.

She couldn't take being that close to him. Laura stood. She walked a short distance away and said, "Before my husband died, we found out I can't have children." She blew air from her lungs. It felt as if she were going to drown in the pain of having to tell Clint her horrible secret. "After we found out, he hated me. Charles wanted a son." She kept her back to him.

Laura couldn't stand the quiet that her words had

brought about. Even the birds had stopped singing their morning songs. She turned to look at him. "Clint, I can't give you sons. If you marry me, there will be no sons to run your ranch in your old age." Her lips quivered, so Laura pressed them together.

"I see." Clint stood and walked toward her. "And you think that if we can't have sons, I won't love you anymore."

Tears burned and stung the backs of her eyes. A knot grew in her throat big enough to almost choke her. She loved Clint and now fully expected his rejection.

He leaned his forehead against hers. "Can I tell you a secret?"

What? He was going to ignore her secret and tell one of his own? All Laura could do was nod.

"Even women who can have children don't always have boys. I don't know if you've noticed, but my child at the ranch, she's a girl." He rubbed his forehead against hers. "Not a boy."

"But if you marry someone else, you have a fifty-fifty chance of getting a boy to carry on your name," she protested.

He sighed heavily. "Laura, I'll be honest with you. Part of the reason I have fought so hard not to fall in love with you is because of Martha. I was so afraid you would die of an infection, too, if you gave birth to a child. But I had come to the realization that fear is no reason not to love. God is in control of everything. So I had to trust that He brought you into my life and He would take care of us."

Laura took a step away from him, but Clint pulled her back.

"I'd rather have the woman I love by my side than

take chances on a boy that may never be." He pulled her close and buried his face in her neck. "Laura, I don't care about having a son to carry on the Shepard name. I care about you. I want to spend the rest of my life with you. What can I say that will make you understand?"

Laura remembered Elizabeth's words: "I think you should tell Clint Shepard that you love him and that you cannot give him a son. If he says he doesn't need a son, but a loving wife, believe him." She smiled.

Clint lifted his head. He studied her face for a moment and then smiled. "Is that the look of a woman who is about to say, 'Yes, I'll marry you'?"

Laura nodded. "Yes, I'll marry you."

He whooped so loudly that Hope jerked away. She looked from the man who was holding her to Laura. "Mama!"

Clint slid Hope into Laura's arms and then spun them both around. "You won't be sorry, Laura. I will love you forever and ever."

She believed him. Clint already knew she couldn't have children, and yet he still wanted to marry her. Laura said a silent prayer of thanks to the Lord for sending Hope into her life. If the baby hadn't been left on her doorstep, she would never have taken the job to be a nanny to Grace, and she wouldn't have met Clint. Then she said a special thanks to God for sending Clint into her life. He was the perfect man for her.

Epilogue

Two Years Later

Clint paced the floor. What was taking so long? He looked to where Hope and Grace sat on the floor playing with their blocks. They seemed unaware or unconcerned that their mother was about to give birth in the bedroom.

Camelia looked up from her sewing. "Clint, settle down. First-time babies often take a while."

He frowned at her and walked to the hallway entrance. Hearing nothing, he walked back to the living room. Was that a baby's cry? Clint hurried to the entrance again. Still no sounds of a crying baby could be heard.

A knock sounded at the front door.

Clint walked back and opened it.

"Is our new grandbaby here yet? We came as fast as we could." Elizabeth puffed as she hurried into the room.

Camelia laughed. "No, but not because Clint hasn't checked every two minutes."

The girls squealed and ran to their grandparents. Shortly after the wedding, the Maxwells had adopted Grace as their own. They all gave and received hugs while Clint hurried back to the hall entrance. He had begun to think of them as his in-laws.

"Would you like a cup of coffee or tea while we wait?" Camelia asked Elizabeth, laying down her sewing.

"I'd love some tea," Elizabeth answered. She hung her sweater by the door and followed Camelia to the kitchen. He heard Elizabeth ask, "How long has she been in there?" just before they disappeared into the other room.

The little girls followed, asking for cookies.

John sat down and sighed. "I still can't believe that our Laura is going to have a baby."

Clint looked at him, thinking the man must be senile. For the last six months that had been all he could think of—Laura was going to have their child.

He remembered the day he'd taken Laura to the doctor. She'd been sick for days, and he'd feared she had developed some kind of infection. The doctor told him that Laura didn't have an infection but was going to have a baby. His first reaction had been relief. Then it dawned on him that Doc had just said she was going to have a baby.

Clint had been horrified. The doctor had sat him down and threatened to slap him if he didn't snap out of it and act happy. For Laura's sake, he'd done just that, acted happy.

Laura seemed unaware of his fear. She was thrilled beyond measure. With the help of Camelia and Elizabeth, she'd been working on the little nursery for months. First painting the room, a soft yellow, then buying the perfect baby crib. She, Camelia and Elizabeth began making baby bedding, clothes, blankets and knitting something they called booties.

Clint grunted. "I just wish it was over with." Fears tore at him. Fear that she'd die giving birth. Fear that she might have an infection like Martha and die a few weeks later. How many times had he made her promise not to die? He'd done so halfheartedly. But deep down, the fears still ate at him.

John stood. "Have you thought of baby names yet?"

"Laura has thrown out so many names, I've lost track." Clint went and sat down, but he made sure he could see into the hallway, just in case the doctor needed him.

"Elizabeth said she thought you might name her Rosebud, if she's a girl and Wade, if he's a boy." John's gaze moved to the kitchen. He leaned forward and whispered, "Did you really agree on the name Rosebud?"

"No, I suggested Faith."

John slapped his knee. "Then you insist on Faith."

Clint tried to laugh. "Faith it is."

The old man's face grew serious. "Poor baby."

"Poor baby?"

John sighed heavily as if saddened. "Yep, that child will have to carry the name, Rosebud Faith Shepard for the rest of her life." Then he burst out laughing.

Clint stared at him with a frown. Why in the world would they give the baby such a long name? The old man was losing it.

When he calmed down he said, "You don't really think she's going to let you tag on the name Faith, do you?"

His head felt as if it were going to explode. Clint

shook it and stood, just as the door to the bedroom down the hall opened.

The sound of a squalling baby filled the house. Camelia and Elizabeth rushed from the kitchen, followed by the little girls.

Clint's eyes grew wide, and he looked to Camelia for guidance.

"Go on." She waved him down the hallway. "You've been waiting all day for this moment."

Elizabeth clapped her hands. "But don't forget about us out here. We want to know if our grandbaby is a boy or a girl."

Clint hurried to the bedroom door.

The doctor grinned. "Congratulations, son. Mother and child are doing great."

"Thank you."

He hurried inside after the doctor to where Laura lay propped up on pillows. She held a squirming baby boy on her chest. His little face was red, and his tiny arms were flailing about.

Loud cries filled the room.

Laura smiled up at him. "Isn't he beautiful?" she asked over the baby's cry. Then she pulled the baby closer to her, so that he could nurse.

Quietness filled the room. The baby snuggled close to his mother, content at last.

Clint reached out and touched the boy's head. He smiled at Laura. "Do you still want to call him Wade after my pa?"

"Of course, I do." She sighed happily.

The doctor clasped him on the shoulder. "They are both healthy. And there is no sign that Laura will develop any infections. Relax, Clint, and enjoy your family. I'll tell the grandparents that we have a boy and we're calling him Wade." He slipped from the room to give them some privacy.

Laura looked up at him with big eyes and smiled. She sighed tiredly and said, "God has been good. We are both fine. Thanks to Him I didn't die on you."

Clint responded by kissing the top of her head and saying, "No, you didn't die. I love you, Laura Shepard. You're the best nanny and mother a child could have. Not to mention the best wife for me." He silently thanked the Lord for helping him overcome his fears, one event at a time.

* * * * *

If you enjoyed this story,
pick up these other stories from Rhonda Gibson:

PONY EXPRESS COURTSHIP
PONY EXPRESS HERO
PONY EXPRESS CHRISTMAS BRIDE
PONY EXPRESS MAIL-ORDER BRIDE
PONY EXPRESS SPECIAL DELIVERY

Find more great reads at www.LoveInspired.com

Dear Reader,

Thank you so much for taking the time to read this book. I hope you enjoyed it. Clint and Laura's story is my last book for the Love Inspired Historical romance line. I'm going to miss writing for this line but know that God has other plans. If you enjoy reading my historical novels, please know that I have more coming out, and you can learn about them by going to www.rhondagibson.net.

I love hearing from my readers, so please feel free to write to me at rhondagibson65@hotmail.com or send a note to: Rhonda Gibson, P.O. Box 835, Kirtland, NM 87417.

Until we meet again,
Warmly,
Rhonda Gibson

We hope you enjoyed this story from
Love Inspired® Historical.

Love Inspired® Historical is coming to
an end but be sure to discover more
inspirational stories to warm your heart
from **Love Inspired®** and
Love Inspired® Suspense!

Love Inspired stories show that
faith, forgiveness and hope have the power
to lift spirits and change lives—always.

Look for six new romances every month
from **Love Inspired®** and
Love Inspired® Suspense!

ROMANCING THE RUNAWAY BRIDE
Return to Cowboy Creek • by Karen Kirst

After years of searching, Pinkerton agent Adam Halloway is finally on the trail of the man who destroyed his family. Then tracking the scoundrel throws him in the path of sweet, lovely Deborah Frazier. Can he trust in love—and in Deborah—when he realizes she's hiding a secret?

A COWBOY OF CONVENIENCE
by Stacy Henrie

Newly widowed Vienna Howe knows nothing about running a ranch, yet now that she's inherited one, she's determined to make it a home for herself and her daughter. Ranch foreman West McCall wants to help—can his plan for a marriage of convenience lead to something more?

ORPHAN TRAIN SWEETHEART
by Mollie Campbell

Orphan train placing agent Simon McKay needs Cecilia Holbrook's help when his partner suddenly quits. The schoolteacher agrees to help him ensure all the orphans have been safely placed with families in town...but keeping her heart safe from Simon won't be so easy.

HANDPICKED FAMILY
by Shannon Farrington

The Civil War is over but the rebuilding in the south has just begun. Newspaperman Peter Carpenter arrives seeking stories to tell...and the widow and child his soldier brother left behind. After pretty Trudy Martin steps in to assist, Peter's search for family takes a turn no one expected.

Get 4 FREE REWARDS!

We'll send you 2 FREE Books <u>plus</u> 2 FREE Mystery Gifts.

Love Inspired® books feature contemporary inspirational romances with Christian characters facing the challenges of life and love.

FREE
Value Over
$20

SPECIAL EXCERPT FROM

Love Inspired HISTORICAL

*After years of searching, Pinkerton investigator
Adam Halloway is finally on the trail of the man
who destroyed his family. The clues lead him to
Cowboy Creek and a mysterious mail-order bride
named Deborah. She's clearly hiding a secret—could it
be a connection to his longtime enemy?*

Read on for a sneak preview of
ROMANCING THE RUNAWAY BRIDE
by **Karen Kirst**
the exciting conclusion of the series,
RETURN TO COWBOY CREEK.

"You're new. A man as picture-perfect as you wouldn't
have gone unnoticed." The second the words were out,
she blushed. "I shouldn't have said that."

Adam couldn't help but be charmed. "I'm Adam
Draper." The false surname left his lips smoothly.
Working for the Pinkerton National Detective Agency,
he'd assumed dozens of personas. This time, he wasn't
doing it for the Pinkertons. He was here for personal
reasons.

She offered a bright smile. "I'm Deborah, a boarder
here."

Her name is Deborah. With a D. The scrap of a note
he'd discovered, the very note that had led him to Kansas,
had been written by someone whose signature began with
a *D*.

He ended the handshake more abruptly than he'd intended. "Do you have a last name, Deborah?"

Her smile faltered. "Frazier."

"Pleased to make your acquaintance, Miss Frazier. Or is it Mrs.?"

She blanched. "I'm not married."

Why would an innocuous question net that reaction?

A breeze, scented with blossoms, wafted through the open windows on their right. In her pretty pastel dress, Deborah Frazier was like a nostalgic summer dream. Adam's thoughts started to drift from his task.

He couldn't recall the last time he'd met a woman who made him think about moonlit strolls and picnics by the water. At eighteen, he'd escaped his family's Missouri ranch—and the devastation wrought by Zane Ogden—to join the Union army. There'd been no chance to think about romance during those long, cruel years. And once he'd hung up his uniform, he'd accepted an offer to join Allan Pinkerton's detective agency. Rooting out criminals and dispensing justice had consumed him, mind, body and soul. He couldn't rest until he put the man who'd destroyed his family behind bars.

That meant no distractions.

Don't miss
ROMANCING THE RUNAWAY BRIDE by Karen Kirst,
available June 2018 wherever
Love Inspired® Historical books and ebooks are sold.

Inspirational Romance to
Warm Your Heart and Soul

Join our social communities to connect
with other readers who share your love!

Sign up for the Love Inspired newsletter
at **www.LoveInspired.com** to be the
first to find out about upcoming titles,
special promotions and exclusive content.

CONNECT WITH US AT:

Harlequin.com/Community

 Facebook.com/LoveInspiredBooks

 Twitter.com/LoveInspiredBks

LISOCIAL2017